THE NUDIST

Sarah May works in television and lives with her son in
London.

Sarah May

THE NUDIST COLONY

V

VINTAGE

Published by Vintage 2000

2 4 6 8 10 9 7 5 3 1

First published in Great Britain in 1999 by
Chatto & Windus

Vintage
Random House, 20 Vauxhall Bridge Road,
London SW1V 2SA

Random House Australia (Pty) Limited
20 Alfred Street, Milsons Point, Sydney
New South Wales 2061, Australia

Random House New Zealand Limited
18 Poland Road, Glenfield,
Auckland 10, New Zealand

Random House (Pty) Limited
Endulini, 5A Jubilee Road, Parktown 2193,
South Africa

The Random House Group Limited Reg. No. 954009
www.randomhouse.co.uk

A CIP catalogue record for this book
is available from the British Library

ISBN 0 09 928956 3

Papers used by Random House are natural, recyclable
products made from wood grown in sustainable forests.
The manufacturing processes conform to the environ-
mental regulations of the country of origin

Printed and bound in Great Britain by
Cox & Wyman Ltd, Reading, Berkshire

In memory of George Gowans and
Elizabeth Maude, with love.

To and For the beloved.

ACKNOWLEDGEMENTS

My sincere thanks to . . .

Rebecca Carter, editor and collaborator, for making this book fit its cover, for her persistence and enlightenment.

Malcolm Imrie and Martina Dervis for trusting me in the beginning when I only fed them scraps.

Mikaël Garandeau for being more grown up than he pretends.

Jonathan Taylor for praise before I learnt to say thank you.

Lastly, to Jennifer and Jeffrey Hutchinson for permitting me to lie.

I

1

He met Ludwig, or rather Ludwig met him outside King's Cross station when the chauffeur slammed on the brakes so hard that he poured Scotch over his crotch and the lady's handbag on the seat next to him slid on to the floor.

The smell made Ludwig think of hot toddies, the speciality of a Jamaican who used to work for him. Hot toddies were given to dissidents, traitors, blabbermouths, cry babies, minors, anyone who threatened the brutal structure and unchronicled morals of organised crime. Once they uncovered them they were tied to a chair, often in their own front room, and then had half a bottle of Scotch poured over their crotch; good Scotch. Wesley (who was the blackest wog he had ever seen) would light a cigarette and smoke it as an egg timer, giving the alcohol time to soak through the man's trousers and underpants.

They were never gagged, and often morons with dyslexic mentalities became articulate, eloquent even. And the wog, Wesley, would always say, 'stop being so melodramatic', as if 'melodramatic' was a new word he had only just learnt that made him feel grown-up.

While they were talking (or crying) Wesley would go and fill a container with water, then he would put his lighter to their crotch. Ludwig had to be seen to watch and the sight always brought on his back pains. Often the man's chest and face burnt in the backdraft. But no one got blood on their hands, no taboo was broken, and no one who was given a hot toddy had ever failed to take his own life afterwards.

Ludwig dabbed at the wet patch between his legs with a clean handkerchief.

'We hit him,' the chauffeur said.

'We did?'

He respected his chauffeur as he did all anatomically disfigured men. Douglas had a wooden leg and a glass eye. He also had family and considered himself a well-treated man, a lucky man, a man who had nothing to complain about.

'Sorry, sir.'

'Well get him out of the traffic. It was definitely a him?'

'It was.'

Douglas would have trouble bending down Ludwig thought as he watched him try to tuck up the ends of his overcoat so that they wouldn't trail on the wet road. He had never enforced a 'cap', it was something Douglas had bought out of his own salary. He watched him walk back to the car between the hedonistic horns of the jam that was now forming, carrying a young boy across his arms. He stood for a while in front of the headlights wondering what to do with the body, and in the end opened the passenger door opposite Ludwig.

'Sir, there's a blanket on the back shelf, could you put it across the seat. He's filthy.'

Then he laid the boy across the back seat and Ludwig ended up taking his head in his hands and putting it on his lap.

'Is he dead?' Ludwig whispered.

'No.'

They drove off.

'He had a small Swiss Army knife on him,' Douglas said, taking one hand off the wheel and feeling in his pocket.

'Perky.' Ludwig sniffed the boy's hair and hands. 'He's been eating fish and chips. Very recently; stinks of them.'

The boy shook all over twice.

'Heroin addict,' Ludwig observed.

'Difficult to tell in the rain. Rainwater makes some people turn grey on the spot.'

He watched as the boy flung an arm across his face. There was a brown smudge down one side where he had lain against the wet road.

'How old are you?'

'Fourteen.'

'Name?'

'Aesop.'

The boy hadn't looked up at him yet.

'Are you hurt?'

'No.'

'Not hurt anywhere at all? Broken?'

'No. My head aches.'

'Let me see your eyes.'

'No.'

'Any family?'

'Brother.'

'Do you live with him?'

'Yes.'

'What does he do?'

'Don't know. Listens to the radio.'

'Does he love you?'

The boy turned his head towards Ludwig's belly.

'More than anything. More than his girlfriend.'

'Do you go to school?'

'No.'

'Let me see your eyes.'

5

'No.'

'Where do you live?'

'Hackney.'

'In a shitty little flat with rotting carpet. You stink of rotting carpet.'

The boy had fairly long hair, black fingernails and wore a ripped bomber jacket. The unwashed body wearing unwashed clothes was flatly rather than sharply unpleasant.

'We ran you over.'

'Was it you?'

'Yes. Don't you think it was good of us to stop?'

Ludwig tried to pull the boy's arm away, but he wouldn't let him.

'Leave off.'

'I've fallen in love with your name.'

'It's not my fault.'

'If you come home with me I'll cut your hair, seeing that nothing else is injured or of interest. I trained as a hairdresser years ago; I'm still good with scissors.'

He looked up to see Douglas watching him through the rear-view mirror.

'Do you want to come home with me and let me cut your hair?'

'My brother's expecting me.'

'You can tell Douglas where your brother lives and he'll take us there, then we can ask him. What makes you think your brother will be at home anyway?'

'He'll be waiting up for me.'

'Does he do that all the time?'

'Sometimes.'

'Tonight might be one of those nights when he's got better things to do. Like going out with his girlfriend.'

The boy took his arm away from his face.

'I knew they would be green. You know green's an unlucky colour to get married in.'

'Yeah, I heard that.'

'Not from your mother though.'

Ludwig rested his hand on Aesop's hair.

'What were you doing?'

'I was with some friends.'

'If you come home with me I'll cut your hair for you, and I promise you won't ever have to kill a man.'

'I wasn't going to kill anyone.' Aesop tried to laugh and sit up, but then saw Ludwig's face.

'I know you weren't, but what I'm saying is that you won't ever have to.'

Ludwig wouldn't let the boy walk. He made Douglas carry him indoors to the downstairs bathroom and sit him in the wicker chair, telling him to take his jacket off and bin it. He took his own suit jacket off as well and rolled up his shirt sleeves before taking hold of the scissors which he kept by the sink to trim his own hair every morning. The special water sprayer seemed to impress the boy who sat very still with his head down while Ludwig gave him an uneven conscript's cut.

'Look at you now.'

2

The woman in the white coat whose belly his face had been in close proximity to for the past ten minutes drew back.

'For some reason it stops where your hairline begins. Your scalp's pure.'

She stared at Ludwig's forehead for a while then went to sit down at her table with its institutional spotlight.

'Is that my case file you're writing in?'

'No, just a notebook. Something I scribble in. I would never remember anything written down formally in that question/answer format,' she explained.

The room was like all the others he had been in here, not unlike a kitchen, but then all treatment rooms were the same. The chair was a cross between a barber's and a dentist's and rose out of the floor in the centre of the room. There was a sink and disproportionately large unit for the flushing away of unspeakable excrescences by the window. At least it was a room with a window, but this didn't alleviate the smell of the lino floor. A lino floor was a washable floor, not even blood stained it, and lino was a smell that anticipated both legal and illegal forms of violence.

Dr Achilles was one of those professionals who kept the tools of her trade unashamedly on display on a trolley; they weren't put away in cupboards and drawers with that overfriendly modesty some doctors were trying to introduce. The only slightly restrained gesture in the room was the corner of a curtain that she had obviously hurriedly tugged across the large mirror above the sink.

'I didn't think more senior doctors had to wear the white coat any more.'

'I like it. I like the coat. I've earned the right to wear it and I'm a believer in uniforms. You don't have to designate yourself.' She put her pen down. 'Especially as a woman.'

'Oh.'

'I'm going to start you on a series of fortnightly treatments, but if you want this upgraded to weekly ...'

'Will that speed the cure?'

'We agreed we wouldn't mention the word "cure".'

'Are you allowed to speak to me like that?'

'I never censor myself, Mr James. I'm used to dealing with children. I usually work with children; I prefer them.'

'I don't know much about children. I don't know any children.'

'Childhood was a state we were all in, Ludwig,' she said abruptly, using his first name not only because he was sat down, but to make her point.

She came and stood over him again.

'You're the first white man I've ever seen with the borealis.'

'That's the Indian name.'

'How did you know it was the Indian name?' She brought her hand down on to his shoulder and he noticed that she wore no rings, or any jewelry in fact. 'It's the only name,' she finished.

'So you've been in Brazil too.'

'Yes, it's one of the reasons I'm treating you now. But

I've never been to Jara.' She walked away from him back over to the desk, leaving him lying alone in the chair, not even expecting a comment this time.

'Can I get out of this chair yet?'

'If you want to. I hung your coat on the back of that door there.'

'I was supposed to begin treatment with Dr Blackthorn.'

'He went north to open a clinic directly related to his research.' Her voice sounded soft because she wasn't concentrating on it.

'He won't be coming back to the Hospital?'

She looked up at him.

'I thought you had been given correspondence and a briefing session on this?'

'No, nothing.'

'I don't think he'll be coming back. Definitely not.'

When he climbed out of the chair his clothes felt strange to him, as though the chair had stripped him bare and he had been lying naked for the past twenty minutes. When he took his coat off the peg, it hung heavy on him. He watched as she leant over the desk, swinging slightly on her stool, her breasts rubbing the wood. A good portion of his face (scraped that afternoon) lay in delicate if blotchy shreds in a shallow tray of liquid in front of her.

'Do you mind if I pull this cover off the mirror?'

For the first time she looked embarrassed.

'I don't want to walk out on to the street bleeding.'

'I'm sorry, I thought . . .'

'It's all right, it was a . . . delicate . . . thing to do, even if it looks a little haphazard.' He lifted the cover of the curtain off the mirror. 'I'm very familiar with me. I'm one of those people who like themselves, who are really able to like themselves,' he said without belief.

He knew she was watching him watch himself.

His face was the same as it had been that morning. Every time he looked at it he saw the forest, a forest whose greens were so dark they were black, and so light they were white. Whose canopy bore the footprints of giants; whose trees and rivers, and flora and fauna had both the architecture and anatomy of the world to come.

The skin was red, an inflamed red that made the muscles in the eye ache just looking at it, and covered in welts, not unlike an animal's footprint. As if a beast thought to be extinct or never to have existed at all – a gryphon, or phoenix – had stepped on his face while he slept. The marks formed a pattern of irregular similarity that only nature was capable of making. His eyes had never scared him before, but now when he looked in the mirror they were the only thing that made him afraid. Because they hadn't changed; because they didn't bear any traces of what had passed. He put his hat on.

'Do you like a man in a hat?'

'It's a nice hat.' She was standing up now.

'Have you noticed how men hardly ever seem to wear hats any more?' He was about to make a self-effacing comment, but stopped himself just in time, remembering that he always left a better impression on people when he didn't. 'What made you choose dermatology, Dr Achilles?'

She put both her hands in her pockets as if searching for something. It was the first time since he had entered the room forty-five minutes ago that he had seen her smile. 'It's the only branch of medicine where people are able to contract disease without actually becoming ill. Even the shadow is infected, but still the body doesn't succumb; it separates the two-dimensional from the three-dimensional.'

She was opening the door for him and he could see that she wanted to cross her arms but was stopping herself.

He took the door from her. 'I'll think about those extra appointments you want me to want.'

'Thanks. Thanks very much.'

Ludwig left the Hospital for Diseases of the Skin which was tall and painted grey. It could have been gothic if it had been brave enough. There was Douglas standing by the side of the car ready for him. He noticed that after attending the clinic, Douglas patted him lightly on the back as he stooped to get into the car. Now it was a gesture he would always come to expect. He had a hard enough time trying to work out what Douglas meant to him, without worrying what he must mean to Douglas, which was far more of a responsibility.

'It was snowing while you were inside.'

'It was? Well, it hasn't settled.'

'It might try again. Are you warm enough?'

'Thank you. Yes.' He pressed his hand against the window. 'Dr Blackthorn isn't going to be treating me.'

'That's a shame.'

'Why? I never met the man. They didn't say anything to me prior to my appointment. On any occasion. Surely that's unthinkable. I simply opened the door and he wasn't there. Dr Achilles was sitting waiting instead, knew everything about me.'

'Was Dr Achilles a woman?'

'She was, yes.'

3

Aesop sat down in the black barber's chair while the woman in pink overalls moved backwards and forwards behind him. Ludwig was sat in the waiting area, his coat pulled tightly over his legs, reading a copy of *Woman's Own*. Every now and then he would look up and smile into the mirror at Aesop, who would grin back, fidget, then look nervously about him. He sensed that Ludwig was getting impatient with the woman in pink, that he expected her to know that he was hoping for a better performance.

Aesop didn't want her to get shouted at. He liked the way the white collar of her overalls looked against her skin, and the brave purple of her long strong nails. Eventually she pushed a small metal trolley over, which had a basket of cotton wool balls on it, a bowl of water and a black revolver lying on its side. She stood behind him with her hands pressed against the back of the chair.

He looked out of the window at the car parked there; the car that was going to take him home.

'No,' he shouted, pushing his elbows into the back of the chair to propel himself out of it.

In one all-embracing movement, the beautician dressed in pink grabbed his neck with her right arm and pulled his head on to her scented breast. With her left

13

hand she scooped up the revolver from the trolley. Aesop noticed that Ludwig looked up from the *Woman's Own* magazine and smiled again, but without catching his eye. He felt the muzzle of the gun against his left ear, then she pulled the trigger and stepped back.

He lay in the chair; still alive. The beautician laid the gun down on the trolley, then soaked one of the cotton wool balls in water. Aesop was surprised, when she pressed it against his ear, to find that it was warm.

'The salt in the water will act as an antiseptic,' she said, fighting with the word 'antiseptic' as if it were something to aim for. She obviously felt that it should have an affinity with the overalls she was so proud of.

'Is he bleeding? I told you, I don't want to see a speck of blood on him, not a speck.'

'Course he isn't, there's no veins in the ear are there. It's very plain,' she said, taking hold of Aesop's ear and looking at the gold stud.

'So?' Ludwig said, aggressively.

'I thought it might be a hoop, or have a diamond in it. Or that it might even have been an "A" for Aesop.' She started to laugh.

'Well it isn't, it's just twenty-two carat, which is more unplated carats than you'll ever see in a lifetime.'

'For fuck's sake. Why didn't you tell me I was getting my ear pierced, I never wanted an earring. I don't like jewellery.'

'Course you do, you've just never been given a chance to wear any before, in peace and quiet, in your own time. You'll enjoy your earring.'

'Your ear might swell up a bit at the beginning. What do you think?'

'It looks all right, better than I thought it would.'

'Do you think he looks bad?' Ludwig said turning to the girl, who was checking the scissors in her overalls pocket.

'No.'

'I like your nail varnish,' Aesop said at last, turning to her.

'You do? Thank you.' She tried to appear shy, to affect a look she had seen, or read about somewhere, but couldn't even begin to pretend that he was treading on her toes.

Ludwig laid his hand on the back of Aesop's chair before the girl was able to.

When they got back in the car Aesop knew from the way Douglas was looking at Ludwig through the rear mirror that he was misbehaving in some way and it pleased him to think that he had the ability to make Ludwig unpredictable. He cupped his hand over his ear, and despite the throbbing he could still hear the sea.

4

So he became, without searching for it or wanting it, Ludwig's spiv. He travelled the commuter trains at regular and irregular hours, and was never allowed to take taxis, only ever public transport. He travelled with his legs apart and a mobile phone on the seat between them, pretending to read the *Sun*, frowning. Wearing designer jeans, shirts, and chelsea-boy pullovers with small round necks.

His posture promised a capacity for unlimited violence (which had so far been restricted to spitting) and, as well as the earring that still shone in the sun and a knuckle duster of a Rolex watch, he wore a gold chain bracelet on his left wrist with his name engraved on it: AESOP. This was in case he should ever forget it, in case he should ever get lost. It gave him hope in his early-hours belief that the world was still big enough to get lost in.

And because he had only ever been in love with a one-eyed fading turquoise bear that his brother had picked up at Brick Lane market, it was relatively easy for him to maintain (despite his connection to Ludwig) the appearance of being untouched and to an extent untouchable. He never went out of his way to engender privacy between himself and any woman, not knowing what to do with them in confined spaces. He gave his number to individuals in crowded public places, only ever agreeing to meet with them before dark. It was the closest he got (or wanted to get) to intercourse, watching the skin on the back of a girl's hand re-shape itself as he penned his number over it, feeling the bone beneath the Biro point. He could give his number out up to ten times in one night, and the pen wrote differently each time depending on the skin. On blacks he had to use the palm of the hand. Some girls, older or drunker than others, lifted their shirts and let him write on their bellies, around the button. He had once been asked to do an inner thigh, but refused because it was too dark to see.

Aesop had enough of his overheads paid to keep him from the shabbier, down-at-heel side of crime: perfume sold from a suitcase, arson attacks on local curry houses, raids on amusement arcades, irregular non-fatal knife attacks etc.. And enough responsibilities (or at least the suggestion of) to keep him from boredom, the demi-god of destruction. In exchange for having his life housed and paid for, he had to donate small regular bits of it to Ludwig: trips to the cinema, attempts at under-age drinking, half-hearted dates with half-hearted girls. These became accounts which Ludwig listened to avidly as if Aesop were describing Ludwig's future and not his past.

He wasn't Ludwig's servant, or sidekick, and he wasn't called upon to directly participate in anything. He was given things to do, people to call, trains to ride, and liked the word 'protégé'. But his brother said that that was all wrong: there was an 'official' word for boys like him, they were spivs. 'Spiv' described the relationship without defining it; the lack of reason that made people speak of love. And why shouldn't they? His brother said that some men had spivs instead of dogs, and some men had them instead of children, and read him a description from the dictionary over the phone one night.

17

Spiv – a man characterised by flash dress who makes a living out of illicit and unscrupulous dealings.

'So let's take a look at you,' he said and gave one of those laughs of his that tasted of salt.

Ludwig gave him a flat to live in. Flats were communal, he said, and – more importantly – what Aesop was used to. In Whitechapel, which was no longer the home of Jews and their bloated kosher restaurants. The new immigrants – for all their garishness and unlikely combination of colours – failed to make it exotic. They had lost any legacies they could lay claim to in their efforts to keep warm, and the second generation had a deadpan dullness to them that was almost grimy. It was one of those places that had always been derelict, a place of exiles and exile.

Aesop was allowed friends to stay because few children trust their own company enough to want to live alone and because all children are afraid of the dark. Carte blanche (as Ludwig knew) was a black hole to the average juvenile. Too much freedom was detrimental to children, it gave them the time and space to realise the difference between misdemeanours and crime.

Friends used his room to bring girls back to, and his flat was nothing more – ultimately – than a bed with four walls. Aesop would often sit on the end watching them, happy to sleep in the wet patches afterwards, to share the bed with them and their unborn children. He hated sleeping alone.

And in the morning he would pull the net curtains back to show the others in bed the minarets of the nearby mosque that could be seen through the dirty glass.

'Can you believe it? Can you believe that? We could be anywhere.'

By the end of the week the sheets of the bed were tainted with the things that prevent a body from being naked. The pillows were greasy from the different oils and sprays that had been used in hair the night before, and sometimes the stains were the unnatural colour of dyes that had been sweated out during love. Lipstick (the reds and pinks of very young girls) was often smeared across the sheets so heavily it looked as if they had been eaten. Occasionally he uncovered traces of blood which made him feel apprehensive about the truth of sexual mythology; and once, tucked in at the end of the bed, a fake eyelash. On Friday mornings he would pull a chair up to the side of the bed to study the geography of intercourse and lean over to smell the heavy sweet smell that bodies which had known each other left behind.

Tasha, the cleaning woman Ludwig had hired, came once a week on Fridays. It was the only day he ate properly. She would bring him food to make his breakfast (he liked to think from her own wages) and give the sheets their final veneer of the week – smoke from frying meat. Every week she called him a dog and asked him if he wanted to die in his own filth.

He liked the impression the stinking sheets gave as Tasha leant over to strip the bed, and often sat back against the wall so that he could watch her face as she uncovered the histories that had been enacted, from the frugal to the sumptuous.

'No wonder you so tired,' she said, but she never laughed, her huge pink lips just folded over themselves and made her look worried. 'What would you do if I wasn't taking these off to be washed? What would you do? Sir, I'd hate to be Girl Friday.'

The day she found the lipstick print on the wall she took the Lord's name in vain and said, 'What did you do to her? She must have been eating the wall.'

'She ripped my Iron Maiden poster. Can you get me another one?'

★

19

Tasha drove her own car. Maybe Ludwig bought it for her or loaned it to her because, every Friday, she had to cross from Whitechapel to his house in Notting Hill where she took all Aesop's laundry, as instructed, inside its basket and stood it in front of the fireplace in the main room.

'That you Tasha?'

'Is, Mr Ludwig.'

'Did you cook him breakfast this morning?'

'I did.'

'And did he eat it all?'

'Certainly did. Ate like a dog. Can't even tidy up his own face afterwards. Had to tell him to go and get in the bath I ran him.'

'Did you wash him?'

'No, sir. He's got to do something himself.'

'Had he tidied the flat at all this week?'

'Now he's not going to is he, not when he knows you're paying me every Friday to go and do it for him. He'd rather die at his own hands, from disease.'

She emptied the laundry basket out on to the rug, the 'Turkish' rug – Ludwig couldn't be any more specific than that. The first time he had asked her to do it he had noticed the flush spread through her arms, neck and face, the 'flush' being a symptom of squeamishness, but there wasn't a trace of this to bruise her skin any more. He hated squeamish people, they were the kind who would kill their own mothers to save themselves.

'Anything unusual?'

Tasha poked around, as if looking for something edible.

'Clothes. They stink of smoke and that stuff he sprays himself with from a can.'

'I bought him some decent splash-on but he says he won't wear perfume.'

'Of course he won't.'

'The school locker-room stuff is as close as he wants

to get. It reminds him of washing powder and a mother's hands.'

'His clothes ain't that bad. He's proud of those. Apart from the smoke he's immaculate.'

Ludwig brushed the palms of his hands over the laundry. 'Clothes are so much softer when they've been worn against a body.' He looked up at her as she tried to straighten her back. 'And the sheets?'

'You should see them this time.'

Ludwig enjoyed their complicity. He never would have had this with a white woman. White women had the audacity to judge even when they weren't being paid. It was their lips in particular he couldn't stand, the way they grew thin and twitched like a cat's arse. Mean lips, lips made mean by being forever afraid of having their kisses rejected. Their tongues worn grey through the spreading of indiscreet and malignant gossip.

Tasha weighed about fifteen stone and was happy to wear her slippers outdoors. As excited as Ludwig when they got to the sheet, her eyes and mouth went wide.

'That boy's been busy this week.'

They took a corner each and stretched the sheet out until it was explicit and taut. Ludwig looked down.

'He has.'

Tasha lifted it to her nose. 'I found a print,' she puckered her lips up, 'like this, pink, half way up the bedroom wall.'

Ludwig gave the sheet a last shake before folding it so that the scents rose. 'They love him. Did you find any-thing else in the flat?'

'No, Mr Ludwig, he's been clean – or clever. No, really, only hash.'

'I can't stop him smoking.'

'And that's all. You can smell it, and it dirties the nets, but that's all. Only the dope. That's what makes him so sloppy.'

21

What he couldn't see looking at the sheet was Aesop sat in his pants and T-shirt on the end of the bed, in the orange light of a London night, his back against the wall and the duvet tucked over as much of his feet and legs as possible — if the position of the lovers allowed it. He didn't hear the girls' 'What's wrong with him? Why does he get to sit there?' Or the friend's reply, 'Shut up. He can do what he likes, it's his flat,' acknowledging to himself, in his gruffness, that he still felt more comfortable, and his behaviour more justifiable, within the presence of another male. At fourteen, the lover didn't want to be left entirely on his own with a woman because he didn't yet trust the fact that afterwards he could remember nothing at all of the final two minutes. He didn't want to be left alone with someone capable of eating him alive.

The sheet told Ludwig nothing of the whispered exchange between the two boys lying in bed in the late morning, once the girl had left to go to school or work.

'What's it like?'

'You saw.'

'But what's it like?'

'It's different each time, in the beginning, but then afterwards it's always the same.'

'Like what?'

'Being eaten alive.'

Douglas walked in carrying Ludwig's coat for him.

'The car's ready.'

'Yes, I'm coming. Douglas, would you just put this on the bottom of the stairs.'

Ludwig noticed the glass eye shifting slowly as he handed him the sheet. Douglas's mouth tightened slightly, and he didn't take his driving gloves off.

'Do you have the time for this?'

'It's only once a week ... Well take it, it's not a winding sheet. Nobody's died in it.'

Douglas shut the car door on him. He had never yet caught the tail of Ludwig's coat in it.

'Do you remember, Douglas, the way one's upper lip sweated merely at the sight of a girl's wrist?'

Douglas smiled. 'The size of her little finger compared to your own.'

'Being able to circle a waist with just one of your arms.'

'Realising that a length of thigh was little larger than one handspan.'

'The sight of a girl in underwear lying in a single bed . . .'

'. . . on sheets your mother had just washed and ironed . . .' Douglas sighed.

'. . . under a duvet whose cover you had had since you were twelve.'

'Nothing but time to yourself. Time to yourself.'

Douglas was referring to his wife, but he had no idea who Ludwig was talking about.

5

'We're here,' Aesop said, but Douglas had already stopped the car.

He realised, as he stepped out, that Douglas wasn't afraid. He was taking off his gloves and unbuttoning his coat. Ludwig, conscious of the time Douglas spent waiting (often indefinitely), had brought him a gadget, a small-screen television that he could balance on top of the steering wheel and peer into. More often than not Douglas preferred to listen to tapes that his wife recorded shows on from the radio. 'The Archers' and others. Nothing made him laugh like the radio.

'I'll go and get Knobby,' Aesop said.

'Who's Knobby?'

'He's a security man for some of the big auction houses.'

'Why do I need him?'

'You don't, but your car does. If I don't get Knobby, I'll come out here and find you sitting on nothing but an armchair from a three-piece suite. So I'll go and get him. Have you got ten pounds?'

'I have not, no.'

'That's what Knobby costs.'

'Then I'll just go and park somewhere else and you'll have to catch up with me later.'

'Ludwig said you had to wait for me and take me back. I know he did.'

Douglas gave him the ten pound note.

'Phone me if you need me,' he said.

'I haven't got the mobile on me.'

'You know you're meant to carry it — switched on — all the time.'

'I keep forgetting how to switch it on,' Aesop shrugged.

Knobby had a flat in the same block as Aesop's brother, but preferred it beneath the tower in the space planners had proposed to build a car park in. It had been one of those dehydrated gestures demonstrating what little they understood of the capabilities of children. And the place was crawling with children. Knobby said that it was the only place where they outnumbered the rats. They went there to learn to fight, to handle weapons, to be ready with stooped backs and flickering eyes when the world came to find them.

'Hey prizefighter.'

'Knobby.'

They pushed their heads together and rubbed each other on the back of their necks. This was permissible.

'Your brother said you'd gone.'

'He did?'

'Yeah.'

'And nothing else?'

'No. That was it, that you'd gone.'

He noticed Knobby looking him over.

'He just said it, not because I'd asked him or anything.'

'Whitechapel.'

'Not bad,' Knobby said, his eyes on the bracelet and watch.

'I'm going to see him now. Is everything all right?'

'Apart from having to work Sundays, it is.'

'Will you take this, I've got something I need you to mind.'

25

'I can do that. Where's it parked?'

'You'll see it outside.'

'I will?'

'You will.'

'I like your hair short. I never pictured you with it short. But I like it like that, it makes you look taller.' He didn't mention the earring.

Knobby was allergic to sunshine. He could barely stand rooms with windows in them, but for a car he would do anything. Every time he lay under a car, he lay there like a convict under rain.

Aesop was learning something about smells. In the car on the way over (even with Douglas's glass eye staring at him in the mirror) he saw the way the stairs turned all the way to the twelfth floor and the way the mesh criss-crossed inside the windows at each landing. He even felt the chipped wood of the banister beneath his hand, could see the letters carved into the painted metal doors of the lifts, and the way his own front door looked as he stretched the key towards the lock. But the smell of the lino, that was something he had forgotten to remember. The look of it, yes, but not the smell. After passing the bins by the door outside, his first experience of homecoming at the end of the day had been olfactory. Lino. Olfactory memory has a direct, blunt access to private history. It's the least deliberate act of memory, the most intrusive and the most truthful.

He took off the watch and bracelet and put them in his pocket.

'Jake? Jake, it's me.'

'I saw you arrive; I heard you coming. The door's open.'

James Cagney was on the television, all five foot of him with that face of his that looked like a caricature of itself. Deirdre was in the bathroom which, through some unaccountable never to be rectified error of construction, was almost twice the height of the rest of the flat. Aesop stood and listened as she sustained one of those high notes he often heard escaping from passing cars, or caught on the commercial breaks.

'I don't know how her voice doesn't get the shakes singing like that,' he said to his brother.

'She was trained.'

'She was?'

'Course.'

Even though the television was on, Jake was sat at the table, staring at the radio.

'This is a new station. Plays nothing but music though. I bet their signals are coming from Vauxhall, Battersea. Can you hear that? You think it does?'

'It does.'

He started to lay the table with the cutlery he had in his hands.

'I thought I'd do us some dinner.'

'Right.' Aesop thought of Douglas outside, unsure how long he was 'legally' allowed to keep him waiting for. Not because he was afraid of Ludwig, but because he was afraid of Douglas.

'Deirdre's singing at Las Palmas tonight; I thought we might stay in.' Jake looked up at Aesop, feigning a stiff neck so that he could tilt his head back and roll his eyes.

'Jake, I can't. Not tonight. I only really came to collect some things. From my bedroom. Some posters and some tapes I think I left.'

'That's all right.' He had to get up after that. 'So he's calling you in.'

'No, I just thought I might as well get my last few things.'

'Why didn't he come with you?'

'I thought he would. I don't know why he didn't.'

'You better go and get your stuff then.'

His bed still hadn't been made. It looked like he had either just got out of it or just died in it. The duvet cover had robots on it.

'Jake? Jake, can I take the duvet cover?'

James Cagney raised his voice so that Aesop couldn't be heard and, in the silence that followed his question, he decided to leave it behind.

Three of the walls were covered in wallpaper that felt as though it had been sculpted in sponge or rubber. His brother had whitewashed it annually. It was difficult to imagine ever being able to brain anyone (or even yourself) against it. Jake had once said to him that there was something fundamentally violent about destroying someone's ability to do violence. Destroying the promise of it. The fourth wall was covered in wallpaper that had motorcyclists performing improbable stunts across it. Someone had already put some carrier bags in the room (it could have been Deirdre) and in the end he only used one of them. He tried not to rip the motorcyclist wallpaper when he took his posters down, and could feel Deirdre's voice through the palms of his hands when he pressed them against the wall. He remembered Jake describing Deirdre to him and asking him if it was all right if he brought her home sometimes. He said she was black and had the stupidest name he had ever heard of, the sort of name women inherit when they hit sixty.

'Seriously, you wait, when you're sixty there won't be any Lucys, Janes, Amandas, Amys, Lisas, Alisons, Julias. You'll wake up one morning and wonder where they've all gone because you won't know anybody who isn't called Barbara, Deirdre, Cissy, Eileen, Doreen or Margery.'

By the time he finished packing Jake had already put a chicken drumstick on his plate and was stirring the Smash.

'Isn't Deirdre eating?'

'I don't know.'

'Haven't you told her?'

'Why should I? If she isn't here she isn't here. If she misses tea it's her own fault.'

'But how was she to know?'

'By being around. She isn't around so she doesn't know.'

Jake was staring at the radio again.

'Knobby's fixing up some new transmitters.'

'From the garage?' Aesop asked.

'That's right.' Jake put in a forkful of potato with each mouthful of chicken. 'I've had the truancy officers round here.'

'What did they say?'

'That you hadn't been to school for two months. That's a whole term you've missed.'

'It's happened before.'

'Not for that long it hasn't.'

'I'm surprised they bothered.'

'I'm not.'

Aesop tried to sit up straight to make the bellyache go away. He realised that he was pleased the officers had been around and wondered if that's what a murderer felt like when he was finally put on the list of suspects. 'What did you tell them?'

'Mind if I tune in?' Jake knocked his gesture sideways as he leant towards the radio that carried the burden of an untold number of breakfasts. 'I had to file you as a Missing Person.'

Aesop put the chicken down.

'You didn't have to do that.'

'You're fourteen. You haven't been to school for two months. I had to. I said you walked out on me.'

'What about the others? They know where I am.'

'I know they do. They didn't say anything. Just that they hadn't seen you around.'

29

'What if anyone ever follows them?'

'You think they're going to take that kind of trouble over you? As far as they're concerned now you only exist on paper.' Jake leant back in his chair. 'Deirdre, what you singing now?' he yelled.

'Cannabis King.'

'That's a clown's song.'

'Shut up. I can't hear myself sing.'

He turned the radio up. 'You should go to Charing Cross station. They've got your picture up on the wall there.'

Jake was laughing now.

Deirdre came out of the bathroom. As she walked and lifted her arms, vapours came off her, unstoppered, squeezed, depressurised, that changed colour once she applied them to her skin. She wore transparent pantaloons that started just below her belly button and came in slowly but tightly at the ankle. There was a tube of something shiny round her breasts and a bracelet on her arm where a tourniquet should have been. Her lips were an obscene pink, her shoulders supported her earrings and she wore a turban on her head. Wherever there was skin visible she had touched herself lightly with gold glitter.

She never asked if she looked good, she knew she always did.

'Aesop, how are you?'

She was the only person he knew who kissed him on the forehead. Before he moved out she had occasionally moved down to his lips, unintentionally wetting his nose on the way so that he could smell the kiss for a good five minutes afterwards.

'Jake, have you seen that stud he's wearing in his ear?'

'I hadn't, no. Aesop,' he said with false admonition (something that had always unnerved Aesop more than the real thing), 'they'll never find you now. That'll really

30

throw them off the scent.' He laughed.

Listening to him, Aesop realised that he had never heard him laugh when other people did; he never shared a gag. He had heard him say before that people who sat and laughed at the television might as well be donkeys braying in a field. Donkeys. There were very few things on the planet born to be slaves, but they were the one thing that defied any existence above this level.

'I heard you singing. I missed your singing, Deirdre.' This was for Jake, not her, but Jake wasn't going to pick up on it. 'Do you ever stop?'

'Only on National holidays.'

'Like Christmas?'

'Like Christmas.'

She sat down carefully, pulling her chair away from the table.

'Jake, why didn't you tell me you was having something to eat?'

'You weren't around.'

She looked at Aesop. The corners of her mouth were getting wet. 'Did you take my washing out of the kitchen before you started frying that chicken?'

'No. It's ruined anyway. It was all pink.'

'I had noticed that.'

'I hate pink.'

'Mum put all my underwear in with her red velour tracksuit. Man, she's not touching my washing again.'

'Course she is, you'll get sick of handwashing it here.'

'Well if I ain't getting fed I'm going.'

'You're going to lose your hearing, dancing next to those speakers three nights a week. One night you'll leave that club, on the look-out for a bus or a taxi, start feeling cold underneath all that sweat, smell the fresh night air, but you won't be able to hear a thing. Your aural world will have vanished.'

'Right. Whatever.'

Deirdre had some of those pants on that Aesop had seen girls wearing, with nothing but a bit of decorated string that disappeared up their backside. Like a trapeze artist's costume. He remembered watching them at Billy Smart's and wondering how they concentrated on mastering the vertigo when their costume was so uncomfortable.

Deirdre caught him looking and saved her last backwards glance, the quick intense one before she shut the door, for him. He looked down at his food.

'Are you doing anything next week?' Jake asked.

'I don't know, why?'

'You might have to take Deirdre out for me one night.'

'Why?'

'Because I might be doing something.'

Aesop had faith in his brother, and had always based that faith on his hands and lower arms which had veins that raised themselves above the level of skin that was supposed to suppress them. A man who wasn't afraid of showing his arteries to the world was a man who wasn't afraid of showing that he was alive. And those hands looked capable of making a pen speak, a piano play. In fact he was sure Jake did play piano, that they had been somewhere once where there was a piano and Jake had played it, but he had never worked out how.

'I'm on air now six hours every night.'

'That's good.'

'Do you ever hear me?'

'I don't get to listen. I don't have a radio.'

'You don't have a radio?'

'Not yet. Ludwig's buying me one very soon. maybe tomorrow.'

'But you have a TV?'

'Yes.'

'A TV and no radio?'

'I've got a personal stereo to listen to my music on.'

'And that hasn't got a radio on it?'

'No.'

'What cheapskate bought you that?'

Aesop walked over to the window and pressed his head against it. 'It's cold on the inside of the glass too.'

Even though they were muffled by the fog he could see the lights outside, the lights from everywhere, but couldn't see what they were attached to. They didn't belong anywhere in the fog.

'When are you going to get curtains?'

'We're not. Why would I want curtains? I like being watched; to be looked in on. Otherwise I'd have more secrets than I could cope with.'

When he turned round, Jake was holding his carrier bag towards him, resting his body against the open door; he loved talking to people from inside the flat with them outside. When friends came round he would stand and talk to them like that rather than invite them in.

'Jake. That night I got run over. Did Ludwig bring me back here? While I was sleeping, did he come back here to say I'd been hit and that he was taking me home? Did he come to say that to you?'

'Maybe,' Jake said after a while.

'Well did he or didn't he?'

'Maybe. But I was out. And he didn't leave anything to say that he had called.'

Somebody must have left the door open at the bottom of the stairs because the fog was inside; it was walking up and Aesop had the impression that it was looking for the crow's nest, for their flat here on the twelfth floor in particular.

'I'll ring you about next week. You're still on that number you gave me?'

Aesop nodded, and when he tipped his head forwards he could smell Deirdre's perfume or hairspray or something, which had held its own against the cold.

33

'Jake? You know what? If you had asked me once, even if it was a mumble, even if you could barely manage it, but had asked me to stay, you know, stay with you here, I wouldn't be leaving now.'

'Well you know what, Aesop? If you had rung any time that night you were run over, any time at all, just so that I could have had some indication that you were able to see me sitting here looking out of the window with my back to the door because I was afraid I would never hear your key turning in that lock again, then I might be asking you to stay. You showed me no such consideration.'

'But you said you weren't in that night.'

Aesop walked over to the front door, the bag in his hand.

'Nobody ever called, nobody came here,' Jake shouted.

Aesop knew he was telling the truth and yet still couldn't believe him. Even the truth now wasn't enough to make him want to stay. He walked down the stairs into the fog, feeling after a while that he had missed the exit and was going down below ground level. He was suddenly terrified of meeting Douglas on the stairs. Douglas, as it happened, was waiting for him, but Aesop heard him first. He heard the tapping of the leg on lino, the leg that had joints but was still hollow. He had often wondered if he took it off before screwing his wife – or whether he left it on.

He came across him as a hulk of navy blue, the peak of his cap vicious rather than reassuring.

'Douglas. Sorry.'

'The film I was watching finished; I thought I would come and find you. How did it go? All right?'

'All right. Douglas? Can I ask you something?'

The fog was clearing and it was already beginning to snow. Flakes were covering Douglas's navy-blue shoulders and Aesop's head like a bridal veil.

'The night you ran me over. Did you come here?'

'I don't remember.'

And then, as if to test the validity of this, 'Where did Ludwig get his face?'

He half expected to be knocked to the ground and have his cheek wetted with a fury of spittle, but instead Douglas seemed to move closer to him.

'In the forest, when he was in South America. Brazil.'

He thought of asking him about his own peg leg and glass eye, but didn't.

6

Sometimes Aesop went to Ludwig's, and was aware that, when he did, he took extra care with his clothes, and even rubbed his shoes down the backs of his trouser legs to make them shine. His life hadn't thrown many occasions at him. Ludwig almost seemed glamorous to him — or at least his American counterpart would have been.

Ludwig passed him a cup. 'Your fingernails are dirty.'

'The bus always makes them dirty.'

'Well wash them.'

'After this I will.' He started to drink.

'And don't gulp.'

'I can't help it. How the hell do you swallow it otherwise?'

'Push it along the top of your throat, then gently let it slip down. Control your breathing.'

'Why would I go to all that trouble for a mouthful of tea?'

Ludwig had lit a fire that afternoon which brought both the dogs into the room. The dogs, Abelard and Heloise, despised each other and liked to reassure themselves of their mutual hatred by doing it publicly. They were like friends who had known each other since childhood, but had since grown apart and, lacking the

36

imagination to make a formal separation, kept each other company without having either the interests or the happiness of the other at heart.

'They like you.' Ludwig watched Aesop's hand in the fur on Heloise's flank. 'They hate each other.' He realised how much he enjoyed this fact. 'Yes, they hate each other. They feel compelled to keep their eyes on each other every second of every day and yet, at the same time, can't stand the sight of one another.'

'They don't hate each other. They're trying to impress each other that's all.'

'That's not it at all, they hate each other,' Ludwig said sharply. 'See, even when you're not touching Abelard, he knows, and I don't know how, but he knows, just knows, that you're touching Heloise because he can feel it as though you're touching him.'

Through Aesop, Ludwig had discovered that he knew a lot of stories worth telling, which meant that sometimes, after a week, or fortnight, or month, Aesop would have a package to collect from somewhere and bring back to Ludwig, and they would find themselves in the downstairs room at Notting Hill with the curtains closed and Abelard and Heloise by Aesop's feet making his shoes shine with their saliva. Ludwig always sat on a hard-backed dining chair just where the shadows started.

When Ludwig told stories he let his jacket hang over either side of the chair, giving his aftershave greater freedom to move about the room and, if he didn't cross one leg over the other, he put his feet together, so that – Aesop noted – while his toes stayed together his heels crept further and further apart and, towards the middle of a story, he was completely pigeon-toed. It made Aesop feel suddenly worried for him.

'Do you know anything about one of the last men hanged in England?' Ludwig said.

'No. Don't even know when they stopped hanging.'

'He was one of the last ones. Of course by then it was long after the days of public hanging, open-air hanging. It all took place in a poky room with a trap door in it, more of a machine than a venue.' He looked at Aesop. 'Put your shoes back on, your feet stink.'

Aesop left them off.

'There's Larry, the condemned, sat in his cell, morning of the hanging and who do you think's standing there? Standing at the door?'

'No idea.'

'An eight-year-old kid who clamps him up in irons before he's had a chance to speak. And the first thing he says to him, straight up, is, "Sorry I'm not dressed properly. My dad took ill last night so my brother said I had to take his place."'

Aesop liked the fact that Ludwig put on all the voices. They had never bothered to put on the voices at school the few times they had read to them.

'And Larry says, "How old are you?" and the boy says, "Eight." The only thing Larry can think of to say to this is, "Have you ever done this before?" The boy thinks about it, then smiles and says, "No." So there's Larry walking along and, although he's probably thinking I could slip these irons over his head and wrap them twice around his throat, he doesn't, and he keeps so close to the boy that he's forever tripping on his heels. So there they are walking up this corridor—'

'Where's the corridor?'

'Wormwood Scrubs. Have you ever been to Wormwood?'

'No.'

'Not even outside?'

'No.'

'Well I have, and I know the corridor. Anyway, they get to the end of this corridor and go up a half flight of steps and the boy knocks at the door on the landing. A woman with one of those candystripe aprons opens it. The boy says, "I need to ask dad one last question." So Larry walks into the flat, the warden's flat. Very naturally. You won't ever have had the opportunity of noticing this, but wardens feel very uncomfortable around people who have never been accused or condemned of anything, very uncomfortable, so the warden wasn't displeased to have the condemned man in his flat. He knew how to talk to him.'

Aesop could almost hear the footsteps. That was something he had noticed about Ludwig's stories. Afterwards, he often heard sounds that reached out of the story and stayed with him.

'Inside the flat there's a television set with a cloth over it, a green tiled fireplace, and a table laid for tea. Real tea. The teapot on the sideboard is the size of a diver's helmet and on the sofa, reclining, the lucky man endeavouring to move and consume.

' "You're bloody disgusting doing that so near the table," the woman says as she starts to butter the rolls.

' "Shut up," the man says, bent over his right foot which is sitting in state on a black plastic pouf. He seems to be changing a dressing on his foot, which he has to keep dabbing with cotton wool because it's weeping. Larry knows from looking at him that, if the woman starts to complain again while he's putting the new bandage on, he's likely to plough her sideways through the window.

' "Gout," he says looking at him. "Some days it's so painful I have to fucking piss myself in that armchair over there," and he points to an oversized chair opposite.' Ludwig smiles at Aesop here, even though Aesop can't picture it.

'He didn't say that.'

'He did. Then he says, "I'm sorry," – that's Larry. So there they are in the warden's flat discussing the invention of the flush. "The loo's too far away. Stupid invention that – the flush. Whatever was wrong with a chamber pot?"

' "You weren't the one who had to empty it," the woman said and she just got the cups and saucers off-loaded on to the table before there was a howling bang from above followed by a squeaking that set the china on the dresser rattling.'

'The trap door,' Aesop said.

Ludwig nodded. ' "Tom's always sharpish," the warden says. "Does that bang every day?" Larry asks. "Not every day, but sometimes more than once a day." And the warden's wife says, "That's the privilege of being an Executioner's wife, you see. The flat comes with the job." "You live below the room?" Larry asks, and she says, "Directly – that way he gets to keep his ear on them. Check whether they're doing a good or bad job."

'The warden who carried out the executions rarely left the Scrubs. As soon as he stepped outside, you see, he said he felt like a murderer. He didn't feel like that inside, but outside he was stripped of his rights, of his privilege to take another's life within sight of the law.

'He says, "Did you get your meal this morning?" Not because he was genuinely concerned with Larry's meal, he was just a real stickler for doing a professional job, for the order of things. That they should happen as written. The only problem was, Larry hadn't had his meal.

'So he says, "I didn't actually, no."

' "So do you want something now?" the warden says.

' "Have I got time?"

' "We've only got the one room. It'll be another ten minutes at least before they cut him down." He looks up at the ceiling.

'So Larry asks for a scone, and the warden says he'll let him get away with the pronunciation this once because it's part of his last request.'

This makes Ludwig laugh.

'The boy notices that he eats the scone with his right hand and that the link between the cuffs is just generous enough for him to hold his left hand under his chin and catch the crumbs, stopping them from going on his mum's carpet.

' "Is your elder son not available today?" Larry puts on his high-pitched polite voice. He does the gentleman criminal very well. In fact he was probably one of the last.'

'Did you know him then?' Aesop asked.

'Might have done. And the warden says, "He's done that one we've just heard. He's got to meet his girlfriend now." Letting him know that family comes first.

' "Oh I see," says Larry.

'Then the boy comes and stands in front of his father who says to him, "Now don't forget to use two hands to pull the lever down or the floor won't gape fully, and if it doesn't gape fully, this blighter's going to have a slow descent. And I'll be listening to the bang so make it sharpish." He puts his sock back on and starts to shuffle to the tea table, nodding at Larry as he sits down.

' "Sorry, what shall I do with the crumbs?"

'The wife holds her apron out and he scatters them into it.

'The room upstairs is very bare and one of the walls is a window where – you know – people are allowed to spectate from.'

'Was there anyone there?'

'I don't know, you'll have to ask . . . no I don't think so.'

'Larry's sad now and tries to crack a joke. "What were you speaking to your father about? Lengths of rope?"

' "Yes, actually."

'Then the boy drags this chair over and stands on it so that he is the same height as him and tall enough to fix the hood over his head.

' "Dad says it's best to keep the handcuffs on because then you're not tempted to struggle. Is that all right?"

' "Perfectly," Larry says. Smoothly, like that. "Perfectly".

'The boy then helps him to stand directly over the crack, and to make things look as symmetrical as possible, he's made to stand with his left leg one side of it and his right on the other.

' "Aren't you supposed to ask me to forgive you?"

'And the boy says, "What for?" He has trouble operating the floor lever but he won't give up easily and he's determined to pull more than "sharpish", but then Larry remembers the most important thing of all—'

'The boy killed a man single-handed and alone?' Aesop interrupts.

'Killed is a bit strong,' Douglas said coming suddenly into the room.

With the door now open, Abelard got up and wandered closer to the fire and Aesop noticed with interest, as the dog stretched, that its cock had recently grown larger.

'You said I was to call you at five o'clock,' Douglas said, obviously cross that Ludwig hadn't remembered. 'Jerry's selected the people he wants for the music video.'

Aesop had never seen Douglas indoors before. In the car and walking to and from the car, but not properly established indoors. He realised with some surprise that it was likely Douglas had an office here, but couldn't work out what it was he did in it, unless it was Douglas who sent him out on all the courier jobs.

Jerry, who turned out to be a record producer, lived within walking distance. He was the only person Ludwig knew who did. As they walked, hailstones the size of a baby's clenched fist pounded down on them so that they tried to tuck their heads down between their shoulders.

'You should get a hat like mine,' Ludwig said.

'I should not.' Aesop tucked his head in tighter but could barely hear any more because of the water in his ears.

'Come on. What's the matter? Why can't you keep up with me. Is it the smoking? Will you believe me now?'

'No, it's my shoes.'

'Your shoes?' Ludwig stopped, but didn't look at the shoes, he just looked more closely at Aesop's face. 'Why didn't you say?'

'I didn't think. I mean, I was thinking that they was hurting. But I didn't think of saying nothing.'

'Well you should have. We'll have to get you some new ones.'

They walked on, but Ludwig didn't pace so hard.

The house was white and set back in its own forgotten garden. Inside there was a woman crying, but the sound was coming from the top of the house. They passed a room lower down where there was a group of people standing round a computer that was emitting a succession of electronic sounds, maddening to those not playing the game. Aesop was aware, as they passed up the stairs, that the people around the computer smelt. The smell of people who never got out of the same old body, let alone clothes. The perpetual rot of the unpicked, the unchosen.

There was a bedroom painted a different colour on every landing and the one he liked best was the dark green one they passed with about twenty hats hanging from the wall and a bed stacked with Victorian dolls. The rooms got lighter the further up the house they went. The kitchen and living space were at the top where a lot of the walls were glass. There were steps going up further still. The crying had nearly stopped, but the blotchy red-eyed whimpering of somebody not ready to give up could still be heard.

A girl with very white short hair crawled backwards out of the oven. She was so tall that Aesop couldn't imagine ever embracing her without first rolling her up. She had bare feet with lots of leather bands on her ankles and a jaded-looking silver dress that hung thinly off her shoulders and faded into her legs.

'Ludwig, I'm sorry.' She pressed herself against him. 'I was having a party,' she started to cry again, 'but because of him,' she stepped back and started to put some oven gloves on, 'I couldn't get round to speaking to people as they arrived. It was going to be a tea party,' now she was crying again. 'But it never started. Everybody left before it even started because of him.' Ludwig stepped back himself before she reached out again. In the end she leant against a tall cabinet and wrapped the oven gloves around her. 'Everything got burnt. There's no food left.'

There was a sofa the length of a ship's mess across the room with eight men on it, men with thick necks and scuffed boots. Thuggish in the most excusable way that got them into trouble, but rarely danger. They were watching ballet on a wide-screen television, not talking as row after row of tutus made their way across the stage, and men in tights with exciting protuberances per-formed sweaty feats without making their make-up run.

'Ever seen this?' one of them said, turning his head round and looking at Ludwig. 'It's the Kirov. The Kirov. It's fucking amazing.' One of the other men said, 'Shush.' 'See. Look at that.' He was still shaking his head as he stood up.

'Is this a kid we can use as well?' he said nodding at Aesop.

'No,' Ludwig said shortly. 'He's got nothing to do with it. He came with me. He wouldn't mind taking a look at your roof garden, actually. Never seen one before.'

'In this weather?'

'Ludwig,' Aesop moaned.

'Go on to the roof. Now.'

'It's straight up those stairs,' the girl said emerging again from the oven. 'And don't mind him.'

Aesop wasn't sure which one she meant.

Outside the hailstones were pushing a barbecue around on its castors – there were even some crumbling August sausages still on the grill. The plants in pots looked as if they wanted to cast themselves adrift and Aesop could see nothing of London because of the hail, not that he was looking to see anything. He sat on one of those chairs with a canopy over it that are built for couples to sit and swing on. The hail had nearly saturated what he guessed had been advertised as a 'waterproof' canopy and the cushions on the seat were wet. The whole thing was living out its destiny and becoming a mould-infested edifice of garden furniture. He doubted, thinking of the men and the crying woman, that it would ever hold a specific place in anyone's memory or that any great happiness had ever been enacted on it, but he liked the sensation of swinging.

He tucked one wet leg under him and let the other dangle over the edge. He didn't look about him, he just stared out straight in front, wondering what the time was, and whether school was out. Admitting to himself, slowly, keeping time with the seat – it was easier to think in motion – that maybe he had always left before 3.30 because he was frightened of seeing it through till then and still having nothing better to do. Then the woman from downstairs was walking towards him, still in her silver dress, barefooted. She was smiling but walking unsteadily. Aesop guessed she had taken something and shut down whichever part of her brain it was she had wanted to shut down, because she wasn't feeling the cold. The hail was pushing the dress hard against her thighs and she lifted the hem slightly, as if to keep it out of the rain. He remembered that feeling, that sudden abhorrence of hurting anything animate or inanimate. On the new drugs you could hear the wheeze of a spider underfoot or the crunch of an ant and it made you wince. It made even the most barely perceptible of acts violently audible. He thought of the time he had watched his brother cut the sleeves out of one of his shirts and had nearly run him through with the bread knife.

'Oh Jesus, that's sweet. That's sweet.' She came and crouched down in front of him, putting her hand between the bottom of his shoe and the ground, moving it up and down and laughing. 'Your foot doesn't even touch the floor yet.'

She put her hand on his knee to steady herself and help herself on to the seat.

'Do you want my coat? Here, have it.' He started to take it off.

'No, keep it. I can't feel the cold.'

'It's minus three. That's what Ludwig said. It's minus three today. You must be cold.' But he knew, right now, that she wasn't and he was glad she was on whatever she was on because he wanted to keep the coat himself. 'You're American.'

'Am I? Oh yes, yes I am.' She leant back and a drop finally found its way through the canopy and on to her face, that Hindu part of a face, between the eyes. 'When I first came to London I used to say just that. And then apologise. You know, "sorry", at the end.'

'How old are you?'

She was shivering now, her whole mouth juddered when she spoke, but he knew that she still wouldn't be feeling the cold.

'How old do you think I am?'

'Twenty-four?'

'Right.' She seemed disappointed in herself but more interested in him and even smiled.

'I'm divorcing him. Him downstairs. You know he hits me?' She watched him as she said that.

She didn't look like a woman who was hit.

'No, actually, he doesn't. But he did this morning for the first time.'

'Where'd he hit you?'

'Nowhere particular. You couldn't really call it hitting. He put both his hands on my shoulders', she suddenly knelt up and put her hands on Aesop and shoved, 'like this, shoved me against the wall. I banged my head. That's why I was crying.' She slumped back down. 'For every bang there's a grey cell lost. And not just lost but irredeemably lost, you know?'

Aesop was asking questions without needing an answer, asking one after the other because he liked the fluidity. Not because he cared – he didn't. He didn't care if the man downstairs (and he guessed he was Jerry himself) had hit her, or in fact even if he had killed her (although he wouldn't have liked to have seen that) because, even though he was happy to share the swinging chair with her, he didn't care if he never saw her again.

'And you know what made me really upset. The fact that none of those people came to help me, came to see – even – what the matter was. When they heard me start to cry.'

Aesop found this hard to believe.

'I helped them,' she said.

'Who?'

'Those people downstairs.'

'How did you help them?'

'Jerry, that's him watching TV, don't mind him – he gave me money.'

Aesop was wondering if she had bought them. Her voice was like her dress, silver, but left a drab impression and it was getting more difficult to understand as her body lost its heat.

'He gave me money to set up a theatre co-operative.'

Aesop nodded, which was something he did when he didn't understand, to stop people asking him if he knew what 'that' was. He realised that the girl thought she had found her audience in him.

'It was for homeless people. That room downstairs, that was my office. I had my own office here and parties, you know, to get people interested, to get their support. A lot of theatres, well-known ones, committed space to me. I was even thinking of touring. I had charities; I had an organisation; I had my own organisation, you know, and that isn't easy to come by. I did that.' She stretched her hands up to the canopy but the contact gave the water collected there the channel it needed and it ran down her arms and over the silver dress turning it battleship grey. She laughed and rubbed her hands over her face.

'All I needed was the people. And I got those. From the hostels, doorways, some beautiful beautiful people. The rehearsal space was booked. You know, rehearsal spaces used by organisations like the National Theatre. On my own, I didn't get any support from him. And sometimes it worked, sometimes they were difficult. And then he got involved saying they could be in his music video. Some video for something. I don't know, they liked him, he'd launched a lot of their favourite bands in the eighties, got a lot of people lifted out of their old shoes, you know, and put up there.' She stretched her arms out in front of herself this time with her palms flat against the hail. 'And he let them know that. But guess what the play was?'

'*Babes in the Wood.*' He remembered a playbill Jake had once shown him outside a theatre in Deptford with some injured football player in the lead role.

She laughed hysterically as if his remark had been calculated just for her, just for the occasion. After a while she even started gasping in a delicate airy way.

'No. But I did write it myself.'

He could tell from looking at her that she wouldn't have been able to take things much further without the interference of Jerry downstairs.

'Shall we get back inside? You're going to be really ill.'

'Do you think so?'

'Look at it, this is hail.'

'I'll be in a fever.' She was getting excited. 'Can people still die of pneumonia? I don't feel cold.'

He tried to get her up, but she was heavier than she looked.

'But then they turned up this morning looking like that. Their faces were like that. You know, like Ludwig's.' She said the last word quietly.

'I didn't see,' Aesop said, but now she had his interest.

'That's why he hit me.' She obviously liked this expression even though it wasn't – literally – true. 'He thought I did it, so they couldn't be in his video.'

'Does Ludwig know?'

'He will now.'

He eventually got her up.

She smiled and led the way back downstairs, treading soggily on the wet tiles with the soles of her feet. The leather bands round her ankles were now black. Aesop quietly took his coat off at the top of the stairs, and put it round her shoulders, worrying (slightly) that others would wonder why he hadn't.

'I'm scared,' the girl said. 'I've never lived without a man before.'

She fell down some of the steps. He offered her his hand because she wouldn't have got up again if he hadn't, but afterwards she kept hold of it.

'Hey, Ludwig,' Jerry was saying, 'I might still use them anyway.'

'You might still use them? After this morning? You

would do that, wouldn't you, especially after this morning,' she said stepping into the room.

'If you don't shut up we're going to miss the finale,' someone said.

'You been outside you dumb bitch?'

She slumped on the stool in the kitchen and tried to eat an apple from the bowl. There was another man in the room who hadn't been there before. Aesop recognised him from downstairs. He was the only one left although there had been others in there. The room had the fetid smells of bodies that start acting like cadavers when they've still got a soul inside them, a sick smell. The man had a jacket on made from a sleeping bag and, across his entire face, an eagle spreading its wings although now the blue and green tattoo had some difficulty keeping its shape over the surface of boils. Aesop watched as Ludwig spread his hand over the eagle.

'Does that hurt?'

The man shook his head, and did the same to Ludwig.

'Does that hurt you?'

'When does it hurt?' Ludwig said.

'When I can feel it growing,' the man answered.

The girl was going blue.

'Amy,' the man said.

Aesop hadn't thought about giving her a name.

'When did you last see them?' Ludwig said to her at last.

'Three months ago.'

'Dress rehearsal,' the man with the eagle said.

Amy smiled. 'That's right, Sean.'

'There was only half of us.'

'They were all right then. Their faces.'

'But a week later, we all . . .'

Ludwig was touching his own face.

'Well, there's not going to be any play. But he gets to

do his video still,' she finished and left the room. Sean followed her.

Jerry shook hands with Ludwig. He used both hands, enclosing his hand and wrist and pulling it towards his belly, the way men used to having their own hands shaken in that way do. A benevolent gesture, the gesture of benefactors or those sharing condolences.

'You'll use them anyway?'

Jerry nodded.

Aesop wondered whether, with faces like that, they now got more money or less money on the streets.

Jerry gave him a mock salute as if it were something he had agreed on with Ludwig, then they left.

The bathroom door was shut and somebody was running water inside. As they passed, it was pulled open forcefully. Amy stood naked in the doorway without posing and the man, Sean, sat holding a towel out across his arms.

'She's getting in a bath,' was all he could think to say.

'It's too hot for me, it burns.'

'Because you've got too cold.'

Sean, unlike the others, obviously came here often.

Her eyes were so wet they looked as if they had just been spat on and they were heavy with intent.

'Ludwig?' She was much more angry than she had been earlier. 'Don't ever bring uninvited guests round again. Ever. You ask first.'

'Amy . . .'

'No, you ask first. Or bring someone who has the courtesy to ask me my name.'

One of her arms disappeared behind her back and Aesop had the impression that Sean was pulling her gently back. She stood on the top of the stairs for a while and her legs were so thin at the top that her pubes looked like something she had got out of the drawer and put on that morning.

51

'Hey you,' she shouted and for a moment they thought that she was going to run after them, but she stayed where she was.

Sean came up and stood behind her.

'Who gave you your face?' he said suddenly to Ludwig.

Amy didn't lean back against him.

'Nobody,' Ludwig said looking briefly at the triangle of hair between the girl's legs as if checking on the evolutionary progress of a species.

'Who looks after your face then?'

'A woman,' he said.

'I think she likes you,' Ludwig said as they left.

'So what.'

'She'll be dead before Christmas unless she falls in love with that man with the eagle on his face, Sean.'

Aesop wasn't entirely sure, from his tone, that he wanted her to.

'Why didn't you give him the name of your doctor?'

'I think she's probably already looking after his face. She might even have given it to him, and she obviously doesn't want him to know her name.'

He looked down at Aesop. 'Do you know her name?'

'Dr Achilles,' he replied immediately.

'How do you know that?'

'I hear you and Douglas, talking. Is she another secret I've got to keep – I've already got bloody constipation.'

'No, not necessarily. I don't think she's particularly interested in hiding.'

7

The cement steps, cleaned and polished by the feet that walked up and down them, threw the music back up into the air so that the sound was always above. Children lined the stairs, holding on to the railings, many of them girls, many of them dressed in saris, some with anoraks over them. They only glanced at Aesop briefly as he passed, his face upturned as well. The sound made the children still and freed them from the usual vibrations of screaming siblings, desperate mothers and pungent odours at odds with their damp, malignant environment. Perhaps they thought it came from the mosque behind the flats, that it was something their fathers, uncles, brothers and cousins knew about but only *they* could hear. They had the preoccupied look of those unable to determine damnation from salvation. Aesop had never seen so many children before and was trying to work out how many lived behind each usually closed door.

Deirdre was standing in the middle of his flat in her silver jacket. Her well-oiled head was flung back, but as she finished her song she brought it forward and, seeing him, ended on a smile. She shut her mouth and vanished.

'How did you get in?' he said.

'The burglar let me in.'

'You're kidding.'

53

'Course. Your cleaning lady. Your cleaning lady, Aesop.
I mean, since when?'

'Tasha? She let you in?'

'She must have thought I was one of your girls.' She
smiled again.

'What if you were, she shouldn't have let you in.'

'Your flat stinks, Aesop. Can't you clean up after
yourself yet?'

'It's all right.'

'And that man pays for this? And Tasha. Now am I
right or am I right?'

'You're right, Deirdre.'

'And your brother told you you had to take me out.
Am I right or am I right?'

'There were children all the way up the stairs when I
came in.'

'There were?'

She went out the front door and looked down.

'They aren't there any more.'

'They were.'

'Maybe.'

'While you were singing.'

'I can make us some dinner you know.'

'I'm not hungry, thanks.'

She put her hands in her pockets, looking at the
furniture, but unable to sit down.

'So what do you think about what your brother said?'

'About what?'

'About you being my chaperone.'

'Your chaperone?'

'About you taking me out. Tonight.'

'He never said nothing about tonight in particular.'

'Well he should have. I'm singing tonight.'

'I know. I heard you.'

'I'm singing in Brixton. Will you come with me?'

If he had had a concept of the word 'plaintive' he

would have recognised it then. It was such a wide open yawn of a question that the tonsils could be seen at the back of it.

'Will you come with me?' she said again.

He had seen belly dancers before in the *Weetabix Wonder Atlas of the World* Jake gave him and at the Turkish restaurant Ludwig took him to where he gave him money to slide down the girls' bellies. He was vaguely aware when he did this – although he didn't like to admit it – that he was frightened of giving them paper cuts. But Deirdre was out of this kind of reach – in a cage hanging from a golden rope. Even the mechanism it was attached to was painted gold, as was most of Deirdre's body, including her face. She was swinging from side to side over the heads of the dancers, swinging faster than her voice which was always left behind, so that when the cage swung back again, it knocked the song out into the audience.

There were girls and boys dressed like her dancing in front of loudspeakers and the place was full of people who spent whole weekends in perpetual darkness, only seeing daylight briefly through the windows of buses or taxis on their way to bed at six or seven a.m. What made the girls who did this so terrifying was that, despite the leagues of legs, the expense of the costume, the hair contorted into styles that challenged their species, it wasn't even pleasure they were in pursuit of. They should have been courtiers, courtesans, but gave themselves the disability of eunuchs.

So he stood in a corner where it was dark, where he should have found people groping, creasing their clothes, joining in nefarious acts of lovemaking, but instead saw only the occasional individual involved in their own solipsistic activities. He almost wished that Ludwig was with him.

55

After a while he realised that the singing had stopped and that the cage with Deirdre inside was no longer swinging overhead. He went upstairs on to a different dance floor where they were playing a different kind of music and where there was a lounge with sofas. She wasn't up there. It shouldn't have mattered, it shouldn't even have occurred to him to look for her, but it did and he was suddenly worried that someone would realise he was under-age. A year ago the evening wouldn't have seemed worthwhile without the promise of persecution, but now it made him afraid.

His arms were thinner than everyone else's and he was only as tall as some peoples' nipples so that lots of them stroked the top of his head as he passed. He asked if anyone had seen a girl dressed as an Egyptian dancer. It was an image most of them found intriguing, but which made them more interested in him than the dancer. No one, however, confessed to having seen her either recently or when she had been in the cage. Perhaps she had already left, leaving him there alone.

He eventually found her at the end of a corridor in the women's toilets which he went into by mistake because he thought someone was following him. She was stood in front of the mirror, washing her hands.

'Deirdre.' He tried not to rush it, but the relief was too overwhelming.

'There you are. I was good. Right?'

'You were. It sounded beautiful.'

'Well I nearly choked on the bloody smoke from that machine. Some bushman of a DJ did that. But apart from all the machinery, all the effects, you could hear me?'

'You were the loudest thing.' He couldn't hear himself speaking he was so relieved; he would have said anything.

'I was loud?'

'Really loud.'

'You want to stay and dance?'

56

'No.'

She seemed surprised.

Outside he didn't offer her his coat, angry at her for making him want to find her. Angry that it had taken so long and that it had made him afraid. It was snowing on her gold arms and belly. The snow was thick in the passageway behind the club and pushed the big metal bins down into the ground. It hid the rubbish, a heavy London snow that had once been capable of burying the stench of offal at Smithfield market and nowadays silenced the roads and stopped people from going in to work and making their computers buzz. Deirdre was gasping with the cold, the way he had heard girls gasp when his friends lay over the top of them. Her mouth was open and purple. It made her look younger.

After they passed the second mini-cab driver (they always waited near guttering whose overflow they walked through to approach people, mumbling) they fixed a rate with the third who was wearing sandals over his socks. He barely looked at Deirdre and didn't seem as grateful as most of them when they secured a fare; in fact he was almost on the verge of derision.

The back seat – a deep-pile nylon fur – was suitably stained. The car looked as though it had been used as a stunt vehicle for a whole string of made-for-TV action films while the inside smelt as if it spent a lot of time waiting to be sat in. There were no stickers or gimmicks decorating the windows or the dashboard, apart from a faded National Trust badge on the back windscreen which made the possibility of it being a stolen car highly probable.

'You was going to make us take a night bus. Am I right?'

'Maybe,' Aesop mumbled.

'I suppose you've got money for this because I haven't,' Deirdre pointed out.

'Suppose I have, yes.'

Deirdre gave the driver Aesop's address. Mini-cab drivers were sullenly silent, as if they had been forbidden to talk to their passengers. They weren't cabbies, they were men who made a living from their cars.

'Can't make much of a living out of this,' Aesop said at last.

The driver smiled and made it clear he didn't want to answer or start a conversation.

'I mean by the time you've bought petrol and everything. Surely all your fare does is pay for the petrol.'

The man smiled again and this time laughed nervously. Aesop realised that he wasn't asking because he was genuinely interested or concerned but because Deirdre was in the car and he wanted to demonstrate that he had some idea of how the grown-up world worked; he wanted to mock the driver. Even though he had no notion of the whole picture, of the facts – that the man was an illegal immigrant who had bought the car second-hand, who owed money on it, whose two children he didn't dare send to school, whose wife was unable to find a corner to bury herself and keep warm in – he knew that the man was afraid of everything.

They stopped. The mini-cab driver watched as the boy got out first and gave him a ten-pound note then stood waiting for the girl, his arms wrapped about him. He would have liked to live at the top of one of those tower blocks. If his brother managed to get hold of papers for him he was going to appeal to the council for a flat and he had his heart set on the top floor of a tower block, any block, as long as it was at the top.

'You live in there?'

'Used to live somewhere like it.'

'At the top?'

'Nearly.'

'You must have been sad to go. Very sorry?'

Aesop shook his head and laughed.

They moved about the flat in darkness, the light coming through the undrawn windows was a vivid orange from the snow reflecting the sky.

'Can I borrow a jumper?'

Deirdre put the one he gave her on slowly and sat down at the table. The flat smelt a bit better after Tasha had been.

'Can you make us something to drink?' Deirdre said.

'Like what?'

'Tea.'

'I can't make tea.'

'Any alcohol?'

'No, not here . . . I don't have beer or anything in the house.'

'Course not,' she smiled, 'you're under-age.'

'It's not that, I . . .'

'I'm sorry for coming back.'

She stood up and went over to the window. 'Bloody awful view you've got.'

Aesop watched her.

'I'm so lonely at the moment.'

He was sure he remembered his mother saying that when she was still alive. In fact, that's all he remembered her saying.

'Not lonely in the sense of there being no people about you, but lonely when a body knows there's no one even thinking about it, when there's no one desiring it. That lonely. I don't know what to do, Aesop.'

Aesop wasn't sure either. He was afraid of touching her in case she touched him back.

'Jake's seeing somebody else. I know he is.'

'He's not.'

He had never thought of this, and wasn't aware until he heard her speak how much he didn't want this to be the case; he needed them to be together. It stopped his brother from being alone too. He remembered being kept away from school day after day because Jake said he wouldn't be able to see the day through from beginning to end on his own. They would walk all over London, but especially down by the river – they both liked the boats – and sometimes they got in to see a film. Other days Jake would sit at the table behind a transistor set, headphones on, speaking about the world he dreamed of, a utopia, which had been the dream of other men, dreams that had had their time and place, like the men who dreamed them. Now unfashionable, and – Jake knew – a safe dream. By the time Deirdre arrived, dominating, scathing, disbelieving, but able to love on a shoestring, putting in a five-day week was out of the question for Aesop, but only then were his absences officially truances. Whatever Jake's personal ambitions, he would be alone as soon as he took a step away from Deirdre.

'Are you sure?' he said.

'Sure sure.'

She wasn't telling him, she was testing his reaction, she suspected an alibi.

'If he is, I didn't know it. I don't know who she is, if she is. I know he isn't doing this, he isn't.'

'I don't know. But he's never in. My mum says you know when someone loves you because when they touch you they leave their fingerprints behind. Well, last night I covered myself in talc from head to toe and there wasn't a fingerprint to be seen. Not even inside. You know what I mean?' She tried to smile. 'Why do you think he's got you babysitting me?'

'He hasn't, he just doesn't want you to be alone.'

'He isn't even jealous.'

'Of what?'

'Of us going out together. Tonight. Of us maybe

dancing together, maybe coming home together, maybe sitting talking together, maybe finding each other.'

Aesop was pulling at the table leg.

'You wouldn't, would you Deirdre? You wouldn't do that to me, would you?'

'Course not.' But her face looked dull as she said it, even though it was painted gold still. 'Sorry I came tonight.'

'No, you needed to.' He felt that he had never sounded so grown-up before, so tall with reason.

'I'm frightened of going home in case he's not there.'

'You can stay here if you want.' He wanted to say it loudly, firmly, to make her trust him, but it came out quietly, discontented with itself.

'I think I will.'

Tasha had just changed the bed, but he still thought he caught Deirdre sniffing at the air. He managed to give her an old Iron Maiden T-shirt which she clutched to herself.

'I don't believe it. I don't bloody believe it. God Almighty,' she said suddenly crouching over his bedside table. 'An Advent calendar. It's years since I've seen one.'

'So?'

'Look, you've even opened the doors. I'll bet you can tell me how many days till Christmas. Am I right or am I right?'

He stood over her to make sure she didn't mess it up and realised, watching her neck curve away from him, that he could kiss her if he wanted. There were approximately three inches between him and Deirdre becoming lovers. He bent forward an inch further and could see that his breath was roughing up the hairs on the back of her neck. What would he be starting? Deirdre turned round surprised, but not unexpectant, and her eyes were leaning towards him. She wasn't afraid. He took a step back.

8

The light in the ward was dimmed to make it look like candlelight, an intimate moving light that acknowledged a right to privacy. It was the only ward at the hospital inhabited exclusively by children. The rest of the building was given over to treatment rooms and administration where colour snaps of unimagined deformities were passed around with the grubby-fingered rapidity of porn magazines. Perhaps a couple of centuries ago, when hanging was public and to get a place you had to arrive the night before, when you used to pay to see the madmen cavort on a Sunday, the ward would have been open and people might have come to stare or pass through it like a gallery, but these sports were no longer permitted. Monsters were allowed their anonymity.

If they had come, though, even now, they would have stared with the fascination reserved for murderers, the fascination with which newsprint details of a child's death are read. The fascination that makes it difficult to find a space in front of the tank at the aquarium where the man-eating sharks are kept; the fascination that turns the lion's cage at the zoo black with spectators at feeding time. The word 'macabre' doesn't justify or satisfy the appetite the imagination has for death, destruction, and suffering, for discovering what it is we are capable of. What it means to be human.

Ludwig noticed that Dr Achilles touched the children even when she didn't need to; she wasn't examining, dissecting, diagnosing, she was by them because she wanted to be close. The younger ones liked to put their faces against her white coat and her back suited having a small pair of arms locked around it. She rested her chin on their heads when they did this, even those who had no hair because there was virtually no scalp left for it to grow from. The older ones – even the teenage boys – liked to put their hands in hers, but they enjoyed her stroking their arms and faces more, if she transgressed this far.

She was touching them to let them know that, even though she knew the name, history and intimate habits of every disease their bodies wore, she also knew 'their' names. They in turn touched her because the hairs on her wrists didn't stand on end when they did. They were eager to be held by her, yet touched her (despite their eagerness) with the frail tentative hands of the pilgrim, the believer. They believed she had the ability to cure them. Some of them believed more in this ability – he saw – under the pressure of her hand than under the lights in her treatment room. Without her touch they would never be cured. She gave them the hope that they would be 'normal', which they presumed was the only way they would be loved.

Ludwig realised, watching her bend, stoop, recline, and talk with them in a whisper (she couldn't stand noise, he noted), that he didn't believe she would cure him. He had never believed it for one moment. He arrived on her doorstep because he had finally permitted his doctor to refer him to the hospital ten years after his return from the Amazon and he had to be seen to follow the usual course of events so that he could continue to live his life without scrutiny. But the truth of the matter was that he was in no pain, did not perceive himself to be suffering (that was something those who met him underwent) and had not thought to seek to be cured. Dr Achilles knew that she didn't have the power of 'healer' over him.

When he was lying on his back in her treatment room beneath the lights that were blinding, he could only feel an elbow, breast, or hip against him. She knew that she had time on her hands; she gave herself totally to the disease and allowed herself to forget his name. She didn't mind teasing him occasionally, keeping up the pretence between them that he wanted to be cured. It enabled her to be brusque with him. On better days, even a little schoolmarmish.

And she wanted to hear about the Amazon, his Amazon, and about the jungle that the disease followed him out of. Session after session at the clinic she pulled another story out of him so that soon he would have none of the Amazon left inside him. Maybe her guided tour round the hospital and this ward was her way of acknowledging that she knew how much these stories cost him. She liked him watching her at work. She liked to be seen in this role, surrounded by those who believed, so that he was able to see how much easier it could be.

The ward was very high up in the building beneath a sloping roof and the noise of the pigeons nesting was very loud. It didn't feel like a hospital, even though it smelt like one. There were no overhead lights; each bed had its own side lamp which cast a masquerade of shadows across faces already disguised as themselves. Not one child had the same disease, and not one of these diseases (most of them relatively common) failed to touch the child's face.

These children liked shadows, and weren't afraid of the dark. It was something they waited for. The only place where a voice and a body didn't need a face. When Dr Achilles left them she said, 'goodnight'.

Downstairs in her office Ludwig was given an ordinary chair to sit on for the first time; he had only ever lain down in there before. She made them coffee from a trolley unlike the one he had already seen in the room on previous visits; there were chocolates on it and the machinery needed to make the drinking of coffee into a ceremony. The chocolates didn't suit her and he wondered if she also kept alcohol on the premises.

'I didn't know there were wards.'

'That's the only one.'

'How long do they have to stay?'

'They don't. Those children on the ward have admitted themselves. Or asked their parents to. They can't stay any longer than a fortnight. There's no reason for them to be here. They receive the same treatment they do regularly in any treatment room, on any regular visit to the clinic.'

She started to push the trolley backwards and forwards as the kettle boiled, moving it like a pram.

'You're one of the few people they've seen up on the ward.'

'But I don't count, I look like them.'

She didn't answer this.

'The only other one, in fact, is a Chinese herbal doctor I use.'

'Do they like him?'

'They like the things he brings with him.'

She didn't ask him how he took his coffee, she just gave him a cup with the milk already poured in.

'So you see there are others worse off than you.'

'Is that why you took me upstairs? I never asked for reassurance on that front. They're younger than me.'

'Have you any idea what it's like at that age, Mr James, not to exchange looks with a girl or boy, not to see them

65

smile when they see you, to know that you won't make someone short of breath by just walking past with your head held at a certain angle, not to be able to sit next to someone in a dark cinema, in the back of a car, or on their bed even, and wonder where they're going to touch you next and what it's going to feel like. They are – most of them – at the age where they are head over heels in love with themselves. They come here because they've braved a term at school looking like they do and can't stand it any longer. They know – even if only subconsciously – that it makes their parents relieved to know they have a week in front of them without having to round a corner of their house, open a door and realise that they've forgotten their son or daughter looked like they did. To be free for a week from the strain of hoping that, one morning, their children might come down to breakfast well again...'

'But they don't.'

'They come here and I allow them to stay in bed for the entire fortnight. Staying in bed during daylight hours is one of the most disorientating feelings. If you're bedridden for a fortnight you feel changed when you at last get up again and leave the bed behind. You're standing. Something which immediately effects the sensation in them of being cured, and gives them the strength they need to return home. For a while.'

This made her smile.

'During the time they are on the ward they receive the prescribed treatment they would usually receive on visits, but when it's time to go they feel they have received more of a "cure". Do you know what it means for them to have to step out of here and walk down into Leicester Square? The winter's bad enough, but in the summer when everyone has a piece of leg, shoulder, neck or back to show, they're the ones that make everyone else feel lucky.'

'But I know all this.'

She looked down briefly at the paper on her desk.

'I heard that you were advised of us and that you were reluctant at first.'

'Maybe I was reluctant. I don't remember. Did you know Dr Blackthorn?' he said.

She paused for a moment. 'Very well.'

'How many of those children will you cure?'

'None of them.'

He suddenly realised that she hadn't touched his face at all today.

'I will cure them temporarily and I will do a maestro's job of disguising what can't be cured. They will all be almost cured. The disease may or may not come back. Perhaps it will leave scars, but there are machines that use light to disguise, heal. Even if they are cured – and sometimes they cure themselves or the disease vanishes overnight – they will always be people who were once ill. If you are diagnosed as having cancer and later cured, you can only ever be someone who has once had cancer, because you've known the disease. These children, this colony of lepers I have upstairs, don't suffer from disease, they live beneath it. They don't know what they look like any more. Perhaps they have mothers who forget to kiss them now.'

'So you introduce leper to leper.'

'I don't run a matchmaking service.'

'What a thought.' He got up. 'Going away for Christmas?'

'I don't know.'

She went over to the window, hands in pockets. 'It's started to snow again.'

They heard the feet, two floors up, running across the newly painted boards as the children ran out of their beds and over to the windows.

Whatever her mood, Achilles always got up from her chair to show people out, as if she wanted to make sure they actually left. Today she shook hands for the first time without her surgical gloves on. She looked hard at him. It was the look of someone committing a face to memory. She had taken pictures with a camera previously, something which had bothered him more than he thought it would.

In the lobby downstairs there was a man waiting. He was walking about as if he had been given a designated area to walk in and, as Ludwig approached, he went to look at the Honours Board.

'Hello,' the man said looking round, but staying near the wall.

Ludwig was about to pass on. The man's hair had grey dust in it, and he looked as if he had been forcibly stretched at some stage in his life, as if there had been a time when a machine aided his growth and his spine now had its work cut out trying to bear his weight and make him resemble something close to other men.

'Excuse me, is Dr Achilles about?'

'She is. I've just been to see her.'

'Oh.' This obviously bothered the man and made his eyes go thick. 'Could you tell me where her room is?'

'On the third floor. She's got her name on the door.'

He didn't go up immediately, but waited for Ludwig to leave.

In the car afterwards Ludwig felt as though he had been talking to a shadow, and looking up at the building found it hard to believe that Dr Achilles and the ward of children were still in there.

Ludwig's back was warm from where Douglas had touched it, helping him into the car. Everything was unsure of itself in the light from the snow. Tonight London from a distance would look – he knew – as if the phosphorescence from the sewers had finally outwitted bricks, mortar and tarmac.

'You got your snow,' Douglas said.

'It snowed last week as well.'

'Somebody heard your prayers.'

'Well, it wasn't a prayer; I didn't want it that badly.'

'Good as, and you got it.'

'Yes I did. I saw it from the window. Do you think it will lie?'

'It will. It's cold enough and thick enough.'

Ludwig didn't want to eat out tonight. Eating out still in all the best restaurants was one of those things he had been very adamant about after he came back from Jara. The waiters, no matter how well-trained they were, couldn't help staring. He watched them fighting with themselves but, in the end, they had to look and it was with the fascination born of repulsion.

The people he dealt with were more wary of him than they had been before because his face rendered threats impotent. It was difficult for them to eat in front of him, difficult for them even to handle their cutlery which they did so awkwardly that they ate like men forced to forgo a place promised them in paradise. They could find nothing on their menus they could even contemplate eating, confronted by him. If negotiations went badly he sometimes took to touching his face, wondering if they thought it was something he had inflicted on himself.

Sometimes when they arrived at a restaurant they were given a different table from the one they had booked, or shown to it too quickly. They were always first to be seated and served. Once they had left he was sure the table linen was taken off – possibly binned – and the chairs removed to the kitchen where they could be bleached. Waiters held menus he had touched away from them, then tried to make it up to him afterwards by asking him if he had enjoyed his food. Telling people that the disease wasn't contagious, that it was interested in him alone, would have rendered him impotent at the table and elsewhere. Instead, rumours of contagion made him infamous.

'Don't go to the restaurant, Douglas. Take me to Aesop's.'

'Are you sure?'

'Tell them that there were some complications at the clinic this afternoon. That should warm their imaginations up a bit. And, yes, I am sure.'

The snow was slowing the traffic down. He enjoyed the disruptive power of the weather: high winds, torrential rains, heat that killed people, and snow. The landscape in the books he had read as a child always had snow in them; snow debilitated the everyday, giving more elbow space for the extraordinary.

'Your children will be pleased,' Ludwig said.

'It doesn't mean as much as it used to, when they were little.'

'Do you tuck your children in at night, Douglas?'

'Course not. I'd be arrested . . .'

'But you used to?'

'When I could. When I was there.'

'Even if . . .'

'When I could be there,' he cut in. 'And when I couldn't, I would phone Maggie and ask her to keep their lights on so that, when I got in, I could go upstairs and watch them sleeping. There's nothing like watching a child sleeping. You know that, even when they're having nightmares, they're always the ones that the nightmares are happening to. It's them that are getting chased, hit, punished, locked up, drowned. Whatever. But they're never the ones doing the chasing. Do you know what I mean?'

Ludwig shook his head, watching Douglas in the mirror.

'In a child's nightmare he never gives himself the limitless power to inflict we do.' Douglas smiled to himself. 'I'd kiss them on the forehead or cheek. Enough pressure to let them know I hadn't forgotten, but not enough to wake them up. I was always the one to turn their lights out.'

Ludwig leant his head back against the seat.

'Was there anything else?'

'No nothing,' Ludwig finished.

9

Before Achilles had joined the hospital, Dr Blackthorn had written letter after letter to her and, among crippled declarations of love and mean-minded attempts at black-mail, he had talked of Ludwig whom he had never met, but who had been the subject of much correspondence. She remembered one letter in particular where he had described Ludwig making as much use of his disease as it made of him. It was almost as if it was what he went into the jungle looking for. He had never asked to be cured. The only thing he had ever asked for was some-thing to relieve the itching at night. The borealis came unchristened by any Western tongue which was why she had to watch it so carefully. She had virtually no knowledge of its nature, its behavioural patterns, its appetites, its ambitions or desires.

One of the things she had realised as a student, and she had noticed this most with cancer cases as well as the more full-bodied terminal diseases, was that diseases often changed their minds. They had their own gestation period, a pre-life, infancy, middle age, and old age, and some decided to die earlier than others. When a miracle cure occurred it was often in a case where an elderly disease decided it didn't have the strength to claim or cannibalise (her word) its host and so died peacefully, leaving the patient carrying the corpse of a terminal disease that no longer threatened his or her life. Alternatively a miracle might seem to occur when a very young disease didn't want to bring its own life to an untimely end and so prolonged the host's death by lying fallow for anything up to ten years before deciding that it had had enough, at which point it would strike the host suddenly dead.

Some diseases were more involved with their hosts than others, but, in the end, they all behaved with the hedonism of children who don't know what it means to be someone else. Those that attacked children were the most vicious, capable of changing children as young as four into adults overnight. But these were the exceptionally intelligent diseases, and the most malignant were the non-fatal.

The non-professional, i.e. the general public, only ever saw disease in this light when it confronted them as an epidemic. Epidemics showed the nature of the beast. Diseases – even within the same family – varied in intellectual and emotional appetite. But Dr Achilles looked everything in the face, keeping in sight the simple fact of their inferiority. Anything that relied on anybody or anything else for survival showed a predilection for weakness. Disease, whatever form it took, needed a carrier; it was unable to stand on its own two feet. It needed its host for survival, an impotence that undermined – continually – its own existence and this was why she wasn't afraid. This was why she was able to touch and lay hands on it without fear.

When Ludwig left later that evening, she remembered Dr Blackthorn saying with a smile that Ludwig was himself 'involved in the skin trade', and before she had had time to react he had held his hand up (in the most nauseating way) to stop her speaking and said, intimately, 'Not in the way you think'.

Dr Achilles worked late at the hospital. All the children were asleep by the time she left and the night nurses were making porridge for themselves and complaining that heating was cut on their shift.

She was tired, which was never something she admitted to, only something she realised, and because of it got on the wrong tube line ending up not at Highgate, but at Hampstead instead, a station she hated (something else she never admitted to) because of the U-bend passageways and pillars that disguised every danger known to woman. There were lifts that took you to street level, a journey that lasted long enough for the amateur or professional alike to decide on murder or worse. Not that she minded murder as much as other things.

Tonight her bags were light; she only had her financial assets and some photos of Ludwig on her. Ludwig had impressed her. Lots of adults, official adults over the age of eighteen, cried in her treatment room, cried because they couldn't go on but didn't know how to stop; or they just cried because the tears stung their faces. It wasn't always their faces, sometimes it was genitalia or other locations, such as one man whose back looked like part of a permanent display of corporal punishment from British naval history.

The shops had stayed open later because of the snow and the season. The hardware store had even uncovered a stock of sledges from somewhere and children had been kept up. People were out, spending money. The snow was thick, so thick that it was already breaking up the routine of things. There were more people than she thought there would be on the heath, and the snow was reflecting the light, giving the effect of daylight diluted in the wrong measure of water.

By the time she had circled the black frozen bathing ponds, the noise of other people had died down and there were no further footsteps in the snow which was already – in some places – up to her knees, making walking difficult. But when she reached open heath and started moving away from the trees where the snow thudded on the branches, she knew she had a shadow and that the shadow had probably followed her from the hospital. He would be sweating in the knowledge that all she had to do was turn her head once over her shoulder and he would be recognised, uncovered. Not that the thought hadn't crossed her mind that he wanted to be discovered. His footsteps were sounding more and more vigorous in the snow.

She stopped. The sky around her was big because of the silence. The falling snow sounded like somebody breathing in their sleep. It covered everything that was glaringly human about the city. It slowed it down, gave it different rhythms, a different timetable, a different clock. The heath, under snow, became a brave, triumphant place, its paths and fences no longer apparent.

'Blackthorn?' she said without turning around. 'This is a long way from Hornby.'

She thought he had stopped when she started to speak and was surprised, when he laid a hand on her shoulder, to find that he had silently reached her side. He was either going to kill her and bury her in the snow or cry. Eyes made foolproof betrayals.

The cold makes the body luscious in a different way from heat. It lets the skin fade to white only to show the raw blue of the veins. It uncovers proof that the body is alive. Blackthorn's eyes became less droll while his nails went an umbilical blue and his lips an obscene red. Red, white and blue. His look was so open she almost fell in love with herself.

'You were following me.'

'I'm sorry.'

'You know I don't like it. You're not even supposed to be here.'

'You never called,' he said.

'What are you doing here?'

'I know that you can't see where exactly I fit into your schedule,' – he was trying to make himself sound reasonable; she started walking again – 'but after giving you Ludwig James I thought I might hear something.'

'Why?'

'I can get you more people.'

'More people? You should learn to ask me questions. I can find my own people; this is my city.'

Although he was obviously feeling the cold, he didn't attempt to pull the large wool coat he was wearing around him. Blackthorn had always glistened, always had an edge to him; she was never sure if glamour was something he strove for.

'You've got a long journey home, Blackthorn.'

He looked at her as she moved away. The snow was falling so thickly now it was all that could be smelt. The brightness had passed and there was virtually no sound. Their hair stuck to their faces in hard-hearted black lashes.

'Don't move. I'll lose you,' he said.

She didn't want him to touch her.

'I need to start walking, I'm getting cold. Don't touch me.'

'Don't leave me.'

'Don't touch me.' She felt the panic, the sudden heat of it shooting about inside her as she tried to run through the snow and, when he finally laid his hands on her, she screamed which was something she had never done before. Even though he didn't step back, it put a wall of sound between them and she could see that the scream hurt him because it wasn't afraid, it was angry.

She was beginning to fall and, rather than helping her, he pushed her further down so that the snow pressed into the back of her head. His body was violently warm.

'I read a story once about a man who got lost in the forest in the snow. He walked round and round in circles the whole night – probably round the same tree – until in the end, just before dawn, he fell asleep in the snow from exhaustion. In the morning he was found by his wife. The tree was less than ten paces from his house.'

'I know that story. That's just the kind of writer you would read. Don't make me your horizon.'

Their breath tickled their gritted teeth as they spoke.

'I remember you,' he said, not taking his hands off her to wipe his hair from her face. 'I remember that night I saw you. I'll always remember you, I'll always see you there.'

The words had no echo; even the heath rejected them. So she filled the night around her with her laughter instead, which came out loud and clear even with him lying on top of her. He always made her laugh. He had once knelt before her, but she had managed to step on his hands with her heels, only moving them when his eyes registered pleasure instead of pain.

'I remember turning the corner.'

'Why do you follow me?'

He looked at her almost tenderly.

'I had my torch on and my beam picked you up coming out from behind those bins; you stepped into that beam and waited for me to reach you.'

'I couldn't see you,' she reminded him.

'You just waited and you had a case in your hand. You looked like a dying man's dream.'

'You have to stop believing in me.'

She could smell his aftershave and was disconcerted to find that she recognised it – worse, that she remembered it. It was something he wore and, other than this, he had no smell. People who smelt had never-ending bodies,

77

bodies you couldn't escape from, bodies that impressed themselves on you leaving sweating stains on the memory; Blackthorn stopped almost as soon as he began.

They were beginning to struggle without knowing to what intent.

As she tried to turn her head away she saw, coming towards them across the snow from higher ground, a man in a long overcoat wearing a scarf that had been wrapped around his neck too many times. He was walking with a stick, a fancy stick made of black with a silver top on it. He was what her uncle would have called an 'Indian gentleman'.

He was picking his way over the snow as if he didn't want to leave an impression on it, but was definitely making his way towards them which was – she knew – a brave thing to do. Unless he was coming not to aid but to abet. As he got closer he started to run. He was one of those people who looked wrong running, but he made good speed. Blackthorn rolled over and lay beside her in the snow on his back, his mouth open. She tried to move away from the coat, worried that she would smell the same as him, when suddenly the man was upon them shouting, 'My dear, my dear,' but because of the snow it sounded like, 'Midas, Midas.' Blackthorn tried to get to his feet but couldn't determine which was sky and which was heath so threw his arms out and abandoned himself to gravity. As he did, the 'Indian gentleman' pulled the top of his walking stick off and this time shouted, 'Midas, don't worry, don't worry,' and, 'Get away, get away.'

A sword came out of the stick; he drew it out triumphantly and with a smile. It was the kind of smile that needed a moustache to become fully accomplished. They all paused and looked at each other, then the Indian gentleman started to scream, 'Run, run' at Dr Achilles. And she ran.

10

Aesop found Deirdre's hairs on the pillow, and a circle of gold where she had pressed her cheek in sleep. She hadn't touched him, but there was the odd trace of gold dust to show that he had fallen asleep in her arms, that he had lain with her arm under his neck and her other arm round his belly, and that his back had pressed against her where her costume didn't cover her. At a glance his spine would look like an object of value, each nobble of bone gold-tipped.

Deirdre had made him warm and let him sleep on the side nearest the wall which was where he felt safest. He put the bedroom light on and there was the gold outline of a body on the bed, like the outlines the police used to show where bodies had died. Despite the bland overhead light it looked like a prince had died in his bed. The telephone rang.

'Aesop?'

'Deirdre, you left.'

'I had to. Don't worry. I wasn't sleeping.'

'What was it?'

'He's not here. I wanted to know if . . . he probably isn't, but I thought he might have come to yours.'

'He's not here.'

'Well he didn't broadcast his show last night.'

'He'll come home.'

'Will he?'

'Course he will. It's his home.'

The last hour was still in her voice: the journey home, the flat with no lights, the door double-locked; the room exactly the same as when she had left it. She had lain on the sofa for thirty minutes listening for the sound of his footsteps on the stairs. Every twitch the building made, every time it breathed, it announced his arrival, until the sounds stopped and he didn't come. She was straining so hard that the blood in her ears began to fill the room with people. Then she had moved over to the radio set.

'Aesop, I need you to find something for me. When I came to your house last night I had some papers with me; it was the script Jake gave me for last night's show.'

'You read his scripts?'

'I read and comment on them.'

'I didn't know he wrote them out beforehand.'

'It doesn't matter.'

'And you help him? He never said you helped him.'

'He's got nothing to hide, Aesop, right?'

'I just never knew.'

'He works hard; all night. I know no money crosses his palms, but he works hard. You know that, don't you.'

'I know he does.'

'Well find me the script, I left it at your place.'

'Leave it, Deirdre, he'll broadcast it tonight instead.'

'What if he doesn't come back?'

'He will. He's probably on his way now.'

'I need to do it now, Aesop. It was meant to go out last night and maybe . . .'

'Maybe what?'

'Maybe he'll be listening. Maybe it's a test, maybe he's waiting to see what I'll do, to see how much it matters to me. He might be listening.'

'I can't. It wouldn't matter if I did find it. It wouldn't

make no difference. I can't read,' he said at last.

'Right.'

'No, I can't.'

'That true?'

'Nothing apart from numbers, my own name, and some brand names.'

'Your own brother brought you up to be a moron.'

'Said I wouldn't need to, said I'd be happier.'

'He did, did he? You know why?'

'No.'

'You can't think why?'

'No.'

'Cause he wanted to keep you all to himself; that's why.'

11

She waited for two hours, despite the memory of the sword-stick, in the knowledge that tall, sprawling men often possess a deranged strength when provoked, a strength that seems to come from an inherent sense of outrage. At 2 a.m. she took the liberty of presuming him defeated or dead and, with relief and a certain sense of pride, she left the flat.

She had a passion for alleyways and could navigate most of this narrower, darker, potent London in her sleep. People came here to enact the bravest of their desires, without the fear of retribution that daylight brought. The alleyways made even the vilest of these seem permissible. It was where people came when they took a step out of everyday life, when they stopped being afraid. Lovers and strangers came to fuck against wet walls, sometimes against their will. Men and dogs came to spray their urine into puddles on the ground. People came to do things it was easier to do here out of the sight of daylight and other people, but within earshot. They came to take their own lives, or each other's. Bodies were left by giant bins overflowing with rubbish. When you came often, you knew who you could meet and when you would meet them.

The snow had kept a lot of people away and made the

alley brighter than usual. There was a strip where it was melting, the strip that lay directly above the Northern Line. Tonight she came looking for Sean, the man with the eagle tattooed across his face. Even in this light she could see the bird's head on his forehead, its beak on the bridge of his nose, its talons hooked over his mouth and its wings spread across his cheeks. In the early days she had contemplated a disguise, but realised that a wig and dark glasses were not only an unnecessary gesture but one that would incite the police to pick her up immediately. As a doctor she would only ever be beyond reproach in the eyes of the law. So Sean and his friends saw her as her patients saw her, only the patients came looking for her, not she for them.

Tonight Sean was teaching an old man to skip with a rope and the old man, who had a portrait of the Queen tied to his back, kept falling.

'Sean.'

They both looked at her.

'Found you has she,' the old man mumbled, seeing Dr Achilles walking towards them down the alley, 'Oh dear, found you, dearie me, and here of all places, here with me, well go on, you, she's found you, I'll keep mum, I will, go on, make the most of it.'

'You should put some plastic over that painting of yours,' she said to the old man. 'It'll get ruined in this snow otherwise.'

'Oh you've found him all right, you've found him,' he said ignoring her, then shuffled off with the rope further back into the alley as Dr Achilles stepped closer and took hold of Sean's face.

'It's really taken hold, considering your diet, your skin tissue, muscles, and your general state of health. It likes you.'

She smelt her fingers briefly before she let them drop.

'Happy? Is my face pretty enough for you?' Sean said.

83

'No, I'm never happy. Was it worth the money?'

'Don't know yet, do I?'

'Well there's going to be another fifty pounds today and one last injection.'

'Fine.' He looked at her. 'So, Doctor, has it been worth the money for *you*?'

'The money and the trouble. I might need to do some further scraping,' she said still looking at his face.

'Ouch.' He stood back in mock terror.

She pulled the blindfold out of her bag and tied it tightly over his head, trying not to touch his stinking hair. He was always very helpful with the blindfold, holding it over his eyes and telling her if he could still see.

Usually four or five cabs passed before they could find one to take them. When one eventually pulled in she gave the cabbie a piece of paper with her address on. Those that stopped were usually the younger ones – they had even had a woman driver once and last week the cabbie had rolled two joints for Sean and called him a lucky bugger. When they arrived he had asked if he could come in and Sean had said, 'You wouldn't want to, mate.' The blindfold covered most of Sean's face which gave them one thing less to look at in the rear-view mirror.

The cabbies listened to too much radio – she found – and had state of the heart theories on Britain. It was very much Britain to them. 'England' seemed to have dropped out of fashion. Tonight's agreed with everything Sean said (and he always had something to say), responding with a 'too right', and again, 'too right', as if the truth were at last being spoken. He said it with a real spitting vehemence, especially after Sean's diatribe about violent clashes between animal rights protestors and homeless people. When they got out the cabby shook his head and said, 'You'll be all right. Good luck to you, you'll be all right, you know.'

They went inside. It was really quite good, even if it wasn't your thing. Not exactly a rip off of the Sistine chapel, but painted so that it was reminiscent of it. Lots of sky, lots of Venus–shell clouds, animals with wings, men with beards, and chariots. There was something about the chariots that made you tilt your head back and open your mouth. The ceiling had been painted by a friend of hers, now dead.

The rough wet shadows on Sean's coat, hands and face made everything in her flat look delicate, even the corner where she kept the photos, tools and samples that you needed to have lived through the twentieth century to bear.

The tray rattled as his fingers grazed the equipment on it.

'Scalpel,' he said holding it up to the light. 'Every household should have one.'

'It's the medical equivalent of the sonic boom.'

'It is?'

'It amputates faster than the speed of sound, leaving you to step into the pain, the realisation, afterwards.'

'Aren't you afraid, living here alone with your scalpel?'

It was a question that a smile was sufficient for and he didn't ask again.

She had a large chair she used for reading in with a lamp above it, and that was where Sean sat. Tonight she gave him a painkiller, not to prevent him from experiencing any pain, but purely because it was part of a professional procedure: it was hygienic and made the process quicker so that she didn't have to give the patient as much attention. She gave it like a dentist, through the inside of the cheek and the needle was so thin it was like fusewire. She knew it hurt him (and she had told him it would) because the eagle on his face raised its beak slightly and frowned. It was as difficult to gauge suffering

85

in a tramp's body as it was in a child's. 'Tramps'. She liked that word; 'homeless' was too specific, a state rather than an occupation. The last time Sean was in the flat she had watched as he took off his boots and ripped his big toenail off, throwing it across the room. As the body deteriorated it seemed able to discard the bits that weren't absolutely necessary. She put a new blade on the scalpel.

Sean lay back staring at the ceiling, convinced that the eyes painted there were blinking.

'Makes me feel dizzy, this, watching all those dirty old men and naked children up there. Do you suffer from vertigo?'

'Vertigo? I haven't heard that word for years. Yes, I do.'

'Do you know why you're afraid of heights?' He was smiling through his teeth as he said this. 'You're afraid you'll be tempted to throw yourself over. That feeling you have in your stomach when you're standing on the edge is the certainty that, unless someone stops you, you'll throw yourself over. You don't trust yourself.'

Then she was next to him, standing above him.

'It's hot in here,' he said.

'I don't like being cold, and I see no reason to be when I can afford to keep myself warm. If you're too hot you can take your coat off, but I'd rather you didn't because you stink enough as it is and it might distract me.' She made a small incision to the right of his ear, then pulled the scalpel across the cheek towards this organ so that the thinnest, most transparent layer of skin curled round the blade like a peeling. There was a lot of blood and discharge from the sore and she had to get him to hold a small urine sample pot below his ear.

'Are you dreaming?' she demanded.

'Always do.'

'Different dreams? Greener dreams?'

86

'Don't know what you mean.'

'Do you dream of trees?' she explained.

'No,' he said shortly, but he didn't sound confused and she didn't know whether he was just saying 'no' because he knew she wanted to hear 'yes'.

He had just wiped the blood already running down his neck away with his sleeve and got the sample pot in place when he sneezed. The peeling settled on the end of her nose where it curled itself around the point.

'I never could do that,' he said pointing at her as she crossed her eyes and removed the peeling with tweezers.

'Try not to do it again.' She laid the piece of his face down in the tray. 'It's got your sneeze on it now and the germs from this may interfere – even if only in a rudimentary way – with the structure of the disease.' She turned to look at him. His eyes were bloodshot; they went bloodshot after ten minutes of being inside under electric lights. He had also started to squint and rub his forehead.

'It's the dust; the dust in here, it's a different kind from outside.'

'I suppose it is.'

He smiled at her. His teeth were brown and his jawline deformed in the way only hardship (like torture) deforms a body – irremediably – but it was a smile because it recognised itself as such.

'Where are we then?'

'London.'

'Knew you would say that,' and he looked down at his lap and laughed. 'Wouldn't think it's nearly Christmas, would you?'

'It's snowing.'

'In here I mean.'

'I hadn't noticed.'

'No tree. Nothing. No decorations. Only unopened

87

cards on the table by the door. Why don't you open them?'

'I will.'

'They'd look nice up there.' He pointed at the mantelplace above the fire, but she didn't answer.

'What sort of person can resist the temptation to open mail addressed to them? Do you want me to open them for you?'

'I haven't had time.'

'I would do anything for a letter. With my name on it. I'm still writing letters, you know. I've got people to write letters to.' He looked up at her again. 'Love letters. But I don't get none back. That's the difficult part. I don't even get to see a postman. You know that's something, I haven't seen a postman in years. Closest I get is you and that white envelope you hand me in exchange for my face. But hand-delivered isn't the same as when you get something man-handled, something somebody's paid to send you.'

She put the blindfold back on as he talked then walked with him to the door. She tried – usually with success – to pick people from the streets who had either left their soul in their mother's womb, or at some later stage pissed it out of their body; ones that didn't talk. Sean talked and had been a mistake; he had tentacles, long tentacles, and all she wanted, due to the unorthodox nature of her work, was a face. Sean – to his credit – was more than this.

'I miss my face. Not looking at it, because they tell you not to do that; I miss getting it touched. There's someone', he seemed embarrassed, 'who used to touch my face, but who doesn't now, who doesn't think to. It won't be long will it?'

She picked up an envelope from the table by the door ignoring him. 'Here, you can take this unopened Christmas card as well, that's one less you have to feel responsible for.'

He put both envelopes in his pocket; he was the only one who didn't open his in front of her, and she knew that he would leave the card in his pocket until Christmas day.

12

'Music? Music?' Jake said, coming through the door of the flat, snow melting in his hair.

Deirdre didn't hear him; she was sitting hunched over his mouthpiece and had completely re-wired their audio equipment. She was wearing clothes he recognised, but that weren't his, and he could see the first knob of her spine at the base of her neck moving as she swung her head from side to side.

'Music?' he shouted at last. He couldn't think of anything else to say, he was surrounded by it. He never listened to it if he could help it, because it distorted things. Which was why he wore earplugs when she sang, and called himself a 'passive listener' if she put music on and it filled the flat while he sat there and had nowhere else to go. She called his hatred a 'dangerous' habit. He could only see music as the generator of false emotions, the spreader of untruths. 'It makes you feel things you don't really feel,' he had said to her once. It was the first properly rounded malignant thing he had ever said to her. They both always remembered it.

She turned around and watched him fall on the sofa. His hair was covering his face and there were wet patches on his orange coat. She watched him for a while, turning dials in a calculating fashion with her left hand, then she went off air and the music stopped.

'I don't know how you do it every night, it's exhausting.'

He watched her face, she was trying hard to smile to stop herself from crying.

'I can't believe you played music on my air waves; I can't believe you did this.' He forced himself off the sofa and started to unplug the wires, pulling the power to sound out of machine after machine, with filthy nails.

'You were testing me. Am I right?'

'No, I wasn't testing you.'

'You stayed out to tune in, didn't you? To see if I would pick up where you left off?'

'The thought never occurred to me.'

'To see if I would take the cue; to see if I would let you go blank tonight or put you out on the air. You were testing me.'

'I forgot about the show.'

'Because you've never forgotten a show. Or missed one. I knew you'd tune in to hear.'

'I forgot about the show.'

'To find out whether someone else jumped in on your waves, or whether I'd keep them busy, and I kept them busy. I imagined you laughing when you heard my voice.'

'I haven't laughed all night.'

'But the only thing I could think to do was play music, dance music.'

'Well why don't you put your music back on and just shut up.'

Then she knew it was like the dream she had had where they argued and he shut a set of double doors painted green on her. And when she opened them his face hadn't changed; he was still angry at her, and she knew that this argument was different. They had argued before, in fact they were always arguing, because they loved arguing, especially with each other. This time it was different because he felt no remorse, and would never feel remorse again. He wouldn't bite his lower lip, go down on his knees and nuzzle her thighs, hold her from behind so tightly she didn't think to breathe, rub his nose in her ear saying, 'Sorry, sorry'. Now when she cried, he would just watch and wait for her to finish.

So she tried not to cry.

'What was I to do? You weren't here. I came home, Jake, and you weren't here.'

'Nothing, you should have done nothing.'

He hated her for wanting to surprise him, for wanting to make him pleased with her, for not shouting at him, and not hitting him. For letting her face light up and not keeping it in check when she saw that he was home.

And to stop himself from crying, he picked her up suddenly, blindly, and held her to him, so that she could smell him. 'I hate myself,' he said rubbing his face violently across hers; 'I hate myself.' She knew that this was the beginning of the end, but that she would hold on because it was in her nature to, and so she held on to handfuls of his hair because it made him easier with her when she hurt him, especially when she hurt him while he was giving her pleasure. While he had his head between her legs and could feel her thighs warming his ears and could taste her on the tip of his tongue before he reached her. In return he was frivolous with her, which was difficult for him because he wasn't a frivolous man, and she nearly mistook this frivolity for the impetuousness of someone in love.

As he came she placed her hands round his throat. He had a scrawny throat and her hands were able to join together around it, as she remembered the emptiness of the flat she came back to at dawn.

She sat curled against him in the morning light, watching him as he winced in his sleep remembering the first time they had met and how she had been somebody then.

13

Aesop had watched *The Wizard of Oz* and now he was watching snooker, had been watching, in fact, since midday, only moving to feed himself or alleviate his bladder and (more infrequently) bowels. He knew he was waiting for Ludwig to arrive, and that he wouldn't go out until he did. He hadn't gone anywhere on his own, or at least of his own free will, for the last fortnight, apart from the despatching of parcels during the day and even this was becoming difficult for him. No, it was more than difficult, it was traumatic. It had taken him an hour the other day to work himself up to leaving the flat, walking down the stairs and one hundred yards to the corner shop to buy a pint of milk.

Last week he almost went to school, but by three p.m. he was still sat on the sofa in his uniform. He remembered the special needs teacher at school who had been in love with him, and whom he used to make cry. Who gave them presents at Easter and Christmas and who had given him her telephone number once in a glaring (and inappropriate) display of courage. He nearly phoned her the morning he put his uniform on to ask her if she would wait for him at the school gates or, better still, meet him at his flat so that they could walk together. What finally deterred him from picking up the phone was the sight of his legs between the top of his socks and the bottom of his trousers when he sat down, and his wrists which left the ends of his jumper sleeves far behind. He had outgrown the uniform, blatantly.

He had no belief or interest in the past and knew when he left anywhere that the space he left behind was soon filled, and that there would be no space for him if he tried to go back. The special needs teacher might or might not still love him, but even if she came to collect him and they walked to school together, there wouldn't be space for him.

When the buzzer finally went, it wasn't Ludwig, it was Deirdre, dressed in her Kwik Save outfit, which didn't bring her down at all.

She waited, kissed him on the forehead then sat down.

'I switched on the radio after you left.'

'You heard me?'

'I did. I heard the music.'

'It was good music, wasn't it?'

'Did he kill you? I lay in bed listening and I was thinking music makes his stomach turn, he's going to kill her. It was good of you, though. Taking on the air like that; I know you won't have heard it from him, but it was good of you.' He watched her twisting the rings on her hands. 'You must love him lots,' he said carefully, realising how much he needed it confirmed. 'I mean you must really love him.' He waited again, but Deirdre got up and went through to his bedroom where she opened a drawer looking for something to change into.

'How much do you love him?'

Then he heard the bed taking her weight and realised that he was glad she was here. He hadn't seen anyone in a while; his friends had their own idea of what 'spiv' meant and stayed clear most of the time. He wondered where they took their girls now. His bed had been clean for weeks and he missed the heady smell of semen that made him feel safe. He was glad she was here. Whatever it meant, he was glad.

She had burrowed down into the bed; only her hair still covered the pillow.

'I wasn't going to do this,' she said from underneath the cover. 'I wasn't going to do this. I told myself not to, but here I am doing it.' She was breathing heavily and wimpering like someone in too much pain to cry. 'He wasn't there. He wasn't there, Aesop.'

He sat there watching her, thinking of the snot that was probably on his duvet now from all that snivelling. And he realised that he felt angry, not just with her, but with both of them. Angry that they couldn't just hold on and keep it together, that they had to go and make trouble for everyone and bring attention to themselves like a couple of kids. They had found each other hadn't they? Something had brought them together, hadn't it? Why couldn't it be left at that, why did they have to put so much effort into changing the order of things, why was everyone so obsessed with happiness? He wasn't on the look out for his, he had no idea what made him happy. He was just glad he had found that there was a country between happiness and unhappiness, even if he didn't know its name.

'I wasn't going to do this, but he wasn't there. You've got no idea what that kind of emptiness is like, it's not even black, and nobody can fill it. I'm right, you know.'

'But he came back.'

'Oh yes, he came back.'

'Well then,' he couldn't help saying.

'Only half back.'

She pushed the covers off her. Her face was blotchy and paler than it had ever been. There were tears still stuck to the mascara on her eyelashes and her lips looked a chewed purple. The eyes were so wet they did nothing but reflect and he couldn't see what colour they were any more. The front of his T-shirt that she was wearing was wet. She tried to tuck her hair behind her ears. Twenty-five seemed ancient to him, something he would never reach, but she didn't look so old now. Her face was screwing up again in the effort not to cry and her nose was dripping on to her top lip which had grown huge.

'Aesop.' She didn't know afterwards why she said it.

To him it sounded like he had always thought somebody drowning would sound, somebody who wasn't entirely convinced that the person they were shouting for help from would save them. Would want to save them.

He waivered for a moment then let himself fall against her. He didn't think to kiss her face which looked too wet, so instead he pushed her T-shirt up with his right hand, surprised that his body knew what it wanted to do, that it desired things it hadn't yet known. The T-shirt got caught around her left breast so he only got his hand round the right one, but her nipple was nearly half the size of her whole breast, and was the most deadly looking purple he had ever seen. The tip of it pushed down hard and filled his palm as he gently squeezed, not because of any tenderness he felt but because he was afraid he would do something he didn't like.

Her belly was warm and he liked the way she held his head in her hands as he kissed her. He was going to be brave, he decided, brave enough to enjoy it; he was going to put her nipple in his mouth and suck it, to find out what it tasted like. He didn't know whether women only had milk in their breasts when they were pregnant, or when they had babies, or whether there was always milk there so he didn't want to suck that hard. He was just beginning to open his mouth, stretching it wider as he got closer, so close in fact that he could see the pores on her skin, when he heard a knock and the outer door opening. There was only one person who had the keys to the flat and that was Ludwig.

He pulled himself off the bed, away from her and walked into the other room.

'Aesop,' Ludwig said.

'What time is it?'

'Late, I know. But I had something to show you, something that couldn't wait.' Not even the great overcoat he was wearing, the one made of beaverskin from Canada, could weigh down his enthusiasm. In his eagerness he had made the classic mistake only lovers are prone to making; he had presumed that Aesop would want to see him as much as he wanted to see Aesop, whose face was bewildered and preoccupied as it caught sight of the white paper rolled in his hand.

'It smells funny in here,' he said, suddenly on his guard.

'I'm sick of people saying that. It's all I ever hear, "smells funny", "stinks", of what?'

'Nothing; nothing bad,' Ludwig said, but he wasn't convinced. 'Just different.'

'And did you leave that door open because you're going straight back out? Cause if you're not, if you're staying, you could at least shut it,' Aesop said with the bravado of someone who knows he's not going to be hit, not this time.

Ludwig looked behind him at the door, then went and shut it. He came back to stand in front of Aesop, still smiling.

'Do you want to see?'

'Maybe.'

Aesop was trying to remember if he had had an erection when he walked out of the bedroom. He couldn't have; Ludwig would have noticed, surely. He looked at his reflection in the window as it projected itself on to the block of flats opposite, so that it looked like the painted head of a dictator spanning a building that had no say in the matter. He couldn't even remember what Deirdre's body had smelt of.

'Well, do you want to see?' Ludwig asked impatiently.

'Be a bit tough if I didn't, seeing as you've come all this way.'

Ludwig wasn't wearing his smile so easily now. Aesop's rudeness, his bad moods, were one thing. He almost enjoyed them, they made him feel affectionate, but this was sarcasm, the most unclean form of anger. He unrolled the poster he held in his hands and Aesop was looking at a picture of himself.

He realised with a sudden tightening of his stomach that it was probably the only photo Jake had had of him. It was a school photo, two years out of date. The photographer had been lucky and caught him on one of the few days he had actually been at school. He couldn't remember Jake filling out the order form or actually buying the photos, but he must have done. He had never seen the photo in the flat which meant that Jake kept it and looked at it in private. He liked the look of himself in school uniform; he had never given it a moment's thought, but it obviously suited him. The photographer – God knows how – had made him laugh. The face was trying to sneer but it hadn't been able to and was laughing instead.

'Where did you get it?'

'You knew about it?' Ludwig said, suddenly feeling, without knowing why, that he had been complacent about something.

'Where did you get it?'

'Charing Cross.' He watched Aesop watching himself. 'And who exactly has the say so to declare you missing, officially missing, like that?'

'Is that what it says? That I'm missing?'

'His brother does, if anyone does. Am I right or am I right?' Deirdre said from the door.

She was dressed, but in his clothes, and Ludwig recognised them immediately. He didn't want to see them on her; it rendered him less powerful seeing her dressed in the clothes he had bought for Aesop.

'But why did he do it?' Ludwig asked.

'To get people off his back.' She nodded at Aesop. 'To get people off our back.' She paused, looking at the back of Aesop's head. 'Maybe he wanted to keep him for himself, out of harm's way. If you're missing, people don't know where to find you to get at you,' she said, pulling Aesop's ear lightly. 'That's you. Not a bad picture. Bet you didn't know Jake and I have one in our bedroom. Isn't framed or anything, but we've got it on the wall near the bed.'

'Shut up, that doesn't fit,' Aesop said quietly.

'Who are you?' Ludwig broke in. 'Who is she?' he said to Aesop, looking again at the clothes she was wearing.

Aesop realised that, whatever Ludwig imagined about the girl he saw, or didn't see, he had never imagined Deirdre.

'Don't worry about me,' Deirdre said. 'I was just keeping him company – he gets lonely here. And he was keeping me company.' She didn't appeal to Aesop to verify any of this like some people would have done. 'Actually, I pop over most days to make sure he opens his Advent calendar.'

Sarcasm, again, Ludwig noted. So that's where he was getting it from.

'And you forgot to open it today,' she said coming to stand by Aesop and pulling his ear lightly.

Aesop felt himself leaning slightly towards her. He wouldn't have thought of doing that, wouldn't have had the desire to, if Ludwig hadn't been watching, and he noticed that, when he did, Ludwig's lips got smaller.

'This is good for me,' Ludwig said rolling the paper up. 'It means you're invisible. There's nothing you can't do now because you're nobody.'

'But you said I wouldn't never have to . . .'

'What are you doing for Christmas?'

'I'm—' Deirdre started.

'Not you,' Ludwig said cutting in, but not looking at her.

'I don't know, I hadn't thought,' Aesop answered.

'Well you can come with me then. I've got a sister . . .'

Aesop stared. The word 'sister' made him think of 'mother', 'father' and a whole host of other shadows he thought Ludwig had never possessed. He couldn't for a moment think what the womb Ludwig had sprung from must have looked like. In fact he couldn't fit the word 'womb' into his history at all.

'She's got family,' he carried on, implying that he wasn't part of it.

Aesop was more moved by this invitation than he wanted to be, not just moved but relieved. He could feel what Deirdre wanted to say when she heard it. They all knew what she wanted to say, but she kept her mouth shut.

'Get yourself ready then. Douglas will drop by tomorrow morning for you,' he said as he walked to the door. 'Are you coming?' he said to Deirdre.

'No, I'm staying. The night.'

Ludwig's lips tightened, but this time he managed a smile as well. 'Fair enough,' he said, but again without looking at her.

14

Blackthorn arrived just as Achilles was leaving the Institute for the day. When she reached the bottom of the steps she walked over to the car parked there. It looked chauffeur-driven, and inside he could see the back of two mens' heads. The man in the back seat must have wound the window down because Achilles stepped forward and put her hand through it, and even waved as the car pulled away. Had he kissed her hand, or shaken it? How could he presume to? How could he dare to? She was left standing on the pavement.

They started their journey, slowly because of the snow, and when they got to Highgate he waited at the girls' school on the corner near her flat, where he waited most nights, until he heard the metallic chimes of her gate closing. But today, crouched by the privet hedge, he heard something he hadn't heard for years, a school bell ringing. A door opened and the street he had waited in night after night was full of the sound of children screaming. He could see them through the gap in the hedge; the younger bodies already aware of the uniform and the specific, expensive combination of colours, while the older ones tried to accomplish a uniform within a uniform, ties worn in a certain way, a certain length skirt, and a certain style of shoes that showed that, whatever it was they were defying, they were doing it to belong where it mattered. Their noses were upturned against the snow and their postures were carnivorous. But after a while the first few bent down and threw their handfuls of snow half-heartedly at friends, trying to ascertain with minimum risk what the general consensus on the snow was.

Two younger girls (he wasn't very good on children but guessed at six or seven) chased each other into his corner, hoods flung back off their heads and filled with snow. They caught each other round the neck and started to squeeze, laughing. As soon as one said, 'I can't breathe,' they paused, then took their positions again, until one of them, her eyes popping out of her head, noticed him.

'Hey.'

'What?' he said defensively, still crouching. They were on eye level.

'How long have you been there?'

'Not long.'

'Since before break?'

'I can't remember.'

'Must have been a long time then if you can't remember. Liar.'

'Not long,' he said again, even more defensively, before they had time to think what action to take.

'Been watching us have you?'

'You looked as if you were enjoying yourselves in the snow.'

They took hold of each other's hands.

'Just us two?'

'No, everyone.'

They paused for a few seconds and he wondered why it was that children never needed to blink.

'Are you the one that's been sending those rude letters to Siobhan in fifth?'

The girl asked the question slowly, but was excited at

the thought of uncovering something.

'I bet he is,' her friend said.

'Of course not,' he put in, feeling that he needed to, and wondering how old Siobhan was likely to be.

'Good job I can't read.'

'I can,' her friend said.

They executed a couple of quick clapping games in a high-pitched chant which sounded as though they were invoking supernatural help, then took hold of each other's hands again. Their coats were falling off their shoulders, and their socks had rolled down round their ankles – one of them had paint spattered on her collar. They had matching mittens with cats' faces on them and fibre whiskers.

'Fuck off.'

Blackthorn stood up.

'She said fuck off,' her friend said, then they ran off laughing loudly.

He was shocked – they hadn't seemed capable of it – and left the corner quickly, as if he had just pissed in it. He thought of the boys at Hornby Young Offenders' who had terrified him on first sight, not because of what they were capable of, but because of what they had already accomplished. And because they wore their prison uniform as they would have and should have worn their school uniform. The female warden, when she had shown him round, had used not the word 'boys' but the collective word, 'children', and he had replied – automatically – 'where?' Coming to think, as he read the case files and drank drinks increasingly undiluted, that children were nothing more than the dreams of adults and that innocence (if it existed at all) was nothing more than malnourished morality. He felt that it would be easier for him to ask them to get down on all fours, wear collars round their necks, bridles in their mouths, and saddles on their backs, and that this would seem neither explicit nor unnatural. He had never felt so afraid for himself before as he did in their company. And he could imagine clearly and without difficulty the two small girls running across their playground now, wearing the uniform worn at the Institute for Young Offenders.

It occurred to him that Dr Achilles must have got in some time ago. Daylight outwitted him temporarily: the lights in the flat wouldn't be switched on yet, the curtains wouldn't be drawn and there would be no shadow. The sun was large and low in the sky, reflecting itself in the windows so that all he could see there was the skyline behind him, and panoramic views weren't what he wanted. He didn't even know if she was there or not. The moon, when it rose, was as large as the sun had been; a Hunter's moon.

Then the lights in the flat came on: she was there. Usually they only came on after the curtains were shut, but tonight the curtains stayed open. The sword wounds across his belly momentarily opened as he realised that, whatever she didn't want to know, she needed to know that he was still alive. She was watching him, and wanted to be seen watching him. They looked at each other and she raised her hands, pressing them against the window. Once she did this her face became much clearer, and when her right hand started to move he thought she was beckoning him, telling him to come inside. He walked towards the gate still looking up at her and his hand was on the catch trying to work out the mechanics of the lock which was suddenly daunting.

'Don't force it,' he said to himself, 'Don't force it.'

Then she was gone and he realised that she wasn't even sure herself if she had made the gesture or not. He stepped back on to the pavement before the gate had time to open.

15

Once Deirdre had set herself up with Jake, she was given all things that shone. Her mother said they were the only things she could bequeath her while still alive: the fairy lights made of every colour glass could be dyed; the plastic icicles; the tinsel; the fairy itself with violently orange hair and sunburnt-looking skin; the can of fake cobwebs with its rusting top, sold when aerosol was still innocent; the chiming angels to put round the candles and the plastic centre pieces which gave a new meaning to the word 'evergreen' but somehow looked less permanent than the real thing. These had marked the beginning and end of every Christmas since the beginning of Deirdre.

As her mother hung, stuck, sprayed, switched on and lit, she invoked the names of everything that was sacred to her personally and the world at large, humming them like a tune known but never learnt. Deirdre remembered how last year Jake, even though he refused to take any part in decking out the flat, had joined in the singing which had meant a lot to her because he hated music more than he hated Christmas.

Today was Sunday and her mother had her Sunday suit on. It was actually a summer suit, but also her Sunday best and she wore it as though she had been baptised in

105

it; with white tights that matched the silk lily sewn to her lapel. She had a peach straw hat on that her hair stuck through, especially round the crown. Whatever the time of year, the hat always made her sweat. Deirdre noticed as she stood behind her with her arms braced for tinsel, that quite a lot of the hairs sticking through the hat were grey and that her mother was beginning to grow that old smell; frailty and loss of memory have their own particular smell.

Up until Jake, Deirdre had always gone to church with her mother every Sunday. When she stopped they didn't talk about it. Her mother understood (it was one of the things she did remember) that men had their own kind of importance; and Deirdre knew that she was praying for her.

'That church misses your voice.'

'I know, mum.'

'Well it can have her back, cause I won't.' Jake had found a new freedom to speak to her in the way he chose, to speak his mind.

'It would, at the drop of a hat,' she said. 'At least her singing makes her money.'

Most of the branches of the tree were so laden with baubles that they were now pointing straight down to hell. There wasn't much naked wall space left either and, if the paper chains and moronic Santas hanging across the ceiling had been made of anything stronger, they would have been life-threatening.

'Shame there's no children to enjoy this,' she said looking at Jake as if this too was something he was incapable of because of a lack of faith, because he wasn't blessed. She touched up her make-up in the mirror above the gas fire which only seemed to warm the wall it was standing against. Her fuchsia lipstick – like her peach suit – she saved for Sundays and she said she painted her lips because she liked to keep her little hole

106

of faith (one of her deceased husband's phrases which he had used to refer to another part of her anatomy) well-groomed. Which was why she paid so much attention to her teeth as well.

'I'll be back after church with the presents.'

'Don't.'

'What you mean "don't", Jake?'

'I said don't. There won't be any presents in this house.'

'What you getting so upset about now? You had better tell me quick cause I'm gonna be late for church otherwise.'

'I don't want any presents.'

'But everybody gets something. Every year.'

'But I don't want any of this.'

'Don't tell me you've sat and watched me up them ladders for the past hour and now you want all this down. Cause it's not coming down.'

'Well I do want it down.'

'I know you've got your own way of saving souls, Jake.'

'I have . . . and I can't do it looking at reflections of myself everywhere I turn. Look at the place, it's disgusting. Turn the lights out and it's nothing, there's nothing there. The biggest date in your calendar is dead without electricity. And you know what?' He picked up a paper-chain that had fallen down from the ceiling. 'It's still dusty, look, caked in last year's and God knows how many other years' worth of dust. Isn't that the most fucking depressing thing? Dusty Christmas decorations? Come on, Deirdre, even you've got to admit that that's depressing. It's dead.'

'It's not dead,' Deirdre said, her Christmas earrings swinging.

Her mother looked at him as she put her overcoat on. She had to put it on herself, neither one of them – despite her age – got it down and held it open for her.

Neither one of them stopped her from climbing up the ladders, from stretching beyond her years to get the angel on to the top of the tree. Neither one of them would walk with her to the bus stop and wait with her in the fog to protect her from the youths that had been forgotten or never baptised who might not just steal her handbag, but have no qualms about spilling her blood either. Neither of them would pick up the phone later to see if she had got back from church safely. And for the first time, looking at both of them, she felt the disgust rising in her stomach, disgust at the prospect of the future. She wanted to be in the church whose new varnish she could already smell, surrounded by people whose geography she understood. She was tired of this. These two were all she had left to look over her death and burial, and they couldn't even be trusted with that. There was only one place for love to be found.

She felt the full weight of herself settle on to her abundant hips and the buttons on her coat squeaked as the body wearing it expanded. Her ankles puffed and she let out a slight belch that had been rising from her oesophagus. She was ready to go.

'There's no turkey this year, I could only afford chicken. And if I'm not round till a bit later tomorrow it's because of the bird. I'll be waiting for it to defrost. It's too heavy to carry frozen.'

'There will be no presents tomorrow and no bird.'

'For you, no. Those can go back to the shop. But for my little girl, yes, she's getting her presents.'

'Jake this is one day . . .' Deirdre started.

'It's my house,' he said listening to himself with a genuine sense of wonder. 'My house,' he said again.

'It's the council's,' Deirdre's mother said, turning round so that the lining hanging out of her coat at the back could be seen. 'And you're a Believer, Jake Whitmore, whatever you say, because I can see how terrified you are. You wake up in the morning trembling and you go to bed at night the same way.'

'And you don't know what it is to be afraid because your world's so small.'

'It can't be that small because you're in it, Jake. Your world's inside mine and there's still room for more.' The hat rose up off her hair as she spoke, the flowers on it no longer looked as though they were made of silk, and her coat curled up at the edges. 'What kind of gospel is yours next to mine?'

'Deirdre, tell her to leave.'

'Mum . . .'

'Show myself out shall I?' she said, the disgust rising again at the way they spoke to her, to each other, and the fact that neither of them would give up their own life for the other. Maybe *she* would, she thought, looking at her daughter. She could see her giving him life. But him? He would be the last man in the boat, because he was the sort who forgot things and so told lies, to himself. He would be the last one in the boat, a blanket wrapped round him, and the oars lost on an empty sea. Maybe he had a faith she didn't understand. The disgust was dying down, but it left a nausea behind she could taste. And now – since he had mentioned it – she could see the dust on the decorations too.

'I'll be round tomorrow with the chicken and presents. There'll be presents for my little girl; presents for her,' she said hotly, thinking, 'there's still time, there's still time', and from somewhere further back came the recollection that she had woken up this morning feeling as though someone had just tapped her on the shoulder and told her that it was going to be the last one.

'Look at her. You've made her forget how to speak,' Deirdre's mother said, watching her daughter.

'You need an exorcist, that's what you need. You . . .' Jake said, getting up to finish his sentence.

109

Deirdre's mother breathed out heavily, then walked across to where he stood and hit him round the head, first with one hand then the other, so that the blows came from her palms laid flat and bare, beating him down into a sitting position as his arms came up to protect his head and his back curved and his knees bent. Deirdre watched her mother from beside the Christmas tree as she pursed her lips and started to sweat under the weight of the punishment she was inflicting. The fuchsia lipstick began to bleed down the cracks in her lips.

She tried to stop her, but got hit herself and ended up standing in the corner where not even the shimmer of the Christmas decorations reached. She hadn't seen the fury for some time; it was the fury that made her mum's eyes shine, born from a sense, not of what was right in the world, but what was wrong. The last time she had seen the fury was five years ago at the age of twenty when her dad had still been alive, and her mother had taken his belt from the trousers he was wearing and used it on her, used it until it broke the skin in some places.

She was hitting him blindly because her hat had fallen over her face, and Jake was crying. Not crying properly because he didn't have the breath to, but they were real tears and after a while he started to say, 'It's not my fault, it's not my fault,' and Deirdre knew that these words were for her and that he felt the punishment was justified.

'That's right, boy, it's not,' her mother said, at last laying off, picking her hat off his lap where it had fallen in her fury and coming to stand back at the mirror so that she could dab at her face with a tissue.

She rearranged the hat and this time, taking no chances (because once the fury was on her it might easily rise up again), stuck some hair pins in to keep it on her head.

Deirdre tried to lay her hand on her arm as she left,

holding the door open for her, but her mother shook it off.

'You don't deserve to be prayed for. Either of you.'

'You will still though, won't you?'

'I don't know any more.'

And she walked off into the fog which had come in and up the stairs as it always did.

16

The garden sloped down towards a small forest and lake. The landscape used to be employed: the old cottage at the corner of the garden had been a woodsman's; the house at the end of the lane a mill, the pond a mill pond. Ludwig said the words 'woodsman' and 'mill' slowly.

'You know what I like about nouns?'

'I might if I knew what they were.'

'They're temporary. They go out of fashion; they render metaphors meaningless.'

Ludwig always made him sullen when he was in one of these moods; but, despite himself, he knew he had the capacity to enjoy being taught.

Ludwig was smoking, something he only ever did outside because it made his face itch too much indoors. The smoke was quick in disappearing the night was so cold.

'We're standing on their croquet lawn,' he said.

'I wondered what all the lumps were.'

'The lumps haven't got anything to do with it; croquet can be packed away in a box. The lumps belong to the moles. He . . .' Ludwig gestured with his head back towards the house, '. . . has sleepless nights because of these lumps. I caught him once with the barrel of a shotgun pushed down one. I was having a pee. It was the

112

middle of the night and I had to come running down in my pyjamas to stop him accidentally blowing his head off.'

'Why did you bother to do that then?'

Ludwig looked at him and laughed.

Aesop could feel the soles of his shoes beginning to slip on the snow. Somebody had let the dogs out because he could hear their panting across the garden and was suddenly afraid of coming across them at night. Animals were different in the dark, no longer pets, no longer owned. Their movements reminded you that you were on their territory; they became baby eaters.

'Those people in there are very unhappy people.' Ludwig offered Aesop the last of his cigarette, but not as he would have done to others as a threat or torment because Aesop had never been afraid or disturbed.

'You said I had to give up.'

'Well I'm giving you this one, so it's different. Anyway it's Christmas. Make it your last.'

'They seem happy enough. I liked them.' He blew the smoke out. 'I like your sister.'

'But you're not supposed to,' Ludwig said, not stopping to think.

'Why not?'

'Because you're not. Inherently you should be repulsed.'

'They were nice to me.'

'You think they were nice to you?'

'They were. Weren't they?'

'No.'

They knocked hands against each other and Ludwig briefly took hold of Aesop's and shook it. 'No,' he said again.

'I thought I was allowed to like them.' Aesop dug his foot down into the snow.

'Not at all.'

'Well, I'll try and be repulsed. Now that you've told me to.'

'Whatever you've done, whatever you're going to do, whether I'm with you or not, you've done nothing as wrong as those people in there. Those people were born with their heads screwed on the wrong way because they spend so much time keeping their eyes on their own backs. They make it their prerogative to underestimate people. And that woman . . .'

'Your sister.'

'That woman would sleep with a man too old to pee unaided if she thought it would do her any good.' Ludwig started to walk down the hill. 'The girl in your flat the other night. Who was she?'

'My brother's.'

'Wife? Girlfriend?'

'Girlfriend.'

'Well, if you're going to do her, do it before she becomes his wife. Otherwise you'll be breaking one of the Ten Commandments. Come on, I'll show you the forest.'

'Can't it wait till tomorrow?'

'Why? I'm with you aren't I?'

Aesop went down on his heels and started to slide, leaving two dark trails behind him as the snow collected on his shoes.

'I'd rather go to the lake.'

'You would?'

'There might be ice.'

'There will be.'

There was a boat frozen into the bank, but in the moonlight it was difficult to see what colour it had been painted. There was a name on the side as well.

'You know that there are people who would die for you, don't you? They . . .' Ludwig nodded again towards the house, '. . . have to live the rest of their lives without

114

that knowledge. So you don't ever need to understand them. They need your pity.'

Aesop moved away from him out on to the lake.

'Don't walk on it.'

'I want to. It's been frozen for weeks. Didn't they used to skate on ponds and rivers and things?' He made his way to the middle slowly. 'I don't weigh much,' he said to Ludwig then let out a series of sounds that you usually had to loiter at football matches, underneath railway arches, in wastelands or places where street lamps had been smashed and never replaced, to hear; urban incantations.

Ludwig watched him yelp his triumph across the frozen space which seemed vast in this light and the rocks and frozen trees on the opposite bank made him believe that he was in a bigger country than he was. 'Have you ever seen a man drown?' Ludwig called out.

'No.'

'You can't swim.'

'I can,' Aesop shouted back across the lake.

And Ludwig realised that, if anyone was going to feel lonely, it was going to be him, standing on the shore by the boat, not Aesop in the centre. He dropped the stub Aesop had passed back to him and watched the ash spread as it fell.

He had his right foot on the lake when his phone went off.

Douglas was sitting in Ludwig's chair looking out through his front window. The houses opposite went a different white in winter; bluer. He stroked the flanks of Abelard and Heloise, feeling the muscle underneath. A dog's flesh, even covered as it was in fur, suggested an edibility human flesh never did.

The house, he noticed, had become littered with objects bought for, or belonging to, Aesop. And when he

115

came across the odd sock turned inside out, the discarded Game Boy, the fingered cycling magazine, and the transmitter for a remote control car (had Ludwig really bought him that?), he knew that it was Ludwig who had left them where they had fallen rather than Aesop who had forgotten them.

The phone rang and he lifted Abelard's muzzle from his groin and gave both dogs a quick kick (he liked kicking dogs). Ringing phones made him feel pursued, as though someone who had been searching malevolently and for a long time had finally found him. It wouldn't be Ludwig: he was suspicious about phoning his own number. He had once said to him that he was frightened in case the person who picked up at the other end turned out to be himself.

'Hello?'

'Douglas.'

It wasn't his wife.

Nobody said his name like Mack Velli said it, as though they were twins and had been present at each other's birth. Douglas didn't listen to Mack in the same way others did, in the same way Ludwig did, but then he had never loved him.

'How's Ludwig?' Mack said.

'Well.'

'Where is he?'

'With his family. It's Christmas.'

'Are they still alive? I hate it when families are still alive.'

'Where are you?' Douglas said after a while.

'I'm dead.'

Douglas paused, not ruling this possibility out – Mack had always had Lazarus potential.

'So you're not in Jara.'

Mack laughed drily.

'No, I'm not. The puppet emperor had a puppet death.'

116

'Where are you busy being dead?' Douglas said, beginning to feel tired.

'I don't know. I'm lost at the moment.'

'Why did you die?'

'Douglas, I never knew you kept so many questions hidden inside that uniform.'

He heard the metallic click of a small animal's cage shutting.

'A consortium of Brazilian interests want to drag me to a tribunal because of Jara. I think – actually – they want to buy it. But they'll get their tribunal and, although Jara will melt the world eventually, it's only the tip of my iceberg. Death seemed suddenly easier.'

Mack was somewhere hot. He could tell when Mack was somewhere hot because his clothes made his voice vibrate. He hated being hot, and was his most unpredictably violent with sweat on his forehead.

'Aurelius?'

'Ah, Aurelius,' Mack said as if thanking him for the reminder. 'Aurelius believes I'm dead; he knows I'm dead.'

'He does?'

'There was a state funeral.'

'And Ludwig?'

'Ludwig will find out I'm dead.'

'And?'

'If the knowledge only lasts a second, for that second he will know what it means to him for me to be dead. Nothing more. And afterwards, when I'm no longer dead, he should know . . . he has to know . . . what it feels like when somebody disappears.' He paused. 'People are leaving Jara because the emperor's dead.'

Douglas heard the dull sounds of footsteps and wondered who Mack was with if he wasn't alone.

'I need you to organise something for me,' Mack said abruptly as if waking up.

117

Douglas held the dog's head tightly between his knees until it started to whine.

'There's a woman.'

'From Jara?'

'Charlotte Hickham. She's back in London.'

'I don't know her.'

'She was a Sector Four teacher. I don't expect you to know her.'

Douglas could tell he was getting irritated now.

'The problem with Charlotte Hickham,' Mack continued, 'is that she saw me after my funeral.'

He recognised the sound of Mack's rings scraping against wood. It was one of the things he remembered – specifically – about him. That you could hear him sitting in the chairs he sat in.

'Ludwig has a boy at the moment doesn't he?' He didn't wait for Douglas to answer. 'The boy should do it. Tell that to Ludwig.'

Douglas thought he would ring off then, but he didn't.

'And the next time you find out I'm not dead after all, try to sound something close to, if not joy, then relief at least. And remember,' he added, excited now, 'when a family such as mine contributes so singularly to a nation's history, death never means the same thing. It doesn't have that ability to swallow.'

Mack was threatening him which meant that they were both acknowledging – after all this time – that he was afraid of him.

'And Ludwig,' he added loudly, 'Ludwig should go to Jara afterwards.'

'Why?'

'Sector Four's the only operating sector now and I need him to close it down. I need someone to bury Jara. Also he'll be in a state, like you were after his first killing,' Mack reminded him without tenderness.

17

The cars and buses were letting out an evil grey spray as Dr Achilles eventually reached London's last remaining outdoor swimming pool. The water temperature was twenty-nine degrees Celsius she noted registering the chalked up numbers, and the outdoor temperature minus two degrees.

The entrance to the pool was glamorous – black marble – suggesting something private, corporate, even though the pool was surrounded on three sides by council flats. There was heavy snow still on the balconies of the flats and the washing that had been left out was frozen. Although it was dark, the pool was illuminated from beneath rather than floodlit. In the summer people lined the sides sunbathing, but now there was only the snow, which had melted at the fringes of the pool and, further back, was still piled high on the cement – not even the pool's heating system interfered with it.

Dr Achilles stood nearly naked in the centre of the city; a small woman with her feet on cement, surrounded by high-rises, thinking what if there's no bottom to the pool? With the steam rising it was difficult to see. Furthermore she had always known that the entrance to the underworld would be inconspicuous; no statues, no flames, nothing cavernous – no oil paint – but buried in the everyday.

She dived into the water that was as warm as piss. As she broke up through the steam she heard the squeal of an attendant's whistle. No diving allowed. There weren't many swimmers tonight and those waiting at the sides of the pool smiled at each other loyally, even the serious ones that did the butterfly stroke and wore swimming caps as well as goggles. Even the slow, middle-aged women and young girls who didn't like to get their hair wet and who wore waterproof make-up. The lane etiquette wasn't so apparent with the thick steam rising from the heated water. Every time she lifted her face up out of the water the cold reached her very definitely and she knew that if she were to keep her head above water for too long, the water in her eyebrows and eyelashes would freeze.

She did the breaststroke down the length of the pool. At the deep end the steam was so thick she couldn't see and it was easier to swim underwater. She swam on her back up the length of the pool and, as she swam into shallower water, there were much longer rifts in the steam and it wasn't so dense so she could see the stars – all of them – and the windows of the flats, some lit, some unlit.

She lost sight of the elderly man in front who she supposed had been told to swim by a physiotherapist. Every stroke he took contorted his body in such a way that he looked as though he were perpetually drowning. The next moment she hit deep water, lost herself in the steam and heard a bang which made her think she had hit her head against someone. At first she thought it might be the drowning man and ducked under the water half expecting to see the twisted grey body making its way to the bottom with relief. But the old man wasn't there. All she could see was a mass of hair that was her own.

She came to the surface and took her goggles off. Then she turned on her back and saw that, although the snow melted before it reached the pool itself because of the heat, further up in the sky by the balconies of the flats and beyond, it was now snowing heavily again. On one of the balconies she saw a man in an overcoat walking. There was a boy trying to keep up behind him and she heard the boy say, 'I can't keep up in these shoes. I can't run in them.'

Then the man turned round and said, 'We're not trying to run.'

And as he turned round she recognised the face. It was Ludwig James, her patient, and she remembered again what Blackthorn had said about him and the skin trade. She carried on down the length of the pool keeping abreast with them in the water; they were high enough up for the steam not to reach them.

Before they turned down the stairs, the boy leant over the side and she wondered for a moment if he were going to jump. He looked straight down at her and stretched his arms out as if to shout, or orate. He opened his mouth then stepped back so that he could no longer be seen.

She swam back up the pool half-expecting to see his face again and wondering – if she did – whether it meant that her life was in danger.

Then she noticed that one of the flat doors was open – the one with the frozen washing still strung up outside – and that snow was blowing in. A few seconds later a bird flew out through the open door, a yellow bird, and she was sure – even though she had never seen a real one before – that it was a canary.

121

18

'I'm not waiting here. I'll pull round and be outside the theatre in ten minutes,' Douglas said, turning round to look at Aesop, who had most of their Christmas presents still spread across his lap.

'He could stay with you,' Ludwig said at last, not getting out of the car.

'No,' Douglas said. 'That's never happened before and it's not happening now.'

'I want to go with you,' Aesop said desperately, looking at the back of Douglas's neck which was bulging as if another thought or another head were trying to make itself heard. He had never heard him say 'no' to Ludwig before, and he waited for the reprimand which never came.

'That was your last chance,' Ludwig said getting out of the car and pulling Aesop out after him.

Douglas leant over and for a moment Aesop thought he was going to catch hold of the bottom of his coat, but he didn't. He was looking for a tape in the glove compartment. 'I don't need saving,' Douglas said looking up, '.'and neither does he,' he added, looking quickly between the two seats at Aesop who was standing on the pavement by the car.

'You could give Wesley a call,' Ludwig said.

'He won't be there. This is too fast for him. Unskilled. He won't take it.'

Ludwig looked at him a moment, then shook his head and crossed the road.

There was always a point, not birth itself, but some time after that, when people began. Ludwig and Douglas had known each other since that beginning, Aesop realised watching them. This made him less afraid of Ludwig and more afraid of Douglas.

The back of Ludwig's coat was spattered in grey slush from the road and, as they passed through the entrance to the swimming pool that was also the entrance to the flats, the girls at the kiosk momentarily panicked at the sight of his face and the thought of it immersed in the public water of the pool.

The cement stairs to the flats had puddles of slush on them and the institutional cream walls reminded Aesop of school. Even though the temperature was sub-zero the stairwells still smelt of urine. Both men's and dogs', which smelt the same when stale. The doors of the flats were painted blue, the sort of blue that had been bought in bulk to inflict maximum punishment on the eyes.

Ludwig was slowing down and not even aware of it. Aesop dropped back as well so that it wouldn't be noticeable. You had to be taught curiosity and he never had been, which was why he hadn't thought to ask questions. All he knew was that a woman had come out of the jungle, Ludwig's jungle, when no one had expected her to, and arrived here in London. He knew that, since Douglas's phone call, Ludwig thought about this woman all the time and had taken to touching his face even more than usual. All Aesop could imagine was a woman with clothes that had rips, torn by design rather than by chance, and with tits like weaponry stuck through the splits and slashes – a cartoon strip from the sort of comic books Jake used to keep by the side of the toilet – and he was trying to work out how he and Ludwig fitted into these newsprint colours, this newsprint world, and why he was scared of the comic-strip girl, when he had the feeling that she should be scared of him.

'Which number?' Ludwig asked.

'What?'

'Which number flat was it?'

'Douglas said fifteen.'

'He did. Right.'

Aesop half expected the woman to look as she did when she had walked out of the jungle, forgetting that a week had passed since then. That was the moment he could see most clearly, as a comic strip.

He could hear the swimmers below (even though he couldn't see any water because of the steam); the sound of limbs trying to accommodate themselves in water.

They came to number fifteen on the corner. It had a string of washing hanging up outside, an old woman's washing, tea towels and some elasticated trousers, now frozen.

'Pick the lock,' Ludwig demanded.

'Aren't we going to ring?'

Ludwig looked at him for a moment.

'I thought illiteracy was your only disability.'

'What's illiteracy?'

'Just pick the lock. Quietly.'

Ludwig was whispering now and, as Aesop bent down to pick the lock, spread himself around him so that he couldn't be seen.

'Done?' Ludwig pushed him back, his fingers to his lips, and went inside.

Aesop wondered whether the other people the girl was expecting were already inside and what his journeys across London, carrying parcels he had never yet thought to open, had to do with any of this.

The television was on, and he thought he recognised the programme. The person living there hadn't changed the decor since the flats had been built in the fifties. There was a cuckoo clock on the wall in the hallway and another clock opposite that had gold metallic spikes to make it look like the rising sun. Next to this there was something that looked like a clock but – he found out years later – was in fact a barometer. There were a pair of worn-out slippers on the floor, some newspapers and one of those wheelie trolleys in red. The wallpaper and carpets were overwhelmingly floral and the light switches were the old-fashioned round ones, and black.

They walked into the main room where they had heard the voices of two women chattering. It was unbearably hot and Aesop was surprised that the thousands of ornaments arranged around the gas fire hadn't transformed back into the raw materials they once were. The girl looked up and he smiled.

She was sitting in one of the chairs in her dressing gown and her hair was wrapped in a towel and steaming slightly. She had blue sponge separating her toes while she painted them, and the varnish she was holding was purple. There was an elderly woman stood near a bird-cage in the corner of the room with a pot of food in her hands. She had wet hair as well and her face and arms were covered in those brown patches old people get on their skin that only old people know the name of. 'I heard you coming in,' she said not looking up from the cage, 'and I thought, what a time to come, just as I was about to feed Bertie, and my granddaughter, Charlotte there, was about to set my hair for me.' She started to cluck at the bird watching them both through the cage.

Aesop noticed a set of blue plastic curlers on the table and the hairdryer next to a plate of digestive biscuits.

Ludwig looked at him and knew Aesop was wondering if they had got the wrong flat. Nobody here seemed to need their help. But the girl – Charlotte – hadn't taken her eyes off Ludwig.

'Who were you looking for? We weren't expecting anyone.' The old woman didn't appeal to her granddaughter, but Aesop noticed that the bird on its perch was swinging slightly from side to side because the hand she had on the cage door was shaking.

'Is there anyone else here?' Ludwig said.

'I'll be honest with you,' the old woman said. 'There isn't. Charlotte isn't well, you see. Her feet were in a real mess and have only just mended, only now. To look at them you would have thought they had been put in a fire. But they're better now. Which means that we can go. We were just waiting for her feet to heal, to get better. So now we're off. We're leaving the flat because we don't want anyone to bother us. We thought we might go to Spain.' She paused. 'I've got a sweetheart,' she tried to feign shyness, 'well, he's an old dancing partner actually, who winters in Spain and we thought we would go there – out of harm's way. Charlotte won't be talking to anyone because she just wants to forget everything.'

The old woman was speaking calmly even though her voice was weak, but after this, when Ludwig still hadn't spoken, she suddenly shouted, 'Do you hear me, Mister? I said we won't be troubling anyone. This is the end.' Then more quietly, and to Aesop rather than Ludwig, 'Look at the scars on her feet.'

The girl was still looking at Ludwig and she couldn't think and didn't know what to do because the varnish was still wet and she had nowhere to put the pot down.

As the old woman clicked open the catch on the door of the birdcage and put the tray of food inside, Ludwig whispered, 'The witness first, always go for the witness before the victim.' And before Aesop even had time to stand back, he had pulled the gun from his coat and shot the woman. The bullet went straight through the cage and into her throat. She tottered for a while then fell forwards knocking the cage with her head and falling across one of the armchairs.

The girl started to cry and was trying to speak. When the cage stopped swinging and came to a standstill again the bird was still on its perch. Aesop had thought, for a moment, that when Ludwig said 'witness' he had meant the bird, but the bird was still alive and the old woman was dead. He looked at the curlers on the table. They were still there, which surprised him.

'What are you doing?' Aesop screamed.

'What does it look like? Stop shouting.'

'But we've found her.'

'I know.'

'And we got here before they did.'

'Before who did?' Ludwig said, turning round and momentarily swinging the gun on Aesop.

'The ones wanting to hurt her.'

'To hurt her?'

Then Ludwig realised that, whatever Aesop's vision of violence was, it still encompassed heroism; his concept of violence was the violence of the just to be enacted in self-defence or against corruption. He had been a bully at school (Ludwig had no doubt of that), but a wincing bully. Although he had a concrete perception of the anatomy of pain, it had been won through perseverance, not enjoyment.

'We came to kill,' he said trying to walk back towards the door, worried that Aesop would decide to run.

'I know,' Aesop shouted loudly, to give himself confidence, trying not to look at the old woman on the armchair. For some reason it bothered him that she had probably knitted the jumper she was wearing for herself. 'I know that now.'

The girl saw, with the insight of the damned, that the

127

boy wanted to save her and that the man wanted to save the boy.

'I am going to Spain,' she said, looking at her dead grandmother and then at Aesop. 'To Alicante. I'm not staying here.' The light from the glass pebbles in the gas fire lit up the earring in his ear.

'You see,' Aesop said turning to Ludwig.

'No, I don't.'

'I left all those children behind, on the brink of literacy, and I was the only teacher left — wasn't that selfish. I couldn't have done that if I had loved them, could I.' She could see how unbearable it was for the boy and wondered if the man might not turn the gun on him. She tried to laugh, but her lips were swollen.

'I didn't know when I started to walk, if I was going to die walking.'

'Then why did you start walking?'

'Jara's going to melt the world.'

'Never let them speak,' Ludwig said to himself, and he knew that she was talking because she sensed that she had a chance and her chance was the boy.

She tightened her dressing gown cord and bent forward to remove the blue thing from between her toes, to calm not herself but them. 'It took me four days to …'

Ludwig pulled the trigger, shooting at the bowed head. He had never shot anyone in the crown of the head before. Aesop looked at him and for a moment, not recognising his face, the diseased face, thought that the girl had somehow shot at him, and that the face was in the state it was because of a gun wound, but then remembered. He started to cry, which was something he had been hoping not to do since the old woman died.

'Ludwig,' he said, then made for him, not out of love, but because he was the only other living person in the room.

Ludwig gave him a brief kiss on the crown of his head, then left the flat.

'Slowly. Do it slowly,' he said as they walked back along the balcony past the other flats. Outside they could hear the swimmers still in the water and the snow was falling heavily.

'I can't keep up in these shoes. I can't run in them.'

'We're not trying to run,' Ludwig said turning round.

And before they disappeared down the stairs, Aesop looked over the edge, as if he were looking at people who were free. The steam was much thinner and there was a woman swimming on her back, her breasts rising up out of the water under red Lycra, her hair spread around her and, for a moment, he thought it was the young girl they had just shot, and felt a wave of relief. But looking at the face again he didn't recognise it. It was a stranger's face.

Douglas was waiting in the road at the bottom of the stairs, not at the theatre opposite as promised. He got out of the car when he saw them.

'What are you doing here?' Ludwig said, surprised.

'Didn't you think to use a silencer? I heard it from the foyer over there.'

Aesop noticed that Douglas was speaking to him, not Ludwig, and that Ludwig was leaning heavily on him, in fact he was nearly suffering his full weight.

'Get him in the car,' Douglas said to Aesop, then to Ludwig, 'You've got to sit up. Come on.'

Aesop walked round to the other side.

'Not you as well,' he said.

Ludwig was no longer speaking.

'Why not?'

'Cause there isn't room,' he said mimicking his voice.

'Course there is.'

'There isn't, and this is the way we're doing it; I'll come back for you.' Douglas glanced down briefly at his shoes. 'You've got someone's shag pile covering those. Get it off.' Then he got in, shut the door and pulled away.

As the car drove past, Ludwig looked slowly out of the window at Aesop, but didn't seem to see him.

So Aesop stood on the kerbside, by the entrance to the flats, his hands in his pockets, waiting. And years later when he thought about himself stood there, he wondered why he had believed Douglas when he said he would come back for him. And almost felt envious of the fact that he had been capable of such a mute trust.

He remembered wishing that Ludwig had left the gun with him, although why he didn't know because what he was most afraid of were the two dead women in a flat somewhere above his head. Whatever he did believe in, he didn't believe that death was what it claimed to be: the end.

Aesop tried to find a patch of pavement with less snow. His shoes were wet through and he couldn't feel his toes. He had his hands in his trouser pockets, but not even his thighs felt warm any more. He could still hear the swimmers, but now they were much further away. He wished he had worn his watch, then he would have been able to keep track of the minutes passing.

He heard police sirens and half thought of running back up the stairs but remembered Jake explaining to him that if a policeman ran down a crowded street chasing a shoplifter or somebody and shouted, 'Stop, thief', everybody in that crowded street would turn round because everyone's guilty of something and most people, however begrudgingly, believe in a day of reckoning. Aesop looked up the street and down; no sign of anyone.

Then suddenly there was music as members of the Salvation Army walked past in their navy-blue uniforms, blowing out 'Good King Wenceslas' through their brass instruments like avenging angels, two days too late. Listening to them play, it was hard to imagine that two world wars had ever been fought. And even harder to forget. That's what Jake once said. He moved his feet again and realised how much he wanted to speak to him, but it was so long since he had phoned that he couldn't even remember the number.

19

Ludwig looked down at Aesop's bed.

'He'll be out in four years,' Douglas said as he walked round the flat with the disrespect of a marauder, moving things with his driving gloves still on.

Ludwig sat down on the bed and lifted the edge of the net curtain.

'Didn't realise he had such a view. You can see the mosque from here.'

'Well, I'm sure he made the most of it,' Douglas said coming into the room. 'He'll be out in four years' time,' he said again.

Ludwig bent over the pillow, rubbing his nose across it to catch the scent of Aesop's head. There was still an indent there.

'He thought we were there to save her. I've never seen him so energetic.'

'Nothing wrong with that.'

'Did I tell you she was painting her nails when we walked in?'

'See . . . women will get over anything.'

'And I could tell from the way Aesop was looking at her, all bent over, fiddling with her feet, that he thought she had stepped out of the jungle straight into that Camden flat.'

132

'If we had known what she was capable of, we would have got rid of her earlier.'

'She came out of Jara.'

'I know. You won't bloody well forget will you.' Douglas kicked some of the clothes on the floor around and checked the wardrobe. 'Didn't have many secrets did he?'

'No. No secrets. Now he has though. I'm his first. He saw me do it. And afterwards when we left, just before I turned to go down the staircase, I heard him behind me leaning over the wall and I thought he was going to jump. You know, jump over it. Because of me.'

'So you like to think. Course he wasn't.'

'He saw me do it.'

'And I've seen you do a lot worse.'

There was a teddy bear tucked in under the duvet, with matted fur and a scar where one of its eyes had been removed. A box of tissues by the bedside with some used ones screwed up on the floor where they had been dropped. On the other table there was a can of shaving foam and a razor still in their packaging. The posters on the walls rippled glossily in the dull light and the fragile stack of porn magazines underneath the radiator looked pathetically unread. There were five telephone numbers stuck to the mirror, but Douglas took these down and put them in his waistcoat pocket.

'I nearly let him do it,' Ludwig said.

'I know.'

'Where's Mack?'

Douglas walked through into the other room and disembowelled the sofa to check that nothing was hidden there. Then he took the bug off the phone and put that in his waistcoat pocket as well before coming to stand in the doorway.

'I told you.' He waited. 'He's disappeared for a while.'

Ludwig unbuttoned his coat and pulled the duvet

133

back as if he were about to get into the bed.

'Look,' he said, noticing the gold outline of a body.

'Strange,' Douglas said, leaning over and wondering how to interpret it.

'You can leave it, you don't need it.'

'We don't know what it might mean.'

'Whatever it means, it doesn't have anything to do with us. Nothing. Maybe he did have secrets after all,' Ludwig said, thinking of the black girl he had seen here.

Douglas was angry. Ludwig could tell when he was angry because his glass eye slid round sideways, giving him a reptilian profile.

Douglas lit himself a cigarette, wincing as he struck the match – he was nervous of fire because of his wooden leg. Then he went to stand by the window and looked out himself as if to check that the mosque really was there. He took the things he had collected from around the flat out of his waistcoat pocket, and laid them on the table, cataloguing them in his mind, then put them away again. When he turned round Ludwig was lying on the bed.

'Get up.'

'I can't.'

'Get up.'

'You'll have to stop smoking, it's hurting my face.'

'I don't care about your fucking face.'

'It hurts now.'

'Well it'll just have to hurt for a bit, cause your doctor friend's not around right now is she.'

He took longer, slower drags as Ludwig began to push his head further into the pillow in an attempt to stop himself from scratching his face.

Douglas moved his feet to one side and sat down on the bed next to him, exhaling the smoke over the back of his head.

'He wants you to go back to Jara.'

Ludwig turned round, his arm over his face as if to protect his eyes from a sunlight only he could see.

'Mack?'

'Mack.' Douglas laid his hand on Ludwig's knee. 'He wants you to close down Sector Four.'

'Close it down?'

'Annihilate it.'

'Traces always remain, Douglas. Especially if there are people involved. You can't prevent traces.'

'He expects you to.'

'Can't Aurelius?'

'Aurelius wouldn't be right. He hasn't been out of Jara for five years – what's left of it.'

'It's pathetic, the efforts put into maintaining an empire, and as soon as it stops being maintained, it disappears. Sector Four doesn't need closing down, it will disappear anyway. One day. Soon.'

'You'll be on a two-year contract, but it may take longer. He doesn't want you visiting the boy before you go. Mack's sending you back to Jara because he doesn't trust you not to visit him. I don't trust you any more either.'

'He's sending me there to die then.'

Ludwig looked up at Douglas and could tell from his face that this (the most obvious of conclusions) wasn't something he had thought about. It shocked him too much to deny it, and even though he hadn't thought of it, it wasn't necessarily untrue.

'It's a two-year contract,' Douglas repeated, intensely aware now of the leg beneath his hand and the warmth of it which signified life. 'You have to go.'

'What about my face; the treatment? It won't get cured there.'

'I think we both know a cure isn't what you're looking for. What would you do without your disease? People might start falling in love with you again; perhaps they will anyway, despite your face. And that's the last thing you want inflicted on you.'

Douglas stood up and looked down at Ludwig lying on the bed and thought that now would be the time to tell him that Aesop had denied none of the charges against him. That he hadn't once mentioned Ludwig's name. But he didn't feel inclined – at that moment – to alleviate another's suffering when he was impotent in the face of his own.

20

It's right, Achilles thought, watching them pick their way in their white towelling robes to the water's edge, that they come to the Holy Land for their cures. Those that can afford them. About a mile north of the Dead Sea mineral works, the world's leading dermatologists had created a health spa exclusively for the diseased. Where they lived for up to two months of the year in the privacy of their own contamination. Where they could bare their deformed bodies to the sun without the cries of others, because the person lying next to them was only slightly better or slightly worse off than themselves.

So they came out of their hotels in this leper colony where no punishments were inflicted, wearing their white robes. Because of the heat they came at dawn, before breakfast, and immersed themselves in water they were unable to infect because they were the only living thing in it. A sea that redefined the colour of death as blue. A blue you couldn't see through, that hid your body from you. She saw their eyes dilate as they looked at the water.

Dr Achilles came here every New Year to work (what were for her rudimentary) miracles, to reassure herself of the democracy of disease, to see the wealthy, even the exceptionally wealthy, humbled before the fact that a

137

cure couldn't be bought if it didn't exist. She only ever spent two weeks a year at the spa, earning enough in this time to continue her research without sponsorship, which would have been too risky an involvement. It was where she had first met Blackthorn, lying on her back in the sea. The meeting, which he had taken days to contrive (he later explained as proof of something), had ended with him crawling screaming on to the beach, his eyes full of sea water.

He had unnerved her, she had to admit. Most of the other doctors working there (permanently or on a consultancy basis) looked on her with a sense of wonder and apprehension. Rumours also persisted at the spa that she was as miraculously proficient at spreading disease as she was at curing it. Blackthorn was the only person who had never looked over her shoulder, who had never looked any further than her, and who had given her the disconcerting impression, the day they first met, that his sole intention wasn't to question her, or worse, but to put his arms under her in a sea that was already supporting her, and carry her out of the water. Blackthorn would know she was here now and she couldn't understand why (despite herself) he hadn't followed her. She was waiting for him.

In the afternoon when the sun was hot enough to become an instrument of torture, or even death, and the diseased were lying in their air-conditioned rooms noticing the most microscopic of improvements, she removed her clothes and walked to the water's edge treading carefully to avoid the birds nesting on the beach. She swam in their sea, lying on her back in the water with mountains on the horizon on either side and with the thick taste of salt on her lips and tongue.

Only this time, whenever she looked down at herself in the water which was cloudy with minerals, she was always wearing a red costume. When she looked up, the sky was grey with snow and there was the face of a boy leaning over a brick parapet, looking directly at her. There were no gun shots, but sometimes the face was so close she had to shut her eyes, and when she opened them again she was terrified that the Dead Sea might have grown and that there would no longer be mountains on either side.

21

The building lay low at the bottom of a rough Lancashire valley that had become a sort of improvised valley of the damned. To its right were an abattoir and hospice for the terminally ill and to its left a mental asylum. These institutes for imperfection were watched over by the man who owned them and who lived on top of the hill in a house built by his ancestors, a lino tycoon, who had been responsible – because of the lino – for the industrial boom that had knocked the town sideways a century ago. Despite the brand-new security systems surrounding the building, it didn't look like an Institute for Young Offenders.

The inmates' histories, like their misdemeanours, were predictable. There were only a few Aesop was genuinely afraid of, in awe of, who had committed crimes that the system would never touch, that not even the newspapers would touch. These were the perpetrators of unchronicled crimes. Other than this there was nobody more guilty or more innocent than the boy they slept next to.

The institute was cleaner than a hospital. Degeneracy, even more so than illness, had to be really scrubbed at, especially when the aim of the hygiene was to disguise the fact that 200 under-age male delinquents were living in close proximity to each other.

Aesop had got into the habit of standing up when people entered a room. Whether they were people he needed to show respect for or people that didn't matter. Like Jake. He stood up in fact for anyone. He discovered – as countless other inmates across the world, across the centuries had also discovered – that, like warmth and food, habits got you through. Habits were bare necessities and, unlike the other more material sort, could be used as a means of measuring – he had a feeling – sanity, but he could have been wrong. When there weren't enough habits to pick up, he went in search of them. Standing up when somebody entered the room was one of the first ones he had been taught. Most of the others he taught himself.

Jake smiled widely as he walked into the visitor's room. It was an embracing smile – one that he had never used before. Aesop knew that his brother had never been as proud of him as he was now, seeing him in his regulation uniform. Pride made his features glow as he took in the scuffed blue shirt and trousers, the heavy boots, the new well-funded yet claustrophobic surroundings. If Aesop hadn't been in his dreams before, he certainly was now.

'How are you?' Jake asked.

'Same.'

'As what?'

'Usual.'

Jake had, in his turn, acquired the habit of rubbing his hands together. 'The number of supporters is growing daily,' he said.

'It is?'

'You should see them.'

'The usual bums from up at the university with too much spare time on their hands?'

'You shouldn't be . . . disrespectful about them.'

'About who?'

144

'The supporters. Your supporters.'

'I'll try and remember that.'

Jake had left Deirdre and London and come north in April. For three months, he had lived outside the boundary of the institute, and others (invited and uninvited) had come to join him. When they visited (usually in groups of five on a rota system) they shook hands with Aesop, which made him think for the first time about the word 'disciple'. Some of them still had paint on their hands from where they had daubed 'Aesop Whitmore is innocent' across countless walls on streets and buildings foreign to them.

There was only one thing Jake had forgotten and, given its fundamental nature, the fact that he had forgotten it was unforgivable. He had never asked Aesop, in private or in public, whether he was innocent. Not because he believed he was – Aesop knew that Jake thought him capable of murder, or maybe not so much thought, but hoped – he just didn't care. Despite the philosophy he had nurtured on the air waves over the years, he had an appetite for violence he was ashamed of. He was war-hungry too.

Aesop sometimes wondered about his own innocence. He knew that his fingerprints weren't on the gun because he had seen the gun in Ludwig's hand (which seemed to him, the more he thought about it, a protective gesture towards him) and the look the girl had given him. The girl knew, even before he had drawn the gun, that Ludwig had come to kill, that he was the murderer. She had looked to Aesop – however briefly – for salvation. She had believed in his potential for salvation, something he had never seen in himself before. But now it didn't matter whether he had killed her or not.

Whenever he was told that he had a visitor, he was overcome, even if only momentarily, with the hope that it would be him, Ludwig. That he would walk from his cell into the floodlit visitors' area, which was like a quarantine annexe, and see a big man sitting there, filling the chair, the room, wearing an overcoat. If that man stood up and held his arms open, Aesop knew for certain that he would walk straight into them. Often when he woke at night, his cell (he called it that even though, because of the ethos of positivism, they weren't supposed to) still reverberated with the phrases from his sleep, and they were always the same: 'Please make him come, please make him come'. But he hadn't. The burden of hope was making him ill. He was addicted to Ludwig in the way people are to those who have betrayed them. He felt that there was an equality between them now; he had never asked for anything and had been given everything and Ludwig, he knew, would be bent double squeaming with the pain of the betrayal. Often in his dreams he saw his cell, and it was Ludwig he saw lying on the bed inside it.

'You should come to the window,' Jake said.

It was his third visit of the week.

'Why?'

'They need to see you. You haven't shown yourself to them.'

'I'm not going to either.'

'Aesop, I know . . .'

'You don't know anything.'

Jake hadn't taken his eyes off his brother since walking into the visitor's room.

'We're getting you out of this,' he said suddenly, as if he were dealing a death blow.

Aesop bent his head further towards the table. The lights in their brightness were blocking all his senses. Not just sight, but getting into his ears as well, obscuring his fingertips, muffling his taste buds, and he suddenly felt unbearably cold. He tried to stand up, as if afraid of being

146

shot while seated, frantically trying to lay claim to something.

'We're getting you out of this,' Jake said again.

The cold quickly spread through him and he was sure his skin was turning blue. He had noticed that these attacks were increasing recently, especially at night and despite the extra bedding he had been given. There were also moments when he could barely hear what people were saying to him. And nobody spoke here, they shouted. Often, mid-mouthful, he lost the taste of the food he was chewing. He made a mental note to confirm to himself that he was ill. Officially, properly ill. His skin was beginning to move slightly, and tighten, and as he wiped his sleeve across his face he realised that his nose was bleeding, tidily but steadily bleeding. Jake was holding his arms out towards him, but he was frightened of uttering the abuse he had ready in case nothing but blood came out of his mouth. Then he fell to the ground.

Jake's body contorted with excitement as he fell on to his knees beside his brother, as if he had been waiting all his life to take another man's head on to his lap. It was an image of solidarity he found sustaining, romantically tragic. Aesop's hair fell over his hands and thighs, and the face looked up into his. The image was provoking and intimate, but he only held on to it for a few moments, then the staff came running across the room from all directions in uniforms more rigid than the prisoners'.

It took a while for an ambulance to be called. If Aesop had been dead it would have been easy, but because he was alive his life was still in their hands and it made them indecisive. Despite the July heat, his temperature plummeted as he was borne outside on the stretcher. Jake ran alongside him, his hand catching at his, trying to maintain a grip it couldn't find. He tried to talk to him, but his voice ran away from him in its insubordinate excitement.

When he failed to rouse Aesop, he started to shout at

the prison officers, the ambulance staff, and, when the other residents in their tents outside the boundary gate heard the voice of their leader yelping in the distance, they came crawling out of their green, red and blue flaps, the scent of injustice heavy in the air, then leapt up gratefully as if the enemy had been sighted at last. In spite of the prison staffs' attempt to detain Jake (and their jostling and grappling excited him more than Deirdre's or any other woman's caresses ever had) he managed to keep up with the departing ambulance. By the time it reached the gates, the supporters of the 'Aesop Whitmore is Innocent' campaign were hanging thickly around them, and had already caught the gist of their leader's outrage, and condensed it into a slogan which they were chanting in unison, finding – in the monotony of the chant – their anger. Jake went running into the middle of them, his boots and trousers covered in dust from the July baked road, his face sweating. He didn't know whether he expected to see Aesop's face at the window of the retreating van, but he certainly never did.

Jake was unable to believe in a natural course of events and thought of the ambulance, as it trailed off up the valley to the nearest hospital, as part of an elaborate conspiracy, something he communicated to the band of supporters whose raised fists, and wide-open mouths with their screaming tongues, he fell into. With Aesop now gone, they were able to apply themselves to the task of setting him free with renewed vigour. The absent hero, even more so than the imprisoned hero, was a cause (in the developed world where they were few and far between) worth fighting for. That evening found them round a campfire in a large circle, their hair, eyes and jewellery shining as they shared the complaints of their rheumatic souls.

*

Things got worse for Aesop at the hospital. The lights there, although as bright as the sunshine outside, seemed to have the obverse effect and he curled up screaming a list of body parts that hurt. While he was waiting in the corridor, they couldn't get him to lie straight until they had piled so many blankets on him that the legs of the trolley nearly broke, and they were frightened the weight would collapse his ribs. But when they peeled the blankets back they were even more afraid of the prison uniform they found underneath.

In the end the Specialist on duty phoned the prison doctor, thinking that his regular attendance at the Institute would throw some light on the boy's ignominious and noisy condition.

'Dr Blackthorn?'

'I'll get him for you.' There was the sound of a housekeeper's slow, important footsteps disappearing, then the phone was picked up eagerly.

'Yes?'

'It's Dr Dewe. We've got one of the boys from the Institute here.'

'He broke out?'

'No, no. An ambulance brought him here. He fainted in the visitors' room. He's barely breathing, screaming that he's cold and his skin has gone blue. I've never seen anything like it before.'

There was a crackle on the other end of the line, then a thin, reedy voice said, 'I might have.'

'So he's not faking it then?'

'I doubt it.'

'Oh.'

This seemed to be the only diagnosis Blackthorn was willing to make.

'You don't mind us offloading him on to you then?' Dr Dewe asked. 'I don't think he should go back to the Institute, and, to tell you the truth, we can hardly put him on a ward. With the press that place has been getting, he's likely to get lynched. If not by them, then . . .'

'No, bring him here. Put him in an ambulance and bring him up.'

'He's on his way.'

Dr Dewe walked away from the phone brusquely. He had orders to give. He hated most of his patients on sight, but as soon as he laid eyes on this boy squirming and screaming in his uniform, as if his body weren't big enough for him, he had to fight really hard to keep back the nausea. He was the kind of boy who performed miracles and disrupted the medical establishment; the kind who came back to life after being proclaimed dead.

When the ambulance pulled up outside Hornby Hall, Dr Blackthorn came running out towards it as if he had been waiting for this moment all his life. And as Aesop emerged from the ambulance, Dr Blackthorn saw, through the pain, the contortions and the discoloured skin, a perfect case of Eastman's Syndrome. Blackthorn's thick arms with their neurotic veins were waving about and his tie was flung back over his shoulder because of the wind that blew – even in summer – on top of the hill.

'Shall we take him indoors?' the ambulance men asked, their white shirts sticking to their bodies in the heat.

'No, no it's not warm enough in there.'

They dropped the stretcher, wondering whether this was a man they should trust, whether this was a man they should take orders from.

Dr Blackthorn danced about from one foot to another, kicking the dust up from the gravel so that it covered his shoes and left faint smears on the shirts of the men. He tilted his head back slowly and took a fish-eye look at the house and its immediate surroundings, and the last thing he saw was the palm house now used by Jack Preston to sustain his grandfather's butterfly collection. Many of his ancestors had jeopardised their lives – and deaths – to bring back plants and trees from continents more vast, even, than those of the British Empire. Now, left to their own devices since most of the staff had been sacked, the vegetation was trying to reassemble that continent from pieces lost to memory.

'The palm house,' Blackthorn suddenly cried, expecting them to share his enthusiasm. 'You know, where the butterflies live,' and he started to flap his arms in imitation of a butterfly.

The men warily picked the screaming boy back up, noticing that he was able to stare straight at the sun, and kept an eye on the man following them, goading them in the right direction.

'Quickly, quickly, we don't have much time. Do you realise how cold it is for him right now?'

The sweat ran down the men's arses, down their faces, into their ears, and on to their lips where the unbearable saltiness of it parched their mouths.

'It's probably about minus ten degrees for him. That's what his body thinks.' At the mention of the boy's body the men started to feel sorrier for him and made more of an effort to get to the palm house.

The handles on the doors were moulded into the shape of swans whose beaks and wings had rusted. As the doors creaked damply open the full weight of the heat inside fell on to the men. The humidity was awe-inspiring and the men cowered under it, unable to believe that God had ever meant this planet to be for them. The smell was overpoweringly swollen, the smell of something about to break or burst. Tropical. Even if the nose didn't recognise the smell, the imagination did.

Aesop stopped screaming and they put him down beneath the thick maternal leaves of a banana tree, then walked as fast as they could, back to their ambulance.

Dr Blackthorn knelt by his side, in the wet soil, keeping his hands over Aesop's head to protect it from the heavy drops of moisture falling from the disturbed trees.

Aesop put his arms out and touched leaves on either side; he couldn't see any sky. It was like waking up and discovering a chink of sunlight in a room with no windows. He believed he was in a jungle and – suddenly, strongly – that Ludwig had been here before him.

22

In 1973, Brazil proved itself one of the few remaining places still able to spawn an empire, built on the melancholic prophecy of a reclusive millionaire, Mack Velli, who bought a stretch of virgin forest that became the biggest piece of privately owned land in the world. Jara; a four-million-acre dream. As Mack once said, 'Sit any Editor-in-Chief from any international broadsheet or tabloid rag down and ask him what he's most afraid of. He'll say "utopia": a day when people stop doing to other people what it is that makes news. But the thing he will never even have thought of is the possibility that the paper the news is written on will run out before the news. By the year 2000 Brazil will be the only country in the world still able to produce paper.' He had dreamed up another fear to give the world.

In the beginning they arrived and slept in their tents and didn't have the courage to call themselves anything more than a settlement. Later, when the canvas the first settlers had slept in was kept in a store house like thousands of Turin shrouds, in Baden-Powell green, they became a colony. By the time the pulp mill and power plant arrived, towed by boat from Japan, there were four cities within an empire whose population count was nearly 30,000; 2,800 miles of private road and 26 miles of private railway, in forest whose trees moved at night, whose valleys rolled over in their sleep and whose rivers failed to navigate their flow by the moon. The empire's working population cleared forest where 300 different species of trees grew per acre to feed the mill producing 800 tons of pulp every day.

The workers came from everywhere; they came by boat, by plane, on foot, some clothed, some naked, but the thing they all shared was the fact that, whatever their own beginnings had been, when they walked into Jara, they stepped into the middle of another man's story. Ludwig James was one of the overseers of this continual stream of labour.

Ludwig remembered time and time again the moment when he stepped into Mack's apartment in Las Vegas, the one people took photographs of – from the pavement, from the roof of the Golden Ticket, from the block opposite – which they would send up with security just to let Mack know that they knew where he was, that they were watching. After spending an hour in the lobby of the apartment before their first meeting, Ludwig had turned to Mack and asked, 'Are the palm trees real?'

Maybe Mack fell in love with him for that.

Ludwig hadn't spoken to Mack Velli for ten years, not since the day he left, when he had taken another man's face with him. There had been no world paper shortage, no fear of one, and no hope of one.

The helicopter landed at the prescribed map reference and Ludwig walked over the brow of the hill. When he had arrived the last time, the first time, there had been a crowd of men to meet him. He remembered looking out through the helicopter window and the only thing that had interrupted the green, which seemed liquid rather than solid, was this thumbnail of a clearing beneath them where a group of men who spoke his language stood. They had had their hands crossed over their heads to protect them from the blades of the helicopter, and their trousers and suit jackets were flapping as if a decree had been issued that gravity should pull in the opposite direction. This time, the second time, when the helicopter rose above him, he was left standing alone in the clearing on the spot where his life had begun.

The space between the hill, the Jara River and the sky was filled with roads, overgrown rail tracks, and a construction that reminded him of the mill. He saw cities with low skylines made of wood, grouped around oversized municipal buildings. He walked down roads whose completion he had missed but whose demise he took part in, kicking at the ruts so that dust skimmed against the corrugated iron buildings on either side. The school buildings here in the Central Sector which had also been unfinished when he left were large but uncomplicated, the interior walls stripped naked. Inside there were benches instead of chairs, an optimistic sign that large numbers had been anticipated. And, worst of all, second only to burning books, abandoned books. Not text books but exercise books, made – he assumed – from paper manufactured at the mill. He looked through a couple. Some of the work was confident, hygienic, while other work was deliberate, laboured over, nothing more than markings. A cramped, crumpled gesture towards social evolution.

Then the rains started, as usual without warning; clouds quickly bruised the sun then there was the roar of drops big enough to hammer a man back into the earth, a violent rain that reached Ludwig's ears with all the fury of a one-sided argument. The violets in the forest needed to be twenty-five feet high to withstand this kind of rain. He became afraid that he was alone, really alone, that there was no one left in the empire at all, that even Sector

155

Four no longer existed. He thought of Douglas in his navy-blue overcoat and braided cap and wondered again if this wasn't part of the plan and that he had been sent to Jara to die.

The rain was driving him into the ground, but he was more afraid of mud than he was of water. He wondered if the small amount of luggage he had brought with him and left where the helicopter landed had now been washed away. He made for the main building that the mill, even in its present decrepit state, was still able to overshadow. They had thought of many names for it and Mack let them sift through them all, from HQ to Central Administration Block (names from wars they had never fought, régimes they had never lived through), until they came out the other side and into his vision, leaving their jargon (which sounded heroic to them) behind. The building became a palace; Velli's palace.

The main doors were already open, as though somebody had just run through them, and inside the rain was even louder, sounding as if it came from below rather than above. As he walked through the palace he had left ten years ago, he heard echoes of everyday familiarities and formalities, the kind spoken on the move, in passing, as coats were put on, hats lifted, backs patted, as if the owners expected to walk through the doors he had just come through and down flights of steps on to six lanes of tarmac with screaming traffic and ranks of waiting taxis. The palace had been the only building in the empire with no signs anywhere inside it, the only one you could get lost in. Ludwig remembered it as a place where happiness could be found; where Mack Velli could be found if you wanted or needed him.

He heard footsteps above him and climbed up the stairs towards them. From experience he had discovered that voices were – however articulate – the least human of sounds. Nothing gave the presence of a human away like the sound of shoes, of a typewriter, of crockery being clashed, unnatural sounds that had to be engineered, created to interrupt the order of things.

As he climbed he pictured a man, dressed immaculately, the only remaining person in the empire, walking in his room alone but purposefully. Maybe Douglas had lied – Douglas and what Douglas said weren't so vivid now – and Mack was here after all. Mack would enjoy the fact that a person had travelled thousands of miles to die; he would have enjoyed planning his death. Mack had a penchant for other people's pain and, with no one else around, he would possibly want to make the most of the opportunity with Ludwig. He would want to make the death slow, but not so slow that he got used to having the victim around and would then find parting unbearable. Ludwig had heard of torturers who felt jilted, lost, when their victims died.

Mack's rooms had always been in the centre of the palace. With his hands on the double doors, Ludwig remembered how Mack had been single-handedly responsible for hierarchy within the empire. It had been the one thing he had really taken to believing: that if there was no hierarchy, men had no expectations of happiness. As he turned the door handles, a man ran round the corner in shoes that looked brand-new, carrying a small black case. In fact, he ran straight into Ludwig so that they both fell into the door.

'My God,' Ludwig said.

It was Mack's personal assistant or 'valet', Aurelius. Ludwig realised that he had never – ultimately – expected Aurelius to materialise. There was only one person he had hoped to find here, and that was Aesop. This was where they should have come. To Jara.

'Where have you come from?' Ludwig said.

'Rome.' Aurelius backed into the room, playing with his hair.

157

'Now?'

'My helicopter's only just landed.'

'Rome Rome? Or Sector Four Rome?'

'Sector Four,' Aurelius said as if he didn't know of any other. 'My God, it's you Ludwig.' Aurelius stared hard at Ludwig's face. 'Can I get you a drink or anything to eat?'

Ludwig could see that Aurelius was struggling to conceal his madness (something he didn't usually bother to do), frightened of upsetting his visitor. He kept looking at the small door at the back of the room that Mack had always made such a fuss of, but that Ludwig had privately suspected hid nothing more than some frivolity he had permitted himself, such as a gold toilet. He remembered how convinced he had been of the existence of the gold toilet. 'Where is Mack?' he asked.

'Mack Velli?' Aurelius said looking worried.

'Of course,' Ludwig said quickly, wondering whether his madness included violence. 'Were you expecting me? I thought you were, even though there was nobody there when my helicopter landed.' He paused, carefully measuring out the accusations, 'and I've seen nobody since.'

'Did you come here looking for Mack?'

'I was told – specifically – that he wasn't here. I thought I was being lied to.'

'He's not here. The cities in Sector Four on the northern bank are still operating.'

'I know, that's why I'm here.'

'The cities in Sector Four . . .'

'You've already said.'

Aurelius walked over to the desk and put his case on it, suddenly changing his tone. 'But then empires are always coming to an end aren't they.'

'I didn't hear anything when I walked through,' Ludwig said, ignoring him.

'Well it was raining, you can't even hear you own

footsteps in that rain. And you're wet. Here.' Aurelius helped him out of his suit jacket and shoes. 'Don't worry about Mack. Did you have any luggage?'

'I left it where the helicopter landed.'

'Then it will have been washed away or stolen. Talk about a city within a city. You wouldn't believe how many Indians have been living here without our knowledge. The population is almost double what we ever accounted for.'

Aurelius opened the case. There were silk ties inside which changed colour as they caught, alternately, sunlight and electric light. 'They were in the sale, but I got a further discount because I bought in bulk.'

Ludwig ran one through his hand.

'They're beautiful aren't they? Do you know what this one reminds me of? It reminds me of peacocks. And that I miss them.'

'They don't have peacocks in Rome then?'

'I don't know,' Aurelius said, confused, 'I've never been to Rome.'

With those words he certified himself, and Ludwig felt cold at the thought that Mack might have handed the task of murdering him over to Aurelius. There was something hit and run about being murdered by a mad-man that made death a wasted experience.

'What are you going to do with the ties?' Ludwig asked as Aurelius gave him the concerned expression the mad employ when they question the sanity of others. He remembered Aurelius before as always running, his dogged fervour, his dogged loyalty.

Aurelius was closing the lid of the case when the door at the back of the room opened. He straightened up and closed his eyes, but didn't turn round as a young girl of about fifteen walked into the room wearing nothing but turquoise pants and a pink T-shirt with the words 'I ♥ Vegas' written on it. She looked quickly at Ludwig then at the back of Aurelius, but he didn't move so she came round to stand in front of him.

'French Rose,' she said, and Ludwig could tell by the expression on Aurelius's face that he expected to see a lotus flower unfurl in the palm of her hand which he took and pressed against his face. 'You promised that you would get me more French Rose.' She showed her chipped nails half to Aurelius, half to Ludwig, unsure who was most likely to come up with the goods.

'She's got a thing about nail polish.' Aurelius smiled.

'I'm on a two-year contract,' Ludwig said, feeling the need to re-establish order.

'You can't be,' Aurelius replied, pulling the girl towards him by the waist and taking hold of her hand to inspect the nails in closer detail. 'There isn't that much left in Sector Four. You know why they get chipped don't you? She bites them.'

The girl looked away from Aurelius towards Ludwig, her eyes opening wider and wider until they stuck wetly to his face. 'Borealis,' she said quietly.

Ludwig nodded instinctively at her, and he knew when he heard her speak it that she wasn't afraid of being in the forest at night. 'Who is she?' he asked Aurelius.

Aurelius had all the makings of a pimp, a talent he had never exploited until now, only for love to cripple it. Ludwig envied him Jara – which he now had the run of – with all his heart.

'She's Beatrice.'

Ludwig nodded at her again; she made him think of a small child he had once surprised in Mack's bed clutching a doll.

'Ludwig. The one who made the thunderstorms,' the girl said, coming further forwards, although he could see that she had no more regard for him than she had for Aurelius.

He remembered standing in the same room years

before when electricity was making the sky change colour. Mack had been pressed against the window which wasn't something he usually did: he stayed away from windows out of habit. Ludwig remembered saying to him, 'A tropical storm. Surely you've seen one before.'

And Mack had pointed out to him that this one was without rain and told him that these storms were caused by the backdrafts from the forest-burning fires. That *they* were creating the storms. 'We're making thunder,' Mack had said, pressing himself even further against the glass.

'What are you doing home at this time?' Ludwig heard Aurelius asking the girl under his breath. He saw her wince at the word 'home'.

'Did you get me nail varnish or not. Cause if not I'm going.'

'Yes. Yes. Of course I did.'

Aurelius tried to touch her face, but she folded her arms blocking out the words on her T-shirt and slammed her back against the wall. She brushed some hair out of her eyes and stared straight at Ludwig. 'Mack's dead,' she said. Then she looked at Aurelius. 'Didn't anybody tell you?'

Ludwig realised from the way her arms were folded that she was lying. Aurelius didn't know the truth and the girl made it clear, with one quick, disparaging look and a finger in her mouth, that he wasn't to find out. Even though she clearly despised him on sight, Ludwig knew that she trusted him not to open his mouth.

Aurelius was looking at him, wondering what Mack's death might mean to him.

23

Ludwig left Velli's Palace before midnight, remembering that this was something nobody used to do. Everybody had been afraid of the dark which was never black but green, and daylight brought a relief that most of them hadn't experienced since childhood. He wondered how Aurelius slept, and what he took to help him achieve this state.

Now, walking on a road that barely existed any more, he was aware that this wasn't even the aftermath – that was yet to come. Early Egyptologists who discovered the Valley of the Kings said that walking into the pyramids was like opening the body of someone long dead and finding a beating heart. This faint beating was what had woken Ludwig up and he was sure Aurelius must hear it night after night. Jara hadn't died, it was just moving forwards in a different direction.

The paper mill was no longer lit at night as it used to be. Mack had decided against monumental floodlights in the end, but the lights they eventually wired up were still bright enough – they discovered – to attract people from far back in the forest who would come and stand at the fringes of roads and rail tracks and watch the light all night as if waiting for something or someone to step out of it.

There had been trouble with the lights at first because of the moths – often big enough to span a man's face or more – which would wrap themselves around the bulbs and burn. The sound they made as they died led a lot of the men to believe they had been sent as a warning. There was man, once, who left his window open while shaving and a moth flew in and landed on his face, pushing its furry body along the length of it and wrapping its wings round until they covered the man's ears. The scent it emitted once it realised it was stuck to the shaving cream sent the man wild with fear and he started to slash at it with the razor, cutting his own nose and mouth off and screaming with his throat full of moth, until he bled to death.

There were lights on in some of the huts in the village and Ludwig wondered what the workers did here unsupervised. There was a lot of litter as well. It was an unusually still night. He remembered nights like this in Jara when he had been able to feel his own skin growing. The lamp over the old warehouse was swinging though, and there was something malevolent about this movement without reason.

The warehouse had once been home to the jungle crushers, over-developed machinery that reminded Ludwig of trained thugs. The workers used to fight to get to drive them and their faces, as they tore up the weeds, were triumphant. These were tiny moments of revenge, microscopic acts of violence the men enjoyed inflicting on the forest. The jungle crushers had not only pulled up the undergrowth, that venomous deterrent to any Amazonian venture, but compacted the topsoil as well; to such an extent that not even weeds let alone trees would grow on it afterwards. The jungle crushers were sabotaged in the end, but whether by the two hundred mechanics employed to maintain them or another group no one ever found out. Mack had enjoyed the spectacle;

163

he said that they were one less thing that turned out to be necessary, one less thing to rely on. They reverted to slash and burn methods after this and the men walked into the jungle on their own two feet carrying chainsaws and machetes, felling trees to make way for trees, suitable trees – the sort paper could be made out of. The annihilation and re-planting programme took away the names of the three hundred different species of tree that grew per square acre, redefining them as 'waste'.

Before he knew it, Ludwig was walking among trees. He guessed that it must have been getting on for 2 a.m. because he could already smell the next day in the darkness. He had discovered very quickly, when he first started working with them, that each species of tree was unique and the one he put his hands out towards now was the tree Mack had dreamt of, the tree that had grown inside all of them, filling the empty spaces between vital organs: the gmelina tree. They had planted seedlings by the million, correcting the natural twist in the trunk in order to make it more malleable. This one's trunk, however, was twisted which meant that it had grown instinctively.

When he tried to pass between the two trunks in front of him, he walked into something solid and, putting his hands out, touched something cold strung between the two trees. He passed along to the next two, but the same boundary was there: glass. It took him a while to find the word, even though his hands had recognised it immediately. Once he had found it, he saw the iron framework, faintly binding the glass panels together. He was standing in the horticultural nurseries, built with glass walls and no roof because of the heat.

He followed the glass until the gmelina trees stopped, suddenly, and he smelt something that made him think of higher skies. It wasn't exactly a clearing, it was a different forest where the trees were only waist-high and, for a moment, he wondered whether these trees weren't in fact the same height as the gmelina, and it was he who had grown. These were pine; he knew the smell as soon as he touched the branches and felt the needles. There had never been pine trees in Jara before.

'Fuck off.'

The words carried aggressively and without power. A girl's voice.

Ludwig stopped. Beatrice looked up at him. Her T-shirt looked very white among the trees and he found the words 'I ♥ Vegas' printed on it disconcerting.

Then someone else said, 'Beatrice, what are you doing here getting pine needles stuck in your feet? Come to shit among my trees?'

'Aurelius,' Ludwig said automatically, recognising the sound of his voice.

'What are you both doing here?' Aurelius said, suspicious.

'I don't know. I wasn't looking, I was just walking,' Ludwig answered.

'Well *I* came looking for her, this thing,' Aurelius said, grabbing handfuls of Beatrice's hair and pulling her to him so that she had to put her hands out to stop herself from falling through his chest, 'who was never a child, but an animal. Did you know she used to have four legs? These are new,' he said taking hold of her arms and starting to bend them, but the girl broke free and ran off, both Aurelius and Ludwig catching a glimpse of the metal at her thigh.

'She leaves my bed most nights at midnight,' Aurelius said quietly, although whether as an explanation or threat Ludwig couldn't tell.

'What's this?' Ludwig said, passing his hands over the top of the tree. 'Pine?'

'These are the old nurseries.'

'I know,' Ludwig replied sharply. 'I supervised their

building. They were always too tentative; they should have been the first thing to become derelict, and instead I see they're being maintained. I saw the gmelina. I walked through them; they're growing uncorrected.

'The gmelina brought Jara to its knees,' Aurelius said, defensively. 'We ignored every basic rule: there was no test planting, no diversification, we just burnt and burnt then planted by the million.' Aurelius rubbed his hands over one of the trees, then smelt it. 'Caribbean pine,' he said, smiling, 'and some eucalyptus too. One of the workers discovered these a couple of years before Mack's death. The results of the test plantings have been excellent.'

Aurelius stared into the trees again, his eyes always looking for the same thing.

Ludwig thought of the lamp swinging in the warehouse doorway and the windows in the village huts with light shining from them.

'You can't begin again,' he said, suddenly horrified, and now afraid of Aurelius for the first time since he had arrived.

'We have to.'

'Why?'

'Because we can; because we've found a way.'

'Did Mack know?'

'Of course not.'

'He wanted Jara to finish, Aurelius.'

'Only because he thought it had to. Now it doesn't have to.'

Ludwig looked at him and realised that it was Mack's death Aurelius had been waiting for. 'The paper mill?' he asked.

'We've begun to repair it inside.'

'Do you know why this failed? Do you know for how long Mack believed there would be a world paper shortage?'

'No,' Aurelius mumbled.

'Probably somewhere in the region of eight months. He created all this from a vision that lasted only eight months. He was a believer in his own prophecy for that long. After that he wasn't wrong, just bored; it was time for the next thing. There isn't going to be a paper shortage, Aurelius. You don't need to do this. Jara isn't going to happen again.' He could feel the presence of the other man going limp.

'Mack was an industrialist . . .' Aurelius said. (Ludwig had never heard him referred to as this before.) 'He wasn't a prophet.'

Aurelius ran his palm up and down the glass wall, which was easier to see now it was lighter.

'I don't want you to close Sector Four down,' he said slowly, 'I want you to defy Mack's last orders, I want you to leave Jara to me; to bequeath it to me. It's in your power to do that.'

The smell of the pines got stronger as it grew lighter and the walk back to Velli's Palace seemed suddenly unbearably long.

24

Dr Blackthorn went to the station to meet Achilles and stood across the exit with his station café cup of tea slopping over his shoes as the train from London pulled in. He felt a sudden yawning desolation at the thought that she might have changed her mind or, at the last moment, chosen to disbelieve him, but then he saw her. She was the last to step down from the train, and looked about her with her vacuum-cleaner eyes as if she had been expecting something: a reception party, a group of supporters, or even just a man holding a board with her name on it.

She was wearing a white dress and carrying a small case. He raised his arms and opened them as she got closer, but she didn't slacken her pace, she just carried on walking towards him until she was standing inside his arms and their noses were virtually touching. He didn't dare close them round her, not even in the most professional of embraces. This time their meeting was official, legal, and in many respects (because of the last time) ridiculous. He found himself back within boundaries and she was untouchable once more. She in turn gave her hand to him as if she were drawing a gun and, although he tried to kiss it without wetting his lips first, she still wiped it across her dress as she walked out of the station.

He had discovered over the past two years that there is a certain safety, a certain courage to be found in loving another person absolutely, and in the sure knowledge that they don't love you in return. That they don't and never will. Over the past two years he had taken the most extraordinary plunges into unreason in order to spend time with her, to get her to spend time with him. Once he realised there was no hope, he no longer had to lie to himself (which was a luxury, he decided, not many people could afford) and was able to look the real rather than the ideal side of humanity full in the eye, in all its ever-changing ugliness, and not shrink from it but love it still. For the first time in his life he was able to feel something close to heroic.

Two nights previously, sat by the side of the camp bed they had erected for Aesop in the palm house, he had watched the sleeping boy, carrier of Eastman's Syndrome, and knew that he held in his hands the means to bring her back to him. They would both know what it was he was doing, and the only thing he had in his favour was the fact that he hadn't engineered the whole thing, it had simply arrived on his doorstep one day; as a fellow professional it was his right to contact an expert and have her brought up, because they couldn't very well move the boy.

His power lay in the fact that she wouldn't be able to resist. Even if she said 'no' at first, she would have to give in sooner or later; she had never seen the borealis in its infant state before. He had something in his possession that she would desire which gave him a greater freedom to control her even than if she had loved him. As the attachment grew he would be able to watch her weakness grow until she became nothing but her weakness and he had decided to give her virtually sole charge of Aesop in order to allow this state to develop to the full.

★

Even though Hornby Hall could be seen from the station platform it still took them fifteen minutes to drive there which gave him time to explain to her (in a proud voice) that most of the remaining staff were inbreds and that Jack Preston himself hadn't been up in the day for the past five years; the curtains remained drawn until dusk, when he rose. In fact this reverse regime had been imposed on most of the staff so the whole house rose at seven in the evening. Blackthorn had the place to himself during the day, only sharing the table with Preston in the evenings when he had his dinner and Preston had his breakfast. As far as Blackthorn was concerned it was an ideal arrangement and Preston's idiosyncrasy enabled him to give rise to one of his own: the fantasy that he was in fact owner of Hornby Hall.

'Imagine the space, the facilities, if we were to open a clinic here,' he said running round the front of the car to open the door for her before she had a chance to.

'Yes, I can imagine,' she said looking up at the hall, feeling weary at the barely concealed tone of proprietorship in his voice. She didn't put murder beyond him, but didn't feel inspired enough right then to participate in some feeble-minded killing, the outcome of which would be the property deeds to Hornby Hall.

Inside the hall it was virtually pitch black, as Blackthorn had said it would be, apart from the odd crack of sunlight that had forced itself through carelessly drawn curtains as thick as carpets. As they passed these chinks their bodies were suddenly criss-crossed with light. Draughts blew round corners and through banisters like children without the threat of discipline. Blackthorn was panting in an unpleasantly canine way when they reached the top of the house and he threw the door to her room open as if he were a bell boy showing somebody to their bridal suite.

'What's this?' she asked.

'The bedroom,' he said, putting her case down near the window.

'Where is he?'

'Oh he's not here. He's not in the house.'

'So why are we here?'

He looked about the room as if it had changed since the last time he was there. 'I thought you might want to wash or change or something.'

'Not at all.'

The curtains in this room were also shut and when the door closed they momentarily lost sight of each other, breathing nothing but the dust that rose and fell in the room in heavy clouds. There were no windows open and she could feel dust settling on her sweating face and arms. She put her left hand out to where she remembered the bed head being. Her finger tips were tingling at the thought of making contact with the cold iron, but there was nothing there and her arm fell haltingly to her side, unbalancing her so that she fell back slightly into the curtains whose folds closed around her arms and legs so that she had to put her own hand over her mouth to stop herself from screaming. She was sure that she could hear Blackthorn breathing very close to her and the hairs on her arms raised themselves in expectation of his fingers. The darkness, despite the fact that it filled the entire house from ceiling to floor and door to window, in this room seemed nothing more than opportune.

She listened for the rustling of his damp shirt, for the hairs on his body scratching at his clothes, the metallic click of his belt and fly zip as he moved towards her, able to see where she couldn't. She was also aware that she was afraid of stepping further back into the curtains in case there was no window behind them, just more of the same, blackness. And she could feel from the way the fabric taunted her that the curtains were probably in league with him, that he had discussed this whole scenario with them. She felt, inexplicably, as though she were about to come to an end, then the door opened letting a threadbare light through that illuminated her white dress.

He was standing in the open door, his face radiant with the knowledge that she hadn't changed and that he knew her still; that she still had nothing to give him. It was right that the room should mean nothing to her, that the bed, whose sheets he had put on himself, should mean nothing to her, whose duvet (the only one in the house somebody hadn't died under) should mean nothing to her, that she should ask no questions. It was right that he should continue to provide unflinchingly for her happiness and comfort, without thanks and without hope. It meant that he could give unadulteratedly without ever receiving anything in return.

'Were you hurt that night on the heath? That man . . .' She trailed off, but they were both breathing more easily now.

'Yes.'

'Where?'

'My stomach,' he said.

They knew then that neither of them would ever mention his hand on her gate that night, and how they had both waited, she at the window, him at the gate, for longer than they should have.

She pushed the curtains away from her, angry at the streaks of dirt on her dress. He had been standing nowhere near her.

'Do you want to see the disease now?' he asked.

They were walking in a different direction this time, westwards instead of eastwards, and they had sunk lower. She could smell the unmistakable smell of wet plaster and wood swollen with damp, smells that made her think of the end of civilisation, the loss of reason. After a while they were no longer walking on carpet. They had reached a part of the house where flagstones still prevailed, the underbelly where it was lighter because the walls had at one time been painted white. At the end of the passageway where she followed the moist slop of Blackthorn's shoes, there was a door with a metal bucket in front of it, stacked full of cleaning fluids and cloths. The swans carved into the door handles maintained a faded sort of dignity in the face of this invasion of hygiene.

Nothing about the door had prepared her for what lay on the other side. Even though the light came from very high up, she still had to throw her arm across her face; and the heat was as hot as the darkness in the house had been black. The smell of humidity was an intensely inhuman smell and it pushed itself up her nostrils until they were gaping and unable to absorb any more; the only relief was – she was sure – the faint trace of cigarette smoke.

The palm house was octagonal in design, but because it was so large and the corners unaccentuated, the feeling once you were inside was that you were standing in a circular building, with an intricately layered dome. Where the foliage wasn't so dense you could see beyond the iron framework and glass to the moors and their outcrops purple with August, and the trees in the palm house pushed against the glass to see these infallible remains of a prehistoric northern hemisphere. Inside the trees and flowers were straining and splitting open with an unchecked lushness that made the glass look all the more fragile. Moss and undergrowth sprawled over the Victorian tiled pathway, making the black and white checks look unhealthy.

Achilles could hear Blackthorn behind her trying to tread lightly, but still wanting to make the moment into a gift for her. Then as she came out into the centre of the

173

palm house she saw a butterfly with a wingspan as big as Icarus, its yellow wings dappled with markings that looked at her as if they were eyes, only the body of the butterfly wasn't black and there were no antennae, the body of the butterfly had legs and arms, and was wearing a blue prison uniform. The boy turned around, but the butterfly was still stuck to his back, the upper wings emerging from behind his head, and the lower from behind his back, vibrating slightly. She recognised him immediately; it was the boy from the swimming pool, the one she had lain on her back in the water and looked up at through the falling snow, the one who had leaned over the parapet, the one who had been following Ludwig; the boy.

Aesop didn't recognise her and thought, looking at the dirt on her face and dress, that she had probably been in the palm house for some time, and wondered where she had been and why he hadn't seen her before.

'Is it still on me? The butterfly, the three-foot butter-fly?' he shouted.

'It's on your back.'

'I knew it. Why won't it just leave me alone? I've tried hiding from it but it thinks I'm playing a game.'

'It's curious; you're the only thing in here that isn't a plant or a butterfly.'

'Can't you get it off?'

She could see that the tips of his ears had gone red and that his hands were shaking. 'Just get this fucking thing off me.'

Dr Blackthorn moved quickly forward wondering where the best place to pick up a butterfly was, but it flew off as soon as it saw him coming, raising itself up into the dome where it could look down at the group below.

'I hate butterflies,' the boy said looking accusingly at Blackthorn.

'I know, I know, but there's nowhere else we can put you at the moment that has a temperature that will ensure your condition remains stable. Aesop, this is Dr Achilles,' he said, as she managed again to brush past his outstretched arms.

She hoped that the boy would recognise her now over the formal introduction, but he barely bothered to look as he sat down on his camp bed, littered with cigarette stubs (so she *had* smelt smoke), a personal stereo with headphones, and a shoebox full of cassettes.

'Is this all you brought with you from the Institute?' she asked.

'It's all I've got.'

'It's all we had time to collect,' Blackthorn corrected him. 'We were only allowed a quarter of an hour. Aesop has rather a lot of supporters convinced of his innocence campaigning around most of the perimeter.'

'Campaigning for your innocence?'

Aesop ignored her, staring straight past her legs.

'Are you innocent?' she asked.

He looked up at that.

'You don't know what it is he's been accused of,' Blackthorn said, wryly.

'What are you guilty of?'

Direct questions were a technique that she found worked well with children; they were a sign that the questioner was willing to reveal things about themselves, that they could be trusted.

'I killed two people.'

'You did? Or were you accused of it,' she said, remembering again him running along the balcony after Ludwig complaining of his shoes.

'Two women,' he said, and she noticed the uncomfortable snarl in his voice. 'A girl and her grandmother. Two days after Christmas,' he added, as if this fact was at least equal to the other one.

'Did you?'

He looked up at her, then down again.

'Well, that's not what concerns me,' she finished gently. 'I don't know why you bothered to mention it,' she said, turning slowly to Blackthorn.

'Just to prevent you wondering needlessly why he was wearing prison uniform,' he said.

Dr Achilles shrugged and sat down on the camp bed next to Aesop, not bothering to move the cigarette stubs out the way first, knowing that it was the kind of thing that he would hold against her.

'Has Dr Blackthorn talked to you about Eastman's Syndrome?'

'Yes,' he said impatiently, looking up at him, then at the roof of the palm house and down between the foliage, for the butterfly, in case it was thinking of landing on his back again. She could see that the boy and the man barely tolerated each other and that because of the dislike Blackthorn allowed himself certain freedoms, a professional laxity he wouldn't usually.

'You've become a rare thing indeed,' she said, taking care not to avoid his eyes this time.

'Lucky me.'

'Here, I brought you some information on it. The only written documentation that exists, in fact; there have been so few reported cases in the developed world. I think that people have been looking at it recently as the medical equivalent of the north-west passage.'

He took it, looked at it briefly, then put it down on the bed.

'Read it when you have a moment.'

'While it's still light.'

'Sorry?'

'While it's still light; this place doesn't have electricity.'

'It doesn't need to, it's made of glass.'

'Once it's dark I have to go to bed.'

176

'I told you that I would speak to Mr Preston and get it fixed,' Blackthorn reminded him.

'Well I hope it happens before winter. I'm still going to be here in the winter, aren't I?'

'It's likely, yes,' Dr Achilles put in, finding it increasingly difficult to speak as the sweat on her upper lip gathered. 'From our point of view, it is the ideal artificial environment for you to sustain the disease in, although not necessarily from yours. Until we can come up with something more this will have to suffice. I'm sorry.'

'No, you're not.'

'I am,' she insisted. 'From what we know of the syndrome, if you were to set foot outside the palm house your respiratory system would fail within thirty minutes. The syndrome makes your body temperature fall at ten times the rate of the average man. Life is only sustained if the body is kept in tropical, or ideally higher temperatures. Such as an African gold mine,' she said smiling.

The boy's head was bowing further and further towards his lap and his hair, which hadn't been cut, was falling across his face, but she knew when a drop rolled off the bottom of his chin and on to his trousers, that he was crying, and that it was probably the first time he had cried since arriving at the palm house. It enabled her to move closer to him, and put her arm about his shoulder. At first when she pulled him gently towards her, he jerked himself back, but after a while she brought his head tentatively on to her breast. In order to get him to trust her, she had to demonstrate her ability to subordinate Blackthorn.

'I'll join you in the house in a minute,' she said to him, catching Aesop's hair in her mouth.

'Whereabouts?' He could feel that his old delirium was setting in and that he needed to anchor it by taking control of the details.

'I don't know, I'll find you,' she said, the words falling down the side of the boy's head.

He left begrudgingly, trailing his feet behind him and after he had shut the door to the palm house and was standing once more in the corridor, he had the sudden impression that however black things had been they had only ever been grey in comparison to the black he was standing at the fringes of.

Dr Achilles whispered into Aesop's hair. 'Have they brought you any new clothes?'

'No,' he said, already starting to wipe his nose profusely on the back of his hand. She watched the snot dry and crack.

'Do you want me to go into town and pick you some things up. Do you mind if I do?'

He shook his head.

As he was bent over she quickly pulled at the back of his collar.

'What are you doing?' His hand went straight to the back of his neck as if he expected to find something there.

'Nothing. Checking what size you are.'

'Well you could have just asked. I'm 24 waist, and 32 chest – they're the sizes Ludwig used to always buy me.'

She sat back slightly. 'Ludwig?'

'Yes, Ludwig.'

She didn't ask any more.

'He was somebody who looked after me for a while.'

He started to sort through the cigarette stubs, automatically putting them in order of height.

'I've never been ill before.'

'Do you know I don't think I have either.'

'But you're a doctor.'

'I know, strange isn't it.'

'Somehow it makes you realise that whatever plans you have for yourself, someone somewhere is thinking differently. It makes you feel as though you own nothing, not even your own death.'

'That's the least of your worries.'

'I hate him,' he said suddenly standing up.

She picked up the article on Eastman's she had given him. 'So do I,' she said quietly. 'You should read this you know.'

'I can't. I can't read.'

Here in the palm house he was able to say it for the first time without it mattering.

25

Aurelius lay in Mack's bed with Beatrice beside him listening to the thunder which always scared him the most when it came alone, without the lightning. He turned over and took hold of Beatrice's hand, pressing the palm against his face. The scent of his genitalia still flowered there along the lines of fortune.

The night Mack died, he climbed to the top of the hill that the helicopter Ludwig came in had landed on and sat with his back against a tree near the pool the Indians thought was the entrance to the underworld. Water for them was the only thing that separated this world from the next and a lot of them only knew of the existence of the sea because of rumours they had heard spoken about it. He wondered where they thought the Jara River flowed to.

The next night he went again, but that night the surface of the pool broke like skin stretched over a spine and he instinctively drew his feet back thinking if this is a door it isn't only for us to get in, but for them to get out. A woman rose up out of the water as women have been known to do. Despite the moon and the water her hair was still black and her skin was the colour of wet gum-tree bark. She had a pink T-shirt on with 'I ♥ Vegas' written across her breasts. Beneath it, her nipples were tear-drop shaped; they made her body melancholy. Her feet, stood on the water's edge, seemed big compared to the small tattered turquoise pants she was wearing.

She might have been picked up in the forest by a Sector Four expedition party and then dropped off after a couple of nights, but was more likely to have come from one of the colonists' brothels built before the plots were hallowed by schools and hospitals. He even suspected that this wasn't the first time she had seen him.

When she saw him her back didn't arch and her arms didn't go up to her face. She stood still with her hands curled down the sides of her thighs – it was possible she was carrying a knife. And it wasn't until she stood up that he realised how small she was; measured in years, not more than fourteen. She had unusually long nails with flakes of vermilion still settled in the centre and, above the olfactory roar of the forest, she smelt faintly of urine which disappeared when she got close. Her hair had smoke in it that the water hadn't washed off, and her body was thick with spearmint.

She walked straight out of the pool into his arms and pushed her cheek into his shirt, so that he found himself staring down at the crown of her head, and the small white blot in the centre that was her scalp. She stepped back but took hold of his hand so that he led her back down into Jara with him, a small button mark indented in her right cheek.

Now he had fucked her inside out. He had eroded all his senses through the limited act of pleasuring himself and was now incapable of leaving fingerprints on any-thing he touched; he had no lines left on his hands, he came from nowhere. And in every patch of darkness he walked into, all he could see was a pair of eyes rising from water. Even in his deepest sleep where he no longer had nightmares or dreams but something worse he couldn't call by either name, he heard the brushing the balls of her

181

feet made across the floor as she came in and the quick breath her clothes took as they hit the floor.

Beatrice (his name for her) had never laid a finger on him. She never helped him to undress and her hands never traced any part of him, although her hair sometimes stroked him inadvertently. She only lay on top of him if he pulled her on himself and he had to take his own cock to her mouth by kneeling over her and pushing it in himself, into her mouth that stretched with a belligerence that gave him a pleasure she hadn't intended.

It didn't matter if he couldn't use the word 'love'. They weren't lovers. He had to stoop to half his height to kiss her and, curled behind her at night, he could push his knees up into the soles of her feet. When he woke up in the morning she was always gone, and instead of being able to watch her eyes open, he was left to search the empty bed for hairs that had fallen from her body.

She slept on her stomach – she always slept like that – with her hands tucked under the pillow where she had stashed her pants and T-shirt. These were the only things that belonged to her that she kept here in Mack's apartment. He always had the impression that life, for her, was elsewhere, he just hadn't found out where yet. Often when she didn't come back till late at night he went up to the pool she had first risen from, but he never saw her there again. At first he had questioned her gently, beguilingly, later he had shouted, later still he started to hit her and finally he locked her in, but she still escaped. She walked away from him every time and every time she came back.

She made him cry for himself. He remembered how unsurprised he had been to hear her speaking English, a strange broken blasphemous language. The first time round it made perfect sense, the second time, it was nothing more than nonsense. She never used language to communicate, only ever as a rebuke or as a means of reviling.

The night he brought her back he laid her down on Mack's bed and said, 'You'll have to help me,' as he circled the head of his cock with thumb and forefinger, trying to make it small enough to fit inside her. 'I can't find you.' Often he let his fingers fall around inside her for hours, pulling her up on to him slowly afterwards, and once he stroked himself and her with a feather from dusk till dawn until he felt the onset of death at the anticipation of pleasure, and although her body was covered in a rash by the end she never once uttered a sound. He lay above her night after night crying and shouting, 'Wake up, wake up,' even though she lay there wide awake staring up at him as his lips and eyes grew in orgasm. She denied him nothing, but never joined him. He made love alone night after night and after he had his orgasm he lay back down in the bed next to her and pulled the sheets about him, clawing at them in his sleep like a criminal unable to leave the scene of the crime, forced to watch the corpse of the person he has just murdered rot in front of his eyes. He had been through her and out the other end, and seen the invisible anatomy that can never be operated on, that once damaged can never be mended, never be saved.

Eight months after Ludwig's arrival, Beatrice let out a small cry in the night and Aurelius noticed that her shoulders were scrunched up and that her lips had gone purple. Then suddenly she flung herself on her back and started grabbing blindly at the sheets, pulling them from the four corners of the giant-size bed and trying to tuck them around her. She woke up and looked at him.

'I'm cold.'

She never made statements, they were too expressive, and unnecessary.

183

'So cold.'

He arched his back over her and tried to tuck the sheets in further until she was wrapped up in a cocoon, resting his hand just below her chin.

'There,' he said smiling.

'Not that kind of cold,' she said and he saw – for the first time – real fear in her eyes

'What kind of cold?' he asked, but now he was starting to feel afraid himself.

'Not a nice cold. A cruel cold. I don't like this cold.'

Then she shut her eyes and although he didn't understand, he knew that he had to keep her awake, that he couldn't allow her eyes to close. He left her in the bed as he ran through the other rooms on the floor, Mack's private rooms. Sometimes as he ran he saw disappearing streaks of fire. He was sure he passed pictures like cave paintings on the wall, and scattered down one corridor were red feathers half covering what looked like recent tracks of muddy footprints. There were others living in the building as he had always suspected, and tonight he had startled them on his quest for further bedding that he could pile on top of Beatrice, and all the time as he ran and threw open door after door, the thing he was most afraid of was running into laughter. Even the thought of the laughter made him suspect Beatrice, thinking that he would get back to the room trailing the abandoned bedding behind him to find her gone. But then he heard his name being called, it was barely more than a scream but he heard his name in it. She had never spoken his name before; she had never even asked it, but instead of turning round he ran further until he came to the door of Ludwig's room. The door opened from the inside before he had a chance to get to it and Ludwig was standing there. The room behind him was in darkness and he flinched from the pale light in the corridor.

184

'Beatrice?' he asked.

Aurelius nodded.

'I heard her. I've never heard her before.'

'You didn't think I might be with her?' Aurelius asked.

Ludwig looked at him for a moment. 'I know you don't make her make those sounds.'

They both strained their ears for a moment in case there were more screams.

'I thought you might be killing her.'

'Or she might have been killing me.'

'She wouldn't be driven to that. You barely exist for her, Aurelius. You know that.'

On the way back he heard no running feet and caught no glimpses of brown backs, brown calves or brown heels disappearing round any corners.

'Would you have stopped me?'

'No.'

'Why were you awake then?'

'I thought you might need me.'

'She's very small – she wouldn't take much killing.'

'There's nothing worse than being left alone with somebody you've just murdered.'

'That's what Mack always said to me.'

'It's what he said to me as well.'

'Yes, but you've put it into practice.'

'I've had to.'

'He never did let me graduate,' Aurelius said. 'I never worked with ... skin ... like you did. I never got beyond paper, a desk piled with paper was the ship I sailed my ocean in.'

'It doesn't matter.'

They got to Mack's old bedroom. He could tell that Ludwig was more taken aback than he wanted to be at the realisation that Aurelius slept there; even Ludwig had a notion of the sacred, and the room smelt of something it had never smelt of when Mack was alive.

185

'Were you, then?' Ludwig said, taking his voice down to a whisper.

'What?'

'Going to kill her?'

'Not tonight.'

She had fallen out of the bed and was trying to get back in. Ludwig and Aurelius looked at each other. She was in the position most people assume when they're injured or bleeding to death and for a moment Aurelius wondered if he hadn't in fact murdered her in his sleep.

'Beatrice, you were calling my name.'

'I was?' She looked terrified at the thought. 'There's two of you,' she said as if she were speaking about something more than white men.

Ludwig stayed by the door, but she kept her eyes on him.

'I'm still cold.'

He watched as Aurelius lifted her back on to the bed and lay above her, his feet hanging over the edge.

'Come and look.'

'I don't want you looking,' Beatrice screamed.

Ludwig came and stood by them both.

'Can you see? She's covered in cracks. White cracks. Touch her.'

Ludwig put his hand out.

'You're really fucking ugly,' she said, looking at him.

Aurelius went to hit her but then remembered that it was a violation, a taboo for civilised people to hit those who were ill, maimed, and he rested his hand on her hair instead, but she had seen the sudden need for violence cross his eyes.

Ludwig went to get his bedding, and the only thing Aurelius could think to do in the meantime was dress her in one of his suits so that she could wear that in bed. He was surprised that she agreed.

'Let me put my T-shirt on first.'

186

'You don't need it.'

She lay down in bed while he pulled the turquoise pants up, holding her breath while he kissed her there before pulling them round her waist. As he helped her into the suit he realised that they should have been laughing while they did it. If they hadn't been in Jara, if they had lain beneath a window that looked out on to streets with cars, if the walls had been smeared in orange from the street lamps, if they had lived within earshot of other people's lives, if she had been older. When he looked at her lying there in the suit, he tried to bring up the laughter but couldn't even remember what the first tickles felt like, his lungs and mouth were out of practice. And the strange thing was that it looked as though the suit had once fitted her. It didn't now but it looked as though it once had, as if she used to be older, and bigger, but was now getting younger, growing smaller.

There was the possibility that she might have asked him to stay with her and he waited by her for the next five minutes, occasionally putting his ear closer to her mouth in case she said it without his realising, in case he missed it.

When he left she didn't try to stop him.

'The Sector Four doctor's the only one I'm still sure is here. Is he here still?' Aurelius asked looking at Ludwig. 'Even if he's here and he picks up my call, he won't be here until the morning – he's got the river to cross.'

'I know a doctor,' Ludwig said quietly.

'Here?'

'London. I know that she would come.'

'Why?'

'She would want to see Beatrice. She knows what things that walk out of the jungle look like.'

And for the first time since he had arrived Aurelius looked at Ludwig's face properly. 'Mack had everybody in Jara, even babies, brought to the palace. He was looking for your face.'

'He knew it didn't come from Jara.'

'He knew after that.'

'It came from the jungle.'

'We thought that you would go back in there afterwards. That that's the only place you could hope to find a cure.'

'You know I wasn't looking for a cure. I went looking for this.' He put the palms of his hands on both his cheeks.

'I don't believe that. I don't believe that now. But Mack did. That's why he was more afraid of losing you afterwards – even though you looked like you did, like you do – than he was before.'

The green light from the laptop computer washed itself across the walls of the office so that they felt as though they were in a tank of water. There was a pile of Mack's old records on the desk.

'Do you ever play these?' Ludwig asked.

'I can't.'

It took them two hours to get through to the Hospital for Diseases of the Skin in London, only to get a message back saying that Dr Achilles was away in the north of England. The nurse on duty, isolated under a daylight simulation bulb, her bowl of porridge steaming beside her, did offer warily to contact her. The electronic message from Jara was beyond the boundary of her world.

It was six a.m. when Dr Achilles woke up although the time meant nothing – not even morning changed the texture of the darkness. She had fallen asleep with her computer on, the screen, full of statistics that would keep Aesop alive, still bright when the message flashed across it. So that's where Ludwig is, she thought.

26

The electrics in the palm house were working again, and she often wondered whether Aesop saw her as the woman who brought him light. They had erected something very close to a 'room' around the water fountain in there; an old armchair that was already going brown with mildew around the edges and a desk with two golden sphinxes for legs and a marble top. Aesop had never seen anything like it. At night, lying on his camp bed it rose above him unsteadily like the hull of a ship, as if it expected something of him.

Dr Achilles had managed to get hold of a television, but the humidity made it impossible for them to get any reception and he was sure that their defeat as far as this was concerned was something the plants felt triumphant about, as if they had been mocked when the set was brought in. Now it stood awkwardly on its steel castors, abandoned and without the means to draw attention to itself, but Aesop couldn't quite bring himself to remove it altogether. Over in the corner there was a tin bath that Achilles had found in the old nursery; this was the only way they could find of giving him a bath that was acceptable to his condition. The water was heated and poured in the kitchen along the corridor, then carried laboriously back through to the palm house just as it was

189

getting dark. He always waited until it was dark outside, which was getting earlier and earlier as winter closed in, and then switched out the lights and climbed into the bath.

One night, sitting in the water with his knees tucked up underneath his chin, Aesop realised with an anxiety of wonder that the furniture he had laid about him like a barricade he was forever afraid of being broken down, followed the layout of the flat Ludwig had given him exactly. Despite the haphazard requests he had put in to have furniture put where he thought it would fit best, his mind had been working to a perfectly articulated plan. It made him feel as though he had been stuck in a ditch without realising it. Perhaps this was it and all that most lives comprised were a couple or more ditches varying in width and depth.

The desk was covered with Peter and Jane books, exercise books and flash cards. In the mornings there were three people in the palm house: him, Dr Achilles, and the syndrome. By the evening there were only ever two. Achilles often brought her tea in on a tray so that she could eat it with him before they started their evening's work. Sometimes it only lasted an hour, sometimes as long as three, and it began when she drew the stool up to the desk and clicked the desk lamp on. No matter how light it was still outside, the desk lamp was always switched on and often the pages of the books were cast in shadows and the words danced out of light and darkness, as the butterflies, attracted by the light flew close overheard, the dust and pollen falling off their wings as they flapped, and into her and Aesop's hair.

When he had first started to look at the flash cards he had leant forward hunching his shoulders and she could see before he had even pronounced the letter that his lips were forming the wrong sound. So she went back to the alphabet, the beginning. When they practised 'a', they sat opposite each other, their mouths open and their cheeks pulled back. She always did it with him making him repeat each letter five times until his lips were wet with concentration. He didn't take his eyes off her lips, in case she did something he missed, repeating the sound until the drops of moisture hanging off the iron structure vibrated with the phonetic alphabet.

It wasn't until the evening they reached 'p', when she watched him pronounce it for the fifth time, that she realised. He had never let anybody get this far before; she didn't know why she had been allowed, but it struck her watching his mouth pout flatly as he carried on pronouncing his 'p's, waiting to be told to stop, that he was utterly helpless in the face of it. She wondered if he was at last going to utter the words he meant to say when he leant over the balcony and looked down on to the swimming pool.

After a while he learnt to write the letter and, rather than holding the pencil between his knuckles and trying to crush the lead out of it as most children did when they learnt, he held it gently with a timidity she hadn't expected. She taught him when the pencil had to write its stroke downwards and when it had to write its stroke upwards and his letters soon changed from being fat and crippled into smooth articulate edifices. When he first started he often used to smudge his work with dribble, but had now learnt how to do it with his mouth closed. Sometimes – she couldn't help noting – he concentrated so hard that, even though his mouth remained closed, he got an erection, as if the breath he wasn't allowed to breathe out through his mouth had to find an alternative means of escape. Sometimes he tried to hold it down with his left hand, but it didn't stop him from carrying on with his writing. When the page was still blank, just as he was about to press his pencil into it, he would always sigh, as if he didn't really want to do what he was

191

about to do, but had no choice, as if the act had more to do with violence than learning. Even if she got called away to the phone, she would walk back into the palm house to find him in exactly the same position, his concentration entirely unbroken.

Dr Blackthorn would wait most nights until around ten, then he would slip his shoes off and put two or three pairs of socks on instead. The socks silenced his footsteps on the gravel and prevented his feet from getting cut as he walked around the side of the house and stood against the glass of the palm house looking in. This minor act of surveillance was childish compared to the hours he had spent walking the streets of London.

He wondered whether one of the side effects of Eastman's was a gradual reduction in eyesight because she started every evening by sitting on a stool and holding cards up at the boy, and there was something in the way she held them that indicated that it was an act without weight. After this they read one of the books from the pile on the desk, and he could see the boy drawing his fingers across the pages as though he were following the logic of intricate diagrams and he wondered whether they had actually managed successfully to chart the syndrome. Then the boy usually wrote or drew so that their heads leant together and he had to watch while the boy brushed the back of his neck where her hair swung and sometimes fell down the back of his collar. Desire and immorality – not speech – are what separates us from the animals, Blackthorn thought.

The details, which boiled down to elbows touching, hair on a collar and hands on the back of a neck were the desolate truth that he witnessed every night through the glass, that he crept silently towards with the dejection of a martyr. He was waiting to take hold of the hatred and anger which were still just out of reach. In bed he laughed a curdled laugh to think that the borealis had once been his only hope; to think that he had possessed it. It wasn't so much that he had failed, but that he had overlooked something and he didn't know if he had the energy to retrace his footsteps.

Every morning Aesop saw the fingerprints on the window at the far side of the palm house, and was afraid that it might be the grandmother they had killed. He was never sure why he didn't suspect that it might be the girl but he didn't, it was the grandmother he was afraid of, and every morning there seemed to be more. He fitted his hands into the prints left behind, and even in reverse realised that every night the person – whoever it was – assumed this posture of pain. Sometimes he thought he saw Ludwig standing there watching him at his lessons.

Aesop finished the word he was writing then put the pencil down. Achilles leant forward to have a look and he watched her mouth form the word he had just written.

'It's funny this,' he said.

'You're doing so well.'

'I mean that I'm doing this at all. Now.'

She started to look back through his papers.

'Now that I'm going to die. I'm never going to leave this palm house.'

'Aesop, you're not going to die. Eastman's isn't terminal. Who told you it was?'

'Nobody. I just figured that if this was my lot . . .' He looked up at the fat dripping trees and at her hair that had gone into tight ringlets because of the humidity. 'Because you know', he said slowly, 'that I won't want to see it through to the end, that I just can't do it. You know that don't you?'

Then she knew that the times he had laid his hand on her arm or bent his head towards her chest or even, during the morning's treatment, taken his shirt off in a certain way (as he had lately been doing), he had done it in the hope that when the time came for him to ask her for help she would give it, she wouldn't refuse him, and he needed her because he didn't have the strength to do it alone. That she had become his saviour, but that, like Ludwig, he didn't expect her to cure him. That his learning to read now was a gift and nothing more, something he had foreseen would lead towards the little death he was asking for. He had expected Ludwig to show him the place where life began, but he never had.

'Actually I was thinking of taking you back to London with me,' Achilles said.

'How?'

'I've already started to make several arrangements that would enable me to move you to my hospital.'

'I hate hospitals; they're nothing but places where people perform miracles against their will, where people are forced to save lives that aren't worth saving.'

'My hospital isn't like that.'

'Yours?'

'I can't stay here for ever, Aesop.'

'Neither can I.'

'Which is why you have to come with me,' she said hurriedly, in search of a wild reassurance she had never needed before. 'I can promise you permanent . . .'

'Don't use the word "permanent", and don't make me those kind of promises.'

'Well stop asking me to,' she suddenly shouted, standing up and unpeeling her dress from the back of her legs. The humidity in the palm house made even her anger damp and oppressive sounding, and she suddenly became very tired at the thought of herself. Then she did something she had never done before, she made him afraid.

'You will need to be in London. At the hospital.'

'I don't want to go to hospital.'

'Well if you don't come to mine you might have to go to someone else's. There are several things about the syndrome I haven't told you, that I shouldn't have to tell you.' She paused. There was still time to stop herself, and if she didn't speak would he need her any less.

'Sometimes it erodes the senses — especially in children. It's very rare to contract Eastman's at all over the age of twelve. It's a paedophile — three is its perfect age. In some cases it robs objects of their faculties: the ears stop hearing, the nose stops smelling, the tongue stops tasting, the skin stops feeling and the eyes stop seeing. In that order. And when each sensory organ has been struck dumb, it simply drops off; the body refuses to carry a dead weight, even though it doesn't discard it readily. Have you seen a child with no ears, eyes, or nose, with a stub at the back of its mouth where the tongue once was, and whose skin is visibly dying as it separates itself from the layers beneath until eventually there are no layers left, just muscle. A creature . . .'

He stood away from her as she said this.

'A creature that maintains its full mental capacity but that can neither hear, smell, taste, see or touch, that is left with nothing to verify its existence, and yet is capable of not dying. Even in that state the child can — if it chooses —' she looked round at him, 'stay alive.'

She walked towards the door.

'Where are you going?' he said, afraid that this was the last thing he would hear her say.

She felt lightheaded, never having abused her authority before. It was a dangerous sort of misbehaviour.

'Tonight, nowhere. But tomorrow I'm going to Brazil. You know that.'

She thought of Ludwig and saw him and Aesop again walking along the balcony outside the flats, the blue the doors had been painted flashed at her memory, and she knew that the bangs she heard under water — both of them – were the shots they fired at the two women. Whether they took a shot each, Ludwig shot them both or Aesop shot them both, it didn't matter. She waivered for a moment wondering whether she should tell him that it was Ludwig who rang the other night, that it was Ludwig who had called her to Brazil. She wondered if there had been any love between them.

'Why Brazil?'

'To tell you the truth, from what I could gather on the telephone I think it's another case of Eastman's. You could make me famous.' She saw him wince, she hadn't even wanted to say that, knowing that he would feel more lonely than ever now after she had gone. And she had already inflicted the most memorable of legacies – a nightmare. She had never hurt herself so much before, and had to look away from the desk where the flash cards stood in their pile and the books still lay open, in case she started to cry.

'Don't say that,' he said jerking his hand that still held the pencil he had been writing with.

'I've said it now.'

'Take it back.'

'Don't be so ridiculous.'

'If you do it now, you can take it back.'

'I'm not taking it back, I've said it.'

He walked up to her and took hold of her hand loosely. The light from the desk lamp barely saturated the darkness, the heat felt even wetter in the half light and she could hear the butterflies, moving in their sleep. The fact that animals had dreams had never ceased to amaze her.

'Take it back.' He started to hold her arm with his other hand as well, the one still holding the pencil, and started to rub in a tentative Chinese burn. 'Take it back,' he said more gently this time, but her arm was throbbing and she hadn't noticed before that he was taller than her.

She hadn't expected him to transgress like this and was even more confused when he stopped pulling at her skin and started to run his fingertips over her underarm instead, uncovering his own kind of authority.

'I can't.' She didn't believe in forgiveness.

Then he kissed her tightly, trying to give the kiss without receiving one in return. Pulled away, took a breath, then kissed her again. He held her hair and neck with his left hand, while gesturing nervously with his right as though there was an audience whose instructions he was trying to remember to follow. He tried to find her tongue, but she wouldn't let him past her teeth which she kept clamped shut. He could feel the skin on the end of his tongue getting rawer and rawer as he kept pushing against her teeth, until in the end he gave up, and suddenly slipped his tongue up along the inside of her lip which surprised her so that she opened her mouth and he touched her tongue more gently than he had intended to, with the belligerence of the victor. She watched as he slowed down and his eyes closed, and as he kissed he drew with his pencil all over her white dress so that she didn't find the markings until she got back to her room and took her dress off that night.

'You will come back won't you?'

'Of course. Why?'

'I know that I wouldn't.'

27

The sky was orange, a heavy orange that was going grey at the edges and when the thunder clapped it seemed to come from below rather than above. A tropical storm.

'Do you remember when we used to make thunder? I didn't know until then that there was such a thing as a man-made storm,' Ludwig said.

'Is she coming?' Aurelius asked.

'She only arrived last week.'

'Where's Beatrice? Where's she been all this time?'

'With her. Dr Achilles.'

'Achilles? When can I see her?'

'Soon.'

Then they both turned at the sound of shoes against tiles, the hard but hollow sound of female weight, walking. It was a long time since Aurelius had seen a woman wearing shoes or a watch. She was going to save him.

'Aurelius, this is Dr Achilles.'

The woman took hold of his hand and smudged her palm across it.

'Thank you for coming. It's a long way.'

'Yes,' she said, unconvinced.

'Ludwig tells me that you're a dermatologist and that you run a clinic, a hospital for diseases of the skin.'

'Yes, that's right.'

'Is it true that you hold the last of the smallpox bacteria under lock and key?' Aurelius had never had to contemplate disease before.

She smiled but didn't answer.

'Beatrice has Eastman's Syndrome,' she said. 'It is unusual for children', she paused, 'over the age of twelve to contract this. I've only ever treated one other case,' she finished, thinking of Aesop sat at the desk, his arms sprawled across it as he followed the words in his reading book, words made bright beneath the arc of the desk lamp. And his kiss.

'The child has been isolated. The syndrome only permits the carrier to survive in an artificial environment. Once the disease takes hold it accelerates rapidly. We have put her into a heated room and I was wondering if I could distract you from the thunder for a moment and take you to see her.'

He repulsed her, he could tell. And as she spoke he became aware that she was accusing him, he didn't know of what, but her whole attitude assumed the burden of the guilt that he should be feeling, that she was waiting to pass on to him.

There were traces of orange on Ludwig's face, from the powder she had brought over with her to stop him from itching. Ludwig said that itching was the devil's curse; it was his revenge against bodies that still carried their soul; itching was born of the friction caused when the two rubbed against each other.

He could tell from the way Ludwig and Dr Achilles looked at each other that whatever she hadn't told him, she had told Ludwig. And from the way she looked at it through the glass he could also tell that she wasn't afraid of the jungle.

'Sector Four is the only sector still operating in Jara, isn't it?' Achilles asked.

'Yes, but they've elected their own administrative body. The pulp mill isn't operational any more, you know that.' Aurelius paused to smile. 'They've become farmers.'

'There was a young Indian girl in Sector Four,' Ludwig interrupted. 'She had joined the school that was still running there until recently. Reading the teacher's report – a Miss Hickham?' he said looking at Dr Achilles, 'there is every indication that she was exceptional. Apparently she spoke English as if she was learning it for a second time.'

The room was on the second floor of Mack's building. Thick red open-weave curtains hung over the window which made the corners and shadows of the room pink. There was a badly made bed with two duvets on it and a desk with economics text books on it as well as a volume of Egyptian history. The only other things that made the room look even slightly lived in were a record player in one of the corners and somebody's hastily put-up maps on the walls. The air conditioning in the room had been switched off.

The girl, who had her back to them, had on the navy-blue skirt and jumper, navy socks and white shirt of the Sector Four school. Her hair was plaited, and her left elbow jogged like a seismograph as her hand wrote. The elbow was scuffed and obviously picked at as a nervous reaction to concentrated learning.

Dr Achilles stopped behind the girl and put both hands down on to her shoulders as if about to submerge her in water.

'Beatrice.'

She scraped the chair back and stood up slowly. She stood in front of Aurelius in the navy and white school uniform. She had been found, given a uniform to wear, shoes to polish and a band for her hair. He looked quietly at the bed expecting to see the Las Vegas T-shirt and turquoise pants left in the desperate sheets.

She had taught her fingers how to hold a pencil so that it would write in the right way for her, trained the eyes to look no further than the end of her nose. On the bedside table there was a small vanity case and by the sink a neon toothbrush and tube of paste. He thought, this is what she's contrived to keep from me.

'How are you, Beatrice?' Ludwig said, resting his palm on the crown of her head and letting it slowly run down the length of her hair. The gesture was paternal – grandpaternal, even. 'Are you sleeping well?'

'Yes, thank you.'

'You have enough books?'

She nodded.

Ludwig left the room then and they listened to the sound of him leaving for as long as the corridor held on to it.

'Beatrice,' Aurelius said, letting his fingers touch the buttons on the front of her shirt.

Achilles moved closer to them both.

'Was this what you kept in the plastic bag that you hid when you came in the afternoons. I knew there was a bag hidden. A bag given you by someone. I could have looked in it. There were so many times when I could have looked, but I didn't. I never looked in the bag.' Then he started to laugh. 'And if I had, I would never have believed in a school uniform. A school uniform, Beatrice . . .

'Did she get it from me?' he said, turning to Dr Achilles.

'It's not a disease that's transmitted, as such,' she said, her tone suggesting that it wouldn't be something he was capable of contracting anyway. 'She's a minor.'

'There are no "minors" here.'

'You never gave me your world,' Beatrice said suddenly.

'You never kissed me. You were probably too tired to kiss me after this.'

He thought she might spit on him.

'Fuck off.'

'Beatrice,' Achilles warned her.

'You're too old to plait your hair. Somehow I can't see you sat there chewing the end of your plait. I just can't see it.' And he tugged on the ends of them, his teeth gritted.

Achilles tried to take hold of his arms but he just pulled a bit harder until he had wound the plaits round the palms of his hands, pulling down heavily so that Beatrice's body buckled. Achilles knew she shouldn't let go of him, but she was already standing on the balls of her feet. 'Ludwig,' she shouted, but in the end had to leave them to shout his name in the corridor. Looking back into the room, even with his hands full of her hair, she was no longer sure if Beatrice was the victim, if the victim wasn't after all Aurelius. And she thought of Aesop lying in his camp bed and the ability children had, whether they belonged to you or not, not to feel obliged. Children were never in debt which was why they made such dangerous lovers. 'Ludwig,' she almost screamed, but it was too late. The door to Beatrice's room slammed shut. She didn't even try to force it open, but ran faster than she had run for a long time, still calling out Ludwig's name, her hands over her ears.

Aurelius pushed the chair Beatrice had been sitting on against the door, then traced his fingers along the spines of the books on her desk, averting his eyes from the bed as if it were something uncouth that offended him while she watched him moving about her room.

'Have you read all of these?'

'I have.'

'It's funny, your words . . .'

'What?'

'You don't sound the same.'

'Well, I wouldn't.'

'Not so broken. More finished.'

He could tell that she wanted him to leave, but she was afraid of turning her back on him.

'Now you sound like a child. You were pretending before.'

'Yes, I pretended.'

Then he started to laugh leaning against the wall.

'And where do you think you're going now? Now that you know all this?'

He watched her as she tried to play with her hair, forgetting that it had been put in braids.

'I'm going to London.'

'You might as well be staying here in Jara. You won't be able to take a single step out of your room.'

'I want to go to London,' she said, more wary now, as if it were a possibility that he did still have the power to prevent it from happening.

'You should have said before. I could have taken you.'

'You never offered.' She was starting to shout.

'You never asked.'

'I didn't know how to. How do you ask for those things?'

'You just open your mouth,' he said, grabbing hold of hers and squeezing the cheekbones until he felt her gum and cheeks.

She pulled herself away, her eyes watering. 'You never wanted to leave this place.'

He watched her, more surprised than he could account for that she had known this; that she had known this much about him. He was even more afraid of her leaving now.

'Aren't you hot in all that?' he said, tugging at the jumper and shirt collar, feeling the dip between her collar bone with his two forefingers.

203

'You know I'm not. Aren't you hot in that stupid suit you wear all the time?'

'You don't like it?'

'Of course I don't. Why should I?'

'I think I was expecting you to.'

'I don't like men in suits.'

He laughed desperately at the breadth of her knowledge.

'You know men without them?'

'I know men.'

'You don't.'

His certainty brought her a step closer still so that he didn't need to pull so tightly on her collar.

'You don't know the first thing.'

He started to walk on to her feet so that she had to take a step back then another, then a little more quickly, until she came up against the wall sooner than she had expected and hit her head.

'Dr Achilles,' she shouted.

Aurelius looked worried for a moment.

'She won't come. She's left you alone in here. With me.'

Pressing his thumbs against her eyes, he closed them, then brought his right hand down over the thick material of her school skirt and pushed it up, checking to see if her pants were turquoise. They weren't. Then he slid his fingers over the elasticated edge where the pubic hairs grew out from under and slipped them up inside her. His fingers separated and rubbed along the inside lips.

Then her hand came down heavily on his, knocking it out of her so that his fingers left a wet trace on her leg.

'Don't.'

She had never said this before; never articulated the violation or stopped him.

'Not in these clothes,' she finished.

She was trying with her one free hand to cover all her body, to pull the skirt back down so she could feel it at her knees, to pull her sleeves down to her wrists where his fingers played until they moved to her stomach. He crouched down and pushed the jumper and shirt up, covering her right breast with his hand and her left breast with his mouth so that it was wet afterwards and the shirt couldn't be pulled back over it. Then he laid her down on the floor and let himself fall heavily on top of her so that the wind rushed out of her mouth and she started to cough. He didn't dare undress her and couldn't find the time to undress himself so made love to her for the last time without feeling her skin beneath him.

As he pushed up inside her he pushed her whole body underneath the chair so that she kept banging her head against the door and after a while her hair found its way under the door, sliding across the floor and under the gap. At one point he heard footsteps in the corridor outside and someone tried the door. He didn't think to cover Beatrice's mouth and could tell from her eyes that she had given up. She only winced and let out a squeak as the person outside trod on her hair that had splayed itself out into the corridor.

Afterwards she sat up, her pants still around her knees so that he could see his sperm leaking out of her on to the floor while she concentrated on tying her hair back into plaits.

'You shouldn't have done that.'

'It wasn't the first time.' He couldn't hear himself speak any more as he put his cock gently back into his trousers.

'I'm an emperor's daughter.'

'Of course you are.'

'No, I am.'

He looked away from his crotch up at her. Insanity was something he had never suspected her of.

'Mack would kill you for doing that to me.'

'Mack?'

'He's waiting for you now. He's seen all of this. Everything, every time.'

'Mack?' he said again.

'And Mack's the only person who's able to kill anybody more than once. I've seen him do that.'

'Mack's dead.'

'Mack's not dead; he's my father.'

28

There was a strange fuzzing sound that didn't belong to the dark green of the artificial jungle, and lights – suddenly – that were so bright the glass boundaries of the palm house were no longer there. The lights stayed on full and he could hear the thuds as the butterflies woke up and sent themselves hurtling against the light. They stayed there banging and fluttering against the glass with an urgent fury. The butterflies weren't the only things he felt stirring. The leaves of the banana tree unfurled and let themselves fatten in the light; he felt the pores of the other plants and trees open as well as the moisture of sleep pushed itself out. The flowers, whose petals opened hesitantly, kept a close check on their neighbours and the old soil gave a quick wet gasp.

Aesop went and stood against the window which he had to step back from because the glass felt so cold. After he had been standing there a few moments the light switched direction, swinging on to the hills miles away; the hills where, Dr Achilles told him, the witches had held their sabbaths and sacrificed babies. The thought of the Pendle witches scared him.

The sound was very loud now and he watched as a group of people carrying what looked like a small coffin made their way towards the kitchen door at the side of the house. He thought of the witches again and looked about him for reassurance, but saw himself standing in a cultivated jungle with a miniature collection of debris that could only be called reality at a push. There was a bang as the kitchen door shut, and a little while later he heard footsteps along the corridor leading to the palm house. It was usually difficult to discern any sort of outside noise over the humidity which had a persistent chattering quality that distorted everything else, including human voices. Then he heard the swan's head squeaking as it did when the handle was turned, and the hesitant sound of a man's footsteps. He was worried that it might be Dr Blackthorn. He knew instinctively the man's secret, from the odd moments their eyes crossed and during the times Blackthorn perched on the edge of his bed, on the edge of his desk, not trusting himself to get too close. Then there was the time he said to Blackthorn, 'I'm surprised you allow Dr Achilles to treat me alone.'

'I saved you,' Blackthorn had said in warning.

'You did.'

'I didn't have to.'

From further away now he heard Dr Achilles's voice: 'Aesop.' It didn't move any closer to him. 'Aesop?' And he tried to remember why he had kissed her the night she left. It wasn't to say thank you for what she had taught him, even though he worked hard at it, it wasn't for that; and he was tired of her sitting by him with her needles, her counters, mapping out a body he didn't understand. So had he kissed her in acknowledgement of this violation or because he found suddenly that he could make her eyes dilate and her legs fluid and that he could leave her expecting more. That she would accept anything given to her. He found that he had the power to corrupt, and knew, as he had never known with Ludwig, what it meant to see someone else's life magnified in everyday you.

'Aesop.'

He wouldn't have to go back to the Institute for Young Offenders now if he didn't want to. Because of her. She would take him with her back to London.

'Aesop?' she said a fourth time, more urgently, and he knew the picture she was beginning to see. She was looking in the dark for the smashed window, but couldn't feel any draft and she could see that the bed had been slept in, that the shoes were under it and the clothes in a heap nearby. Now she was turning her eyes upwards; he could almost see them following the iron girders until they reached the spiral staircase where they climbed, not slipping once, to the balcony at the top. There they perused the circumference of the palm house, looking for knotted bed sheets and the naked boy she expected to see hanging from them. As he saw this he realised the sharp pleasure of being the object not only of another's desire, but of another's pain as well.

He heard the wooden sound of the coffin being put down on the tiled path and became terrified for the first time that it was for him. That Dr Achilles had realised the full burden of him, the full horror, and had decided to fill the coffin she had probably had made weeks ago. He had never suspected the existence of a coffin before. Then at the sound of the footsteps getting closer and quicker he stepped further back on to the soil among the trees until the desk lamp was suddenly switched on and the light it threw out was strong enough to cast the shadow of his hiding body across the pavement. He stepped into his shadow and there was Ludwig standing in front of him. The skin on his face looked rawer even than it had when he left him after the killing, as if several layers had disappeared since then.

'Dearest,' he said quietly.

Ludwig stood exactly how he had imagined he would, only he had always pictured him standing up from behind a desk in the visiting room at the Institute. He had even imagined the scraping of the desk as his thighs pushed it away, the arms outstretched and the coat rippling about him as the lining caught the heavy orange lights in there, confusing them. He didn't walk into his arms.

'Where were you? Where did you go?' Aesop said.

What he didn't ask, although it came to him now as the only real question, was why he had left him.

'A long way away. Somewhere they don't have snow,' Ludwig said, his eyes wandering quickly over him. 'I wasn't meant to see you for two years.'

'Wasn't you?' Aesop stepped further into the light. 'Well you're seeing me now.'

Ludwig looked down at his legs and feet.

'What happened to the shoes I bought you? Where's your bracelet?'

'They took them away; confiscated them. They're at the Institute.'

Ludwig carried on staring at his feet.

'What did you think of prison?'

'They don't call it prison,' Aesop said defensively.

'What do they call it then?' Ludwig said more gently.

'I've already said. Institute. Institute for Young Offenders.' His hands found their pockets. 'It's near here. Where was you?'

Aesop wasn't going to tell Ludwig how he had looked out for him at the Institute, in the visitor's room; how he had waited day after day for him to fill it.

'Will you be frank with me?' Aesop asked.

Ludwig tried not to smile. He knew it would rankle Aesop who still had the childish trait of taking himself seriously. People were always offering to be frank with him, but nobody had ever asked him to be frank in return.

'Where was you?'

'Jara.'

210

'That's not being frank.' Aesop was disconcerted; he had expected Ludwig to be more contrite, more full of grief and less full of himself.

'It's the truth.'

'But I don't know where that is.'

'I was sent to Brazil.'

'Who by?'

'I had some work to do there.'

'For Mack? Was he the one who gave you the face?'

'No,' Ludwig said quietly.

'And you were going to work for Mack for two years?'

'Two years, yes.'

'Why didn't you stay?'

'Mack was dead.'

Even though this didn't mean anything to Aesop who had never known Mack, the fact that he was dead disturbed him. Maybe it was the fact of death that disturbed him.

Ludwig tried to hold his arms out again, to vaguely encircle him, but Aesop reached out for the plants instead, taking an aloe leaf into his fist.

'That night, the night we went down to the frozen lake and I walked across to the middle – did you know then?'

Ludwig didn't say anything.

'Did you know what was going to happen?'

'I did, yes. But I had decided then that I didn't want it to.'

'Were you given the choice?'

'No. But I knew I didn't want to.'

'But you did it. It all went ahead. Everything to plan.'

'That's right.'

'You didn't think of stopping it?'

'You can only stop it beforehand, not when you've

started. It's too late then.'

'Did you want to do what you did?'

'I didn't mind. About that. Two women; two people; two people less, more, whatever. Nothing wrong with that. It was the two years, the two years that was so . . . so you've been thinking about it.'

'No,' Aesop said defensively again. 'No, I was just thinking it now.'

'You didn't have much time to yourself at the Institute then,' Ludwig said sharply.

Aesop started to splay his hands out nervously where they hung down the sides of his thighs. Then he saw that Ludwig's eyes were smarting.

'I saw you. I see you in that flat now. Often. You didn't want to do that.'

'I didn't want you to see me.'

'Maybe. But you didn't want to do it. I know you.'

Nobody had ever laid claim to him before.

'You do?' Ludwig said hopefully.

Aesop nodded, his chin out.

'I saw you too,' a woman's voice said and Dr Achilles stepped forward and came to stand next to Ludwig. 'And you looked straight at me,' she said, her eyes on Aesop, her eyes over Aesop. 'I heard the gunshots – both of them – while I was under the water. Then I saw you two. Then . . .' She came closer to Aesop, closer than he had allowed Ludwig to come. He saw the curve of her neck and collarbone and the way it deflected the light.

'I was swimming on my back, the length of the pool, following you, and I saw you leaning over. You looked straight at me.'

'You were wearing a red costume.'

'Yes,' she said as hopefully as Ludwig before her.

'I didn't see you though.'

Aesop looked at them as they stood there blocking the path.

'Brazil. You were both there. Is it him you went to get from the jungle?' he said to her, looking at Ludwig. 'Did you tell him you'd found me?'

It was somehow right that Achilles and Ludwig had both ended up in (or, even more terrifying, came from) the same place and the thought that they already knew each other horrified him.

'Did you tell him?' he insisted taking hold of her wrist so sharply he bruised the pulse point.

'She told me before we left Jara. It's why I left Jara. You're why I left Jara,' Ludwig said blankly.

Aesop felt suddenly exhausted, knowing that between them both there was no room for escape.

The noise of the butterflies grew more distinct as if during the night they had grown tongues and were learning to speak. They could hear the helicopter on the lawn outside starting up again and as it rose into the air the light swept over the butterflies, turning them into something bright, forged, hammered: steel. The light continued to move over the hands and faces of Aesop, Ludwig and Dr Achilles and across the top of the coffin which started to scream as the light pulled away from the dome on the top of the palm house and disappeared.

'What's that?' Aesop said when the screaming didn't stop.

'Come and see,' Dr Achilles said.

The coffin was on the path behind the fountain. It was new: there were no traces of soil or rot on it. The screams were hollow, sound without echo, and loud.

'We'll stand her on her feet,' Dr Achilles said quietly and Aesop watched as she crouched down, her knees sliding across the damp floor, and slowly began to hoist the coffin up by her shoulders without his or Ludwig's help. She seemed stronger than before and not so dry; fuller and wetter. He noticed the cruelty still, but she used to imply it only, now she was letting it run its course

213

without subduing it.

As the coffin was raised into the half-light he noticed the pink vanity case on the floor with a toothbrush balanced on top of it. For a moment there was a dusty smell that was almost narcotic in potential. Then, with a sigh, the coffin came to rest on its feet and the screaming stopped.

There was no lid, only a perspex screen. Dr Achilles kicked the pink vanity case to one side and pressed her face against it. Ludwig made no attempt to move any closer. The sight of the coffin on its feet only made him look more warily at Aesop.

The sound of the helicopter leaving finally died down as a greasy shower of moisture fell on to his head and shoulders. He felt the drops rolling down his face and into his ears as he stared into the coffin. At first Aesop could see nothing behind the glass, and didn't know if he wanted to. He saw the trees around him lazily reflected, and after a while he saw himself. Then he saw a pair of hands pressing against the glass, trying to push through. They looked fluid as if not quite properly formed, brand-new still. For a moment he wondered what his hands were doing there behind glass until he realised that they didn't belong to him. Next he watched as a cheek was pressed up against it. A cheek, like the hands, not fully formed, then a forehead, lips. Then these vanished and he saw the outline of his uniform again and clearly, brilliantly, a pair of eyes.

Dr Achilles unbuttoned her jacket and took something from an inside pocket that looked like the key to a music box. She gave it to Ludwig and went to stand behind the coffin as he snapped the catches off the front.

Aesop expected the hands to press against the glass again, but they didn't. He even lost sight of the eyes, until Ludwig pulled the glass away. Nothing happened although they all stood back in anticipation. He noticed the irritation pulling at Dr Achilles's cheeks as if it were a scene she had either rehearsed or dreamed, only to have it fouled – unexpectedly – by its protagonist.

'Beatrice,' she said sharply.

They watched as a bitten hand curled round the edge of the wood, then another one.

'We're still in Jara,' a girl's voice said sullenly.

Aesop had never heard a voice sound so dark before.

'No we're not,' Dr Achilles responded.

'The helicopter flew in circles.'

The hands disappeared from the sides of the box.

'Of course it didn't,' Ludwig put in not only to soothe her, but to reassure himself.

'We're a long way from Jara,' Dr Achilles added.

Aesop could see that she too was trying to soothe, but with logic rather than instinct. Then Ludwig, losing patience and unable to bear it any longer, put his hand into the box and drew Beatrice out.

Aesop saw a girl the same age as him with drab brown skin, wearing a navy-blue school uniform. Her eyes were so large they looked as though they kept her head and the rest of her body together. She looked straight over him, uninterested, no longer afraid. As if everybody and everything she saw was just something new to despise because she didn't yet have the capacity to destroy it.

'No dangerous animals live in England,' Aesop said suddenly.

'My case,' she said to Dr Achilles, ignoring Aesop completely.

'What case?' Achilles asked, worried, as if everything hung on the case.

'My pink plastic case,' she said, spelling it out.

'Oh.' Dr Achilles bent down immediately and handed it to her.

The girl pulled out a pink T-shirt with the words 'I ♥ Vegas' written across it, and a pair of turquoise pants.

'I told you not to bring those.'

'Well I wanted to.' But she put the clothes away in the bag, looking up at the glass ceiling above, and through it.

'Could be Jara,' she said at last. 'But the stars are different.'

Then as Dr Achilles and Ludwig looked up to note for themselves the differences between the northern and southern hemispheres, Beatrice turned round and pushed the box over, nearly falling with it. Aesop watched expectantly as it fell, hoping that the impact would crack the tiled pavement in half at least, or throw the whole thing up into the air, that the trees would shake until the trust they had in their roots was broken, but there was nothing, only a soft soggy bang.

She looked briefly at all of them, then walked over to the desk where Aesop's reading books were still open, and putting her vanity case on top of them slowly opened it and began to take her treasures out (Aesop didn't doubt that they were treasures watching the way she curled over them). She ignored the fallen coffin.

Dr Achilles and Ludwig looked about them, then at each other, as if acknowledging for the first time that the palm house was only made of glass.

29

Beatrice had screamed because she was terrified that they would never let her out and then when they had stood her on her feet and taken the glass lid away, she pushed herself right to the back of the box whose construction (she knew) Aurelius had overseen (and which was made out of gmelina tree) as if this was the last moment that was hers to own. It was Ludwig who took the glass lid away, not Dr Achilles, who was probably the one to have heard her screaming in the first place.

They couldn't see her yet, not even the boy who had looked right in, but they were all waiting for her. And when she stepped out she smelt something that she thought at first was the scent of her own memory as she felt the familiar thick red-veined heat that only death could alleviate, a jungle heat, with its wet overripe poisonous smells. She felt desolate, not only because there was another place on earth that was Jara also, but because perhaps there was nothing else on earth but Jara. Perhaps these cities Ludwig, Aurelius and Mack spoke of no longer existed; perhaps they came from dreams or fragments of books they had saved. Perhaps they came from nowhere other than Jara, and the whole world was overgrown.

But then looking about her she saw that, unlike Jara, there were boundaries, not only to the sides, but above as well. She was relieved to feel, slowly, a sense of limit being imposed on her, the same limits that had been imposed on the trees, fauna, and butterflies. They were all allowed to exist, but only to a certain extent. Their existence was permitted, not forgotten, which was how, she realised, she had come to look on civilisation: as a complicated system of behavioural patterns. You either behaved or misbehaved, were either congratulated or apprehended. Then there was the area beyond misbehaviour which nobody talked about.

The first person she saw was the boy who had blossom, pollen and other substances in his hair that the flowers had either brushed or secreted on to him. And he wasn't wearing clothes but, like her, a uniform. He must have wanted to comfort her because she heard him saying that no dangerous animals lived in England, when dangerous animals were never something she had sought to escape anyway.

After Velli's Palace in Jara, she was able to recognise the morals behind the architecture of the palm house. The same morals were also behind the larger darker shape that she had seen next to the palm house as the helicopter landed: the house.

She remembered lying in the box on top of the hill overlooking Jara by the pond where Aurelius had first seen her. She could hear the helicopter drumming around her and Dr Achilles pushing Aurelius out of the way in order to be the one to lay the glass lid on top of the box. When Dr Achilles stood back Aurelius lay down on the glass. Once she realised it wasn't going to break she saved her screams, and closed her eyes to the lips that were moving frantically above her face. When she opened them again the lips had gone and he was taking paper out of his pocket, unfolding page after page and

218

pressing it against the glass; not giving her time to read one sheet before pressing the next one down. He didn't even expect her to read the poems in the end, he only wanted to demonstrate quantity. This was all he had time for; to validate the past.

Then he no longer had the energy to hold on to them and the pages, one after another, started to fly into the air. Despite the pulp mill, the factory, it was the first time she had seen so much paper in Jara.

She looked quickly at Aurelius as if he had at last understood something. But the air was full of paper and the back of Aurelius's shirt was being lifted up. His hair was trying to leave his scalp, and she thought that any moment now he would leave the ground altogether, and be taken upwards so that soon she would be looking at nothing but the soles of his shoes. But it wasn't the wind from the helicopter that was lifting him, it was Dr Achilles who had handfuls of jacket and shoulder blades and was pulling him back on to his feet, away from the box.

As they stood the box upright, Dr Achilles, Ludwig and the rest of the group moved towards the helicopter and Aurelius was left standing by himself on the brow of the hill. The tower as big as Babel's that was the paper mill stood behind him and beyond this the flat-roofed turrets and panoramic windows of Velli's Palace, and then the river, wrecked but still able to fulfil its potential.

The third thunderstorm of the day rushed in from the west and broke over them as they hoisted the box up into the helicopter, and she saw people walking out of the forest as if somebody was driving them from behind. They weren't Jara workers or even native workers, and they weren't speaking to each other. They were naked; a nakedness that was worn.

They walked in bands rather than lines, keeping pace slowly. Above the storm she could even hear the jangling of the birds as they rose up out of the trees. It was the biggest hunting party she had ever seen. Nobody was leading them, they were walking collectively. As the birds settled back into the trees she could hear the sound of their bodies moving along the road that led into Jara, like a whisper spoken in all the known and unknown languages of the world.

At the sight of the Indians they pulled her quickly up the last few metres, not caring as the box banged against the side of the helicopter: they thought these people had come for her. Before they laid her on her back and the door shut, she saw the streets of Jara full, crowded with naked people, and half of them were filing steadily into Velli's Palace, not even looking up before they went in.

30

The problem with sleeping under glass was that it was never properly dark. Light became half-light and half-light, light again, but there was always the expectancy that one night it would go pitch dark. This was still a possibility despite the electric light that came through the windows of the house and yawned out on to the lawn, embracing the palm house. At night the house was no longer a house, it was more like a factory because of the lights. And some nights, lying there on his bed, Aesop could almost hear the noise of machines, a host of machines, that ran so smoothly they barely needed to be operated, only fed. The smell of them, that particular smell of working iron, indolent one minute, furious the next, managed to make a small claim for itself even in the dense humidity of the palm house.

Lying on her stomach Beatrice watched the end of his cigarette — that blunt private light — and listened to the quick wet suck of his lips. They had decided silently, unanimously to hate each other, reckoning quickly from past experience that this would be safer. So they lay in their camp beds, almost side by side, with his feet where her head was, needing to speak and trying to decide whether or not hatred would be diluted by speech. Then there was the problem of who should — by right — speak first. Tonight, for once, Aesop didn't have his headphones on, and wasn't shuffling through his tape collection with the mania of a man who's lost everything.

'You wearing your uniform?' he said at last.

'Yes,' she mumbled defensively, but turned to face him. 'Are you wearing yours?'

'Always do in bed.'

'So do I. Now.'

'Why do you wear that school uniform?'

'Because I'm supposed to want to.'

'Do you?'

'A bit. But I won't wear it all the time.'

Beatrice heard the wheeze of the dead cigarette as it dropped to the floor and the scuffle as Aesop looked for the next one. She could tell from the flash of his face as he struck the match that he had thought about it but in the end decided not to offer her one. So she didn't ask him anything more about his uniform, even though he wanted to be asked. He had to sit a little longer on the answer he had all prepared, and it made his conversation carelessly aggressive.

'My real name's not Beatrice,' she said at last, quickly.

'So.'

'It's Nima.'

'I don't care what your name is. Don't give a fuck.'

'That's why I'm telling you. It's like talking to no one, but at least I'm saying it.'

A butterfly half flew, half dropped towards them and she saw the cigarette light waiver near the floor as Aesop pulled the blanket over his head.

'It's gone,' she said, straining her neck towards it.

'They do it on purpose.'

'They do, actually.'

His wrist was the whitest thing she had ever seen.

'There's only two people who know my real name,' Beatrice carried on.

'Who's that then?'

'You. And one other person.'

'Ludwig?' he said quickly.

'No, another person.'

'What's your real name again?'

'Doesn't matter,' she said.

'Yes it does.' His voice was deeper, less careless.

She turned over away from him and the springs (which had already set about rusting because of the humidity) stretched to support her new position. Her hand felt under the bed for the pink vanity case and stroked the top of it.

'Mack told me that Ludwig was the man who made him stand in front of windows again. He hadn't stood in front of a window for a lot of years until then,' she started slowly.

The air between them became very still as Aesop strained to catch every word and she paused to breathe in the cigarette smoke between each sentence, realising that she liked it.

'He came to him, in the first instance, in this dark suit. Immaculate, but dark.' She paused. 'Have you ever been to Las Vegas?'

Aesop laughed and started coughing.

'They don't wear dark suits in Las Vegas. Not then. Apparently. So Mack said. But he didn't care. He kept Ludwig waiting for a long time and, while he was waiting, Ludwig did nothing but sit and stare at the palm trees in reception. Looking them up and down. When he was called in eventually, he complimented Mack on his palm trees. He believed they were real. It never occurred to him that they might not be. Why would you want a fake palm tree? Where would you get one if you did? Why did they make them anyway? Why did a factory exist where they manufactured nothing but fake palm trees?'

'Ludwig said that?'

'No, Mack watched him think it.'

'How old was he then?'

'Young. Mack fell in love with him because of those palm trees.'

'He told you this?'

'He had to. There weren't enough people to go round the things he knew, the things he had to tell.'

Beatrice started to play with the catch on her case.

'Shut up, that's irritating me,' Aesop said shortly. He could tell from the way she was speaking to him that she wasn't expecting anything from him. He thought it would calm him, that's how he liked things to hang between him and other people, but it didn't, it made him nervous.

'That was before his face.'

From the corner of her eyes she could see the hand Aesop held his cigarette in going up to his own face.

'Mack knew him first before his face. I saw him too, before his face.'

She pushed the vanity case back under the bed and pulled the blanket up over her shoulders, and they lay there. She was aware that she was waiting for him to finish his cigarette, but it wasn't this that was stopping her from falling asleep. After a while she realised that he was going to let it burn down to a stump between his fingers in order to burn them as well.

'What happens if we leave? If we leave the palm house and step outside?'

'We'll stop breathing,' Aesop said quietly.

'That's what she told me as well. Just checking. Life is only sustained if the body is kept in a tropical climate,' she murmured.

'So why are you here then?'

'Because she couldn't stay there, could she. Not just for me. She would have got bored after a month, maybe less.

I asked to come,' she added.

Beatrice pushed her face down into the pillow, making a kissing motion with her mouth, then pressed her thumb against her ears so that she could hear the blood vessels making waves inside the drums.

Aesop let out a short triumphant cry as the cigarette burnt his skin, then threw the stub over the edge of the bed.

'Sometimes it erodes the senses: the ears stop hearing, the nose stops smelling, the tongue stops tasting, the eyes stop seeing, the skin stops feeling, then they all drop off. But the child stays alive,' he murmured.

'Is that what she said?'

'Yes.'

'She's lying,' Beatrice said.

Aesop started to get up, then lay back down again. Stiffly. Instead of being reassured, he was more terrified now than ever. Perhaps he had never kissed Dr Achilles, perhaps it was she who kissed him, and he had never realised.

Then they both started laughing at the same time, as if laughing would keep the monsters away. They laughed properly, not the thin-lipped mean laugh they were used to, but a full open-mouthed one. They nearly made the mistake of seeking each other's eyes, but remembered in time.

Aesop fell asleep, afraid of what the girl lying next to him had brought with her into the palm house. He was afraid of falling asleep first in case she gave her night-mares, or – worse – dreams, to him.

But Beatrice was already asleep, standing against a window taller than her, watching the intestines of a storm travelling towards Jara, unravelling themselves as they came. She stood waiting for the first roar then the forest below caught alight and fire began to spread so that in the end the roar came from the fire instead of the thunder, and night came from the sheets of birds that rose up out of the trees as the fire took hold and started to spread, not only outwards, but upwards.

31

By agreeing to meet him at the town's only hotel, Jake knew that the doctor had already made an informal confession. The hotel was severely floral, severely velvet and severely depressing. The furniture, unable to transcend its chips, the carpet unable to transcend its stains. Jake had planned his anger carefully and it involved hospital corridors, trolleys, IV drips, vast swinging doors and the sound of countless feet running across lino. He felt (virtually) impotent in these padded pink surroundings whose decaying hope didn't even generate an ambience of suicide. Nothing was possible here.

A man wearing a shirt and light trousers came into the bar, looked around, noted Jake, then ordered a drink. He stood rubbing his arms nervously.

'Dr Blackthorn?' Jake said.

'Why are you asking me?' the man said, but came and sat down, falling into the chair, his hands between his knees.

'We spoke on the phone about a boy who was taken from the Institute for Young Offenders in July. As an emergency.'

Dr Blackthorn was drinking alcohol, Jake noted, and couldn't focus on anything for long without flinching.

He could smell, faintly, the stench of sick and healing bodies rising from him.

'Aesop,' Blackthorn said slowly, and as soon as he said it he remembered the way Achilles had looked, dragging her suitcase along the station platform. The way she carried it as someone would carry a dead body; the way she made all inanimate things believe that they had once been alive; the way she imposed a little of herself on them. The sight of her in the small tight bedroom at Hornby Hall, with the velvet walls and curtains closing in on her, and her luggage, like human debris from an orphanage, discarded on the bed. He remembered her stood in the centre refusing to grow smaller to fit the room, but afraid and expecting him to take advantage of the artificial night to touch her. There were times when his skin almost left his body he wanted to touch her so much, but he hadn't then. The most untouchable of women; the most touched.

'You're one of the campaigners aren't you?' he said taking in the dark clothes and numerous layers, squinting slightly at the dayglo logo on Jake's T-shirt. 'Is he innocent?' he asked suddenly; it bothered him most of the time and he knew that it might make a difference to Dr Achilles if he could prove he was. He was sure that her fascination (it was 'fascination') was as reliant on Aesop's being guilty of murder as it was on his being a carrier of Eastman's.

'Of course,' Jake said. It had been a long time since anyone had asked him this.

Dr Blackthorn slumped.

'You remember him then?' Jake put in. He sensed increasingly now a refinement or sharpening in himself which had in turn led to a new and frightening intolerance of others.

'I don't have to,' Blackthorn said, swallowing, 'I see him every day.'

'Is he really ill?' Jake asked forcefully, with no concern for Aesop's suffering, only for whether the illness was true or false.

'Yes, he's really ill,' Dr Blackthorn said. 'He's diseased in fact.'

'He's my brother,' Jake said staring at Blackthorn's drink.

'I thought he was an orphan.'

'You did?' Jake said, interested. 'You took him away.'

'Not me personally,' Blackthorn said pettily. He hadn't made up his mind whether to be elusive or not.

'But you know where he is?'

Blackthorn saw Achilles again, navigating her bed-room at the hall in darkness and realised that the stinking young man in front of him offered a new and unex-pected turnstile in his bid to control what had become an uncontrollable situation. Achilles needed to know of this man's existence, and that he, Blackthorn, might choose to give him Aesop's whereabouts. He had never had anything other than himself to threaten her with. She needed to be told now that Aesop wasn't alone, that he had a history to account for, that he had a brother looking for him.

'I just want to see him.'

'You do?' Blackthorn didn't believe him and could tell from looking at Jake that he didn't believe himself either. 'You don't. You would have found me earlier if you wanted to see him. But you need to know where he is. Well you have to understand that he's ill.'

'Don't they have medical staff at the Institute?' Jake said, trying to move away from their knowledge of each other.

'They do; in fact I work there as well as at the hospital, but he's unusually ill, rarely ill. He needs a very special sort of environment.'

Blackthorn noted that Jake hadn't yet asked for a

diagnosis, or even for the disease to be named.

'I do have rights,' Jake whispered, and it was the most tentative claim he had made since setting up the camp outside the perimeter fence at the Institute.

'Unfortunately Aesop doesn't. He belongs to the State; his body belongs to the State.'

'Is he dead?'

'Of course he's not dead,' Blackthorn said thinking that it was the first time he had mentioned death in the context of Aesop. 'He's still being confined, in a slightly more specific way, that's all.' He thought of Achilles's hair, coarser, but lighter, mixing with the boy's, their heads bent in the arc of light and how Eastman's infected all of Aesop's body so it was all of his body that fascinated her. Usually her obsessions were localised: it was a hand that held her, or an eyelid, a face, but never before an entire body, especially a body that disguised its disease. Most of the time, in fact, you wouldn't know it was there at all.

One of the bar staff (of which there were too many), decked out in his fake gondolier's uniform, came and asked them if they wanted anything else to drink.

'Look,' said Jake, 'I was able to see him at the Institute. A murderer's allowed to receive visitors so surely an ill one is. Surely his status doesn't change. Why should he become a confidential matter now? Is his disease more interesting than his crime? Why won't the Institute give me the information?'

'They don't know that there's any information to give. They're doing everything they can to protect Aesop.'

'From who?' Jake stood up. 'I will find him. Brothers are something you put a lot of effort into finding.'

'He has to be kept in an environment with a sustained temperature. If he's taken out of this environment he dies.'

Jake took this information in carefully, then stood waiting.

'It's also very dangerous to proclaim someone's innocence when you don't necessarily believe in it yourself.'

Jake looked down at his boots against the carpet, unable to decide which depressed him the most, and he couldn't work out whether the smell of large quantities of vegetables steaming in stainless steel was beginning to make him feel hungry or sick.

'Why did you come to me?' Blackthorn said, watching him.

'Why are *you* going to tell me a piece of confidential information?'

Blackthorn pressed the empty glass hard against his groin.

'Aesop's being kept at Hornby Hall,' he said quietly, making no effort to move or get up out of his seat as Jake left.

In the months that he had been ensconced there, Jake's camp had grown into a settlement around the old bus shelter on the western side of the perimeter fence. He still slept in the bus shelter which had become the unofficial HQ and, with some old polythene sheeting and bits of fencing, they extended it and made it virtually waterproof. Only a month after he had arrived, a group of travellers had joined him after being thrown out of North Yorkshire due to new council legislation there. They proved adept at tapping into local generators and it was because of them that the camp got sporadic electricity. Jesper, a disillusioned Norwegian, led this group along with a handful of well-spoken A-level students taking a year out before university who had decided to tag along with Jesper instead of going backpacking in Australia. They spent most of the time fighting quietly among themselves as to who would be the first to bear Jesper's heir. A few of them had tried to latch on to Jake, but the sound of the rain dripping on to the polythene sheeting drove them mad, and at night the thought of Deirdre still made him afraid and he talked in his sleep.

A group of socialist workers who had been sitting in at the university in protest against the cut to student grants had moved over to their settlement. Occasionally Jake heard children in the early hours of the morning although nobody knew whom they belonged to, which confused the social worker and the teacher from the local primary school who visited the settlement sporadically with the righteous glow of those who hold the key to happiness. Their tight trousers, big jumpers and overweight earrings didn't disguise their totalitarian visions.

Some photojournalists shared a tent for a while with three men from Durham who had been involved in the miners' strikes years ago (one of them even claimed still to have fantasies about buggering Margaret Thatcher). Somewhere among all of this was Rose who had trained as a graphic designer and spent the last two years trying to persuade mothers with over three children, and often no central heating, not to use disposable nappies. An aggrieved young woman with no grievances of her own, trying to bear the burden of an idyllic childhood. She was responsible for the production of the AESOP WHITMORE IS INNOCENT banners as well as being the unofficial press liaison officer because of family connections with the broadsheets. She had negotiated the printing of thousands of leaflets through a friend of hers who ran an anarchist press. These lay stacked in their packs, unopened, in the back of the bus shelter while Rose organised the chopper drop that would snow protest over the town at some unspecified future date. She helped him to see the disparate groups within the settlement as the legacy of a nation's injustices; she called them a tribunal and made them powerful. Rose recognised in him someone who had studied and

232

believed in but never participated in protest. A believer was never fully a believer unless threatened with martyrdom; protest, like faith, had its own creed.

Jake recognised in her someone who laid claim to working-class roots that went back to Wat Tyler and beyond when in reality she was probably the Archbishop of Canterbury's daughter. He could see that she thought she understood him, that she might love him. But she didn't.

When Jake got back from the meeting with Blackthorn, Rose was kneeling in his shelter, crouched over a banner that read: 'Rehabilitation not Punishment/ Understanding versus Judgement'.

'Rose?'

'Where've you been?'

'Talking with someone.'

'This is their banner,' she said, watching his eyes flicker aggressively over the words. They both knew whom she was referring to: the only group of real dissidents within the settlement who had arrived a week ago. The professionals who hitched from one event to the next, who preferred marches to demonstrations, the national to the local. The rabble rousers who liked to be caught on camera running alongside walls of fire, or scrunched in a ball pounded by men in uniform and their truncheons. These were the serious riot-mongers who ran in Jake's dreams, who he was afraid of, and who only attached themselves to something if they could smell the blood in it. Jake had known it wouldn't be long before they arrived because he had started to smell the blood himself and understood that the need to act on this was like a craving.

'The Institute?' he asked.

'They want to burn it down,' she mumbled.

'Inside there,' Jake said breathlessly, pointing through the wall of the bus shelter in an easterly direction, 'they've got a recreational area the size of a football pitch, an Olympic swimming pool, a library with more multimedia facilities than the one at the university. They've got wall-to-wall carpet, power showers, choice of menu for breakfast, lunch and tea.' He looked down at the pile of cigarette butts by his feet. 'It's a fucking five-star hotel.'

'Why didn't you say?' Rose said, her eyes shining.

'Why should I? This is about failure in the British justice system, not the Institute. This is about innocence. Aesop Whitmore has never been a dilemma. Whatever wrong he has or hasn't perpetrated, and whatever blood fills the creases in the palms of his hands, none of this compares to the persecution he has undergone; he's a victim of persecution.'

She looked at him then went back to painting the banner, giving the words their second coat of paint. 'I know, but it's been months since he was taken away and he's showing little sign of turning up again. People's attention is waning.'

'I've found Aesop,' he said quietly.

She put the paintbrush down.

'Then you had better start spreading the news.'

32

The closing credits came up on the programme Douglas was watching and his wife, who had her hand wrapped closely round the top of his thigh, started to hum to the music. He caught at handfuls of her hair with his arm round her shoulder, closing his fist round it until the ends didn't tickle him any more. He could smell the hairspray she used in it and the fabric softener she used to wash their clothes. They smelt the same clothed, as people who live together do, but naked they were each their own olfactory continent.

'I don't want you to go away tonight, can't you leave tomorrow morning?'

'You know I can't, sugar.'

He had been waiting for her to say that. It wasn't that it meant all that much to him, he just knew that if she didn't say it he would have to punish her for it in some way. He stood up and turned the television off without asking her if there was anything else she wanted to watch. She didn't flinch like she used to. His regime was also hers now and she had put her life in his hands a long time ago.

When he stood up he always pulled at the waist of his trousers to check that his cock and balls were still there and hadn't dropped off while watching the television. He did the same thing when they were out at restaurants, or when he got out of the car. Maggie's feet couldn't reach the floor from the sofa and he watched them as they swung slightly, catching at the pile of the carpet.

He passed out into the hallway where Maggie had her collection of African animals, gazelles, antelopes, elephants, carved in wood that she dusted every other day, and the photographs of their daughters who had both got into university. The two patches of wall remaining were for their graduation photos. He was fond of saying to Maggie's father that he couldn't see the point himself, all they had gone and done was get the council to pay them a grant to screw boys their own age and – he didn't doubt – men twice their age, in the privacy of their own room which came complete with bed, sink, lock and key.

He tugged at the nets as he passed; they were white and he had nothing to complain about there, he just couldn't understand why they had them – the glass in the window was frosted beyond recognition anyway. As he reached the top stair he thought (as he did every time whatever his mood) of what lay there for the police to find if they ever came looking, if it ever came to that. Sperm, puddle after puddle of it; not that you could see it now, but the traces of it (even after all these years) would cover the top three stairs. It was where he and Maggie used to make love before Eliza was born.

They discovered it one night when they couldn't last till the bedroom and he had caught at her ankles before she reached the top landing. When she was full-term it was the most comfortable place for oral sex, with either his face lapping at her open legs or her with her elbows and belly resting on the stairs below sucking at him, even with the wooden leg. They barely noticed the stairs. Joined in the way they were, they looked like a free-standing totem pole. He never walked up the stairs without picking his way round himself and Maggie twenty years younger tentatively trying to find new, previously undiscovered fuckable parts of each other's body.

He closed the door to the bedroom and sat down on the bed for a few moments; Maggie hated creases in the bed and he was wary of sitting on it but suddenly felt very tired. He had made the headboard himself when they were first married and had wanted to put a mirror in it at the time but she wouldn't have it. They had inherited the wardrobe from her parents after they died; an old-fashioned one that still had the shelves labelled with things people didn't wear any more: a section for collar studs, for pyjamas. The wardrobe was called 'the gentleman's valet' and had obviously been a top-seller in its day, and probably the brunt of many jibes from those with the real thing. He looked at himself in the full-length mirror. Vanity wasn't a suitable occupation for the married man, in fact it was a suspicious one. The gentleman's valet was a bachelor's very best friend, almost built to be a companion. But he liked looking at his own reflection and had never shied from it. He just hadn't worked out when he did it whether it made him feel less or more lonely, but he believed that it was every man's business to know himself and so never took fleeting glances, always studying himself in detail.

He took his suit down from the peg – it was the only item of clothing he had ever bought for himself – and put it on. Then he opened the hat box on top of the wardrobe where Maggie kept the hat she wore to funerals. Everybody who was in line to die had done so; the only funeral she was waiting for now was his and she didn't know when that would be although she prayed it wouldn't take her by surprise.

Maggie prayed a lot. She tried to keep it quiet but couldn't conceal the fact that she was a believer. She

237

hadn't slept at night until their two girls were christened. He heard her saying to her mother once on the phone, 'I need to make it as soon as possible, what would happen to the little blighters if we didn't get it done and something happened to them.' He knew she prayed for him; she loved him but she hadn't been capable of saving him alone, because he needed a lot of saving which was why she had married him.

He pulled his gun and holster from underneath the hat where he kept it hidden. He knew instinctively now when he was in a house whether there were firearms on the property or not. A house with guns was a very different place from one without, even if they did look the same. Maggie had never said anything to him but he still couldn't be sure whether she knew or not. He liked the holster – it made his shirt fit better – and as he stared at his reflection in the mirror on the inside of the door he could see past it to the bed where he saw himself and Maggie, both of them younger with less skin on them, and the two girls curled up around them where they had crept into their bed during a thunderstorm. He liked nothing better than to make love to Maggie when it was raining and to see her face lit up with each flash of lightning and then to lie there wetly afterwards waiting for the claps of thunder and the thudding of the children's bare feet on the carpet as they came pounding for safety in their parents' bed which smelt of something they didn't understand but were too tired to question.

'Douglas are you all right up there?'

She suspected him these days of nothing more than some medical deficiency he was keeping from her and knew that she was convinced she would catch him out soon in the middle of one of the spasms she imagined him having.

'I'm fine love, I'll be down in a minute.'

Then he unhooked his overcoat from the back of the

bedroom door and took his cap down, sniffing it automatically to be reassured by the smell of his own head.

She was waiting for him downstairs, her hand already
on the front door and her head tilted up with her right
cheek thrust slightly forward where it anticipated the
touch of his lips that even now after a shared history of
forty years managed, without effort, a quiet passion that
made life – for both of them – worth living.

'See you later love,' she said, her cheek wet now from
his kiss.

'Not for some time.'

'Oh, I didn't realise it was going to be so long.'

'I did say.'

'What's he got you doing now then?'

'Don't know do I? Never do.'

'Well don't let him work you too hard.'

'I won't.'

He kissed her again, on the forehead this time so that
her face was wet from him in two places, then he walked
down the garden path and got into the car parked on the
road outside. They had lived in the same house since the
day they were married. She listened to him clopping
down the path he had cemented himself and smiled as
she thought to herself that she never had been able to
take men with two legs seriously.

Once the car had gone she got the hat box down from
the top of the wardrobe. The gun was gone. He had to
go further afield for his killing these days; she remembered when they were first married, he used to be gone
for as little as twenty minutes sometimes and often the
bed he had just left was still warm when he came back
home, clean but smelling of blood. She knew when the
killing had gone well because he woke her to make love
to her and making love had never felt as right as it did
when he smelt of another's blood, when he was inside
and around her, stinking of a vibrant death. She used to

wonder afterwards whose blood it was, whether it was a man's or a woman's, or even a child's – she couldn't discard this possibility. Perhaps their own children were conceived the night another's died. Maybe it was wrong, but it gave her a sense of balance; he helped her to achieve an equilibrium even though he didn't think she knew about the killing.

She lay back on the bed unsure what to do with herself. The house around her was empty and felt suddenly not so much unfamiliar as useless. She rolled herself up in the top sheet and waited for him to come home even if it meant sleeping through an unaccountable number of weeks.

33

'Curved iron ribs and curved glass weren't perfected until the 1830s, but I still think that the main body of this was built in 1839. The dome – this is an elliptical one – probably wasn't completed until the 1850s, just after the ones at Kew.'

These were the sort of things Beatrice told Aesop, the sort of things she cared about. He listened as he listened to everything she said, but it didn't make anything any more real, and – despite himself – explanations were what he sought. Some nights she hardly talked at all while on others she couldn't stop. Tonight she sat on the edge of the desk, her knuckles holding it tightly as she named every plant and tree under the glass, listing their idealistic English names which had made her smile when she learnt them: palms, cycads, bougainvillaea, sugar cane, coffee, cinnamon, banana, aloe, ivory nut, rubber, bamboo, guava, and the bird of paradise flower. Brought here by Victoria's plant hunters.

She carried on staring straight ahead of her through the glass and over to the hills opposite. Every now and then a butterfly landed on her back and she cocked her head round to look at it, the antennae getting caught in her hair.

They had tried at the beginning not to get used to

each other, afraid of caving in in some way that would make life unbearable if one was taken away from the other, but in the end their familiarity with each other became a physical presence, like a third person.

'She keeps these here,' Beatrice said, curling her foot round the trolley and pulling it slowly towards her.

'I'd noticed.'

The trolley with Dr Achilles's equipment on moved hesitantly over the tiles.

'I don't think she should, the heat can't be good for them and these probably aren't sterile,' she said at last, leaning forward and carefully picking up one of the syringes, wiping it under her arm. She smiled at him and put it back. 'Don't worry, that was mine. Recognised the smell of my blood on it.'

Aesop didn't like these moments. They were precarious and he never knew where they were going to lead. It reminded him of girls at school with gut-splitting laughs who swore and abused at random. These girls had terrified him because they had no notion of consequences. Beatrice too could choose not to although with her it was more of an effort.

When he was in the palm house on his own he used to wheel the trolley under the desk. He could have asked Dr Achilles to remove it, but he knew if he did that that he would have been a step closer to her and he wanted to keep his distance.

Beatrice was pulling the trolley backwards and forwards, her feet curled round the legs.

'It makes a terrible noise, all this metal.'

'Stop it,' he said nervously.

'What?'

'The noise.'

He moved away and sat on the edge of his bed.

'What kind of person would do this?' she said sorting through the instruments.

He ignored her, looking down at his ankles, wondering whether he liked the hairs that were growing there or not.

'There are no details to make them beautiful. Nothing to signify that they're her instruments. How old are you?' she said suddenly, looking up from the trolley.

'Fourteen. I told you.'

'Still?'

He hesitated a moment, 'Still.'

'And I'm fifteen. So I'm older.'

She pushed the trolley over to him.

'What kind of person would leave no less than three scalpels in a room with a fourteen- and fifteen-year-old.'

'Scalpels.' He leant forward, interested. 'She trusts us,' he said quietly, not touching the instruments. He sounded more defensive of her than he had meant to.

'No,' Beatrice said sharply. Then she started to violently push the trolley. 'This is to remind us that we're sick. Very very sick,' she started to shout.

Aesop tried to catch hold of the legs, but she had no regard for him.

'Stop it, she needs these. She might not have any more.'

'Might not have any more? She's got bags of the stuff in there.' She pointed to the back wall of the palm house that the Hall lay beyond.

'But she needs these.'

'Scared for your life, Aesop?'

She picked up the three scalpels then took hold of the legs of the trolley and flung it against the fountain.

'And these', she said cutting the air near his face with them, 'are a dare.'

'What do you mean?' he said leaning back.

'It's our way out, she's giving us an option. They're scalpels, Aesop,' she said suddenly raising her voice again and bringing them down across the palm of her hand.

'We've been left alone with scalpels.' She put her hand against his face – it was the first time she had touched him – and moved it over his cheeks and brow.

He kept still, only moving his eyes to close them so that she could move her hand across. She sat down on the bed next to him, brought her legs together, straightened her back and raised her chin, trying to breathe calmly, as if remembering a set of instructions she had once been given for success in life. Then he noticed her hand curled in her lap and that his face felt tight because the blood, which he could smell very close, was drying on it.

'I know what she has in mind,' she said quietly. 'Two small rooms, well they might not be all that small, but they'll be separate, maybe even in different parts of the building.' She waited but he didn't say anything. 'We'll be allowed anything we ask for.'

'How do you know that.'

'I just know that we will because what we'll ask for will be all the usual predictable stuff which they'll give us – bestow on us to help bring the rest of the world to us. The rooms will be mostly white, not much colour. People will come and visit us, treat us, sometimes it will be Dr Achilles, sometimes others, maybe even Black-thorn, and then they'll leave by the door. But we won't ever get to use that door. Perhaps it won't even be possible for us to see each other.'

'How do you know this? Is this what she's told you?'

'No, it's what I know. I know how she sees things; how she sees us.' This time her voice was a lot closer and her hand went out to his cheek. She lifted her hand off and sucked her fingers quickly.

'Doesn't taste very nice.'

'Well it wouldn't, would it.'

He watched the scalpels in her hand.

'You must have thought about it.'

He had, but he didn't want her to know.

'You have.'

He was already sucking the end of a cigarette.

'How would you do it?'

He lay back on his elbows and said nothing for a long time. Then at last he jerked his head up towards the centre of the dome.

'Up there? Hanging?'

He nodded intently, as if this information might be too much for her.

'How do you see it then?'

He shook his head and the cigarette fell out of his mouth on to the bed.

'I see myself climbing up those stairs.'

'With the rope?'

'With the rope over my shoulders, and I'd tie it to that iron bar up there, make a noose . . .'

'How do you make a noose?'

'No idea, but I'd find out in time. Then,' he paused here, 'then I'd jump into the trees.'

He sat up.

'And after that she'd walk in, and wouldn't be able to find me. She'd lose it all right then, until she looked up and saw me swinging there, all bloated.' He was smiling when he finished.

'Thought so.'

'You knew?'

'No, I just thought you'd have a very clear picture. And that it would involve her. You won't do it,' she added without pausing.

'I will.'

'You won't. It's a coup you want, not a death.'

'I would have, before,' he blurted.

'Before what?'

He could already hear the triumph in her voice.

'Before I got company.'

245

'Oh.'

They were both staring at her hand.

'And you?' he said.

'Maybe. I've got something to do first. But after that possibly. Most possibly, yes.'

They were silent after that.

'Well don't do it without telling me first.'

'I won't,' she said and it was the closest thing to a promise she had ever come to making.

Then he leant over and took the scalpels out of her hand.

'You're so white,' Beatrice said.

'Never seen the sun,' he said.

'Not likely to now either.'

'Who knows.'

This was one of the strangest things he had ever said, and unlike him, unprovocative. It was her he was promising something to.

'Let's bury them,' he said softly.

'What?'

'The scalpels.'

'We could, couldn't we,' she admitted.

'We should. If she's not going to take them away.'

'She won't. Ever.'

'No.'

Five minutes later they were on their hands and knees by the bird of paradise flower scooping handfuls of soil away until they had a trench that would have borne the body of an emperor, let alone three scalpels. They both jumped in at the same time.

'Where does it end?'

'Maybe it doesn't.'

'It has to. There has to be a foundation,' she said frowning, 'otherwise it could blow away in the wind. Otherwise,' she carried on looking about her, 'this jungle is built on English soil.'

'Hallowed ground,' Aesop said.

'What do you know about hallowed ground?'

'Nothing, it's from a hymn someone I knew used to sing.'

'To you?'

'I think it was for me, yes,' he said.

They dropped the scalpels in by their feet and started to fill the hole while they were still standing in it, climbing out when it reached their knees.

'We could put the rest of it in,' Aesop said looking at the trolley.

'No, let's leave it at these, it's damning rather than angry.'

'We're threatening her,' he said remembering the kiss and her flitting open eyes.

The earth was pressed hard where they had knelt on it, the knees of Aesop's uniform were thick with it and Beatrice's socks were full. They noticed it on each other, but not themselves until they went to the fountain to try and wash it off.

'She's in love with you,' Beatrice said pulling her sleeves up. 'She wants to eat you.' Then she wandered off among the trees, forgetting him already as she walked. 'You never ask me any questions.' Her voice came from the far side near the staircase and he wondered for a moment if she meant to climb it so that she could see him from the balcony above.

'I do.'

'You don't. Hardly ever.'

'It's not that I don't want to know.'

'What is it then?' she called out.

A shadow crossed the water in the fountain as the butterfly that liked him the most flew over, and he curled his shoulders slightly in anticipation of its landing.

'Do you miss London?'

'You don't know anything about London.'

'I wasn't saying I did, I just asked if you missed it – that's all.'

'Course I miss it.'

'Were you born there?'

'You know I was.'

'No, you never told me.'

'I thought I did.'

'Where's your brother?'

'I don't know. Same place as before, I expect. Outside the Institute for Young Offenders.'

'What's his name?'

'His name?' He had to think a second before answering, he hadn't spoken it for so long. 'Jake. I've got him here,' he said, and she heard him kicking at the tape collection under his bed. 'Enough conversation to last me a lifetime – my lifetime.'

'Does she know about him?'

'Who?'

'Does Dr Achilles know about Jake?'

'Not about Jake, no. But she knows about the campaigners outside the Institute. That they're campaigning for me.'

'For your innocence.'

'For my innocence.'

'And you don't want them there, do you?'

He pushed his face into his knees.

'I'm not innocent.'

'I know what men and women who have killed other men and women look like. You haven't ever killed anybody.'

The skin that wasn't in the water was already drying. Then she was beside him; she had moved without him hearing her and he jolted as he felt her finger on his arm and afterwards the water running down where she had touched him.

'I did something the last night I was in Jara.'

She had mentioned a man called Aurelius before and he thought she was going to now.

'I was in the room Dr Achilles had set up for me. I know she's going to make my room at the hospital exactly the same.' She put her other hand back in the water as well. 'It was my last night there.'

'You knew you were leaving?'

'She told me, and she showed me the box they were taking me away in. Aurelius had been with me that afternoon; they were always leaving me on my own with him – he knew I was leaving. There were things I had promised myself.'

'I've never promised myself anything.'

'I was going to kill him.'

'How?'

'Big question,' Beatrice said with a quick smile. 'A poisoned arrow tipped with juji.'

'How were you going to do that then?'

'You don't believe me?'

'No.'

'Why not?'

'I can't see it.'

She was going to say something, but then ignored him.

'Juji's hallucinatory. Makes you see things.'

'A slow death?'

'Yes, but not painful. In that sense. Just slow. The things you see when dying make a lot of people think that they're already dead. They think they're getting a fore-taste of what's to come.'

'What do you see then?'

'It's different for every person. You live your life again in thirty minutes – but only the bad bits. Anything wrong you've ever done, anything wrong you've ever dreamt of doing, happens in those thirty minutes.'

'What would Aurelius do?'

249

'Make love to me.'

'For thirty minutes?'

Aesop saw himself crouched on the end of his bed in Whitechapel, afraid, but not surreptitious, watching as friends' bodies, bodies he had grown up with, disintegrated. He remembered lying in the smells they left behind and hearing the echo of sounds that made him feel older and much younger than he was at the same time.

'Over and over again for thirty minutes.'

'Is that a bad way to die?'

She looked intently at him for a moment. 'The only way for him. There wasn't anybody or anything before me. He didn't want to do what he did.'

Aesop almost began to feel sorry for him.

'Mack told me he was a Catholic, and you know the thing about Catholics?'

'No.'

'They're the only ones that kept . . . no they didn't keep it . . . they were the only ones that didn't lose their faith in Jara, that weren't able to lose their faith. They wanted to. Most of them wanted to, and they found ways to – like Aurelius – for a short while, but it always came back to them, it always found them again in the end.'

'Maybe they were glad of it – in the end.'

'Maybe. I think they were. I know that it would have made Aurelius cry. But then he was always crying, there was hardly anything in the end that didn't make him cry.'

'But you didn't kill him in the end, did you?'

'How did you know?'

'You were ill, you couldn't leave your room.'

'Yes, I was ill,' she said as if remembering. 'I decided to kill myself instead. The classic alternative to murdering someone you've dreamt of murdering is to kill yourself.'

'But you didn't do that either.' He didn't sound so convinced despite the fact that she was standing beside him and had her arms in the water.

'No.'

'So nobody died that night.'

'No.'

He watched her hands feeling the stone of the fountain.

'Mack said that I came into the world already dead. There was nothing he could do to me after that,' she concluded. Then she started to rub the palms of her hands up and down the white underside of his arms where he hadn't thought to look for mud.

She was crying. She didn't stop herself shaking, she didn't put her hand to her face to wipe the snot away from her nose or the tears clogging up the corners of her eyes, and he could see in the last light that was coming in through the glass that most of her face was wet in the slightly greasy way that tears make a face wet, and she didn't make any moves to wipe it away because she wanted him to see her fear and her grief. She just carried on washing him.

Then, in their stillness, they heard the sound of feet running along the corridor, and the handle of the door to the palm house squeaking as it was turned. Beatrice let her hands run down his arms and back into the water.

Under the water they found, without even being aware of looking, each other's hands and Aesop felt her bracelet rubbing against his wrist.

34

Dr Achilles walked along the corridor to the palm house on the balls of her feet, her tongue flicking against her teeth as she anticipated his anticipation. Closing the door quietly behind her, she lifted the hand she had opened the door with briefly to her face. It smelt as it always did – of rust – and there were tiny flakes of tainted white paint stuck to the palm. She liked to keep this hand smelling and looking like it did when she went to bed at night; it gave her something to nurse.

Even after only a couple of minutes stood inside the palm house the pages of the book she had brought with her were already curling up at the corners and it made her remember the fate of things from this world that she had taken on her first Amazon trip as a medical student: the books that had evaporated, the records that had melted, the hi-fi equipment that had made sounds they had never been invented to make, picking up frequency waves that didn't exist. The only mistake the jungle made was in destroying them before they had lost their meaning. Even when they were navigating the currents in the centre of the Amazon itself and the river bank on one side was so far away it looked like the horizon, and the other river bank nothing but a reflection of it, she knew she yearned to hear the music the heat had destroyed. Often when she caught herself straining her ears or waiting silently, she knew that she was trying to pick up the traces of this music because she didn't believe in its absence. The jungle took away her belief in machines and made her think that the music would have to find another channel, another means of making itself heard.

She crept round the corner to the point where she usually announced herself and Aesop would look up, his face wide and expectant beneath the light, his body hooked slightly over the left-hand side of the desk so that he could watch her coming. As she leant forward she was aware that her face was pulled back in a smile and that she must look absurd, but didn't care, preferring instead to embrace the freedom ridicule gave her. But tonight he wasn't there.

They were both up to their elbows in water and looking at her not with expectation, but horror.

'Stop,' she said automatically.

They took their hands out of the water, but their faces didn't change expression.

Then she saw the mud and her hand went out for the door. She had a fear of mud. The blacker it was the more afraid she was. Mud signified nothing but burial grounds; it was something that sucked and ate, and didn't allow the dead to turn to dust. It was the breeder of moist life, too much life, churned over again and again to the surface. Men could be – had been – made out of clay. Not moulded out of it, but spat out of it.

She raised her arms to her face, dropping the book and smelling for the first time mud in the palm house. In her mind she had never permitted the soil any strength because of the violent density of the foliage, but now she began to suspect that it sank deeper than she had thought. And here were the children covered in it, and not even afraid.

She took one last look at them – they had moved closer together and there was no light showing between their arms and legs – then opened the door and ran.

She felt a heavy pity for herself she had never felt before and the beginnings of a grief that was black at the edges as well as in the centre and as she ran back along the corridor into the house she could feel nothing but their bodies against her; she was surrounded by the smell of their skin and their skin was nothing more than clay. The walls of the corridor were wet with moisture and no longer a clean solid white, but stained with dirt and bulging outwards so that her hands were unable to reach them any more.

Blackthorn stood in the shadow of the kitchen door listening to her hysterical breathing and watched as she clutched at her knees with each step, brought them up to her chest then gasped as they went down on to the stone flags. She was walking as though wading through mud.

He had always hoped that she suffered from night-mares, but he had never expected them to weigh so much that she suffered them while still awake. He watched her blindly making her way up the corridor, sweating now with the effort of pulling her leg up each step of the way and of having no support (she flinched every time her hands went out for the wall). It was something he had never thought to see, and wondered why it disconcerted him when it should have satisfied him.

35

'You stink and I'd never noticed,' Sean said, burying his nose in the dog's fur. As he leant over he felt the map of London he wore against his chest, inside his T-shirt, crumpling slightly. He had found the dog two weeks ago and the scars on his face where it had tried to attack the eagle tattooed there were only just healing. Sean had tried to cut the rope from the dog's neck when he first found it, to avoid the responsibility of ownership, but the dog had started to howl against the idea of freedom as if it had once been hurt by it in some way.

The dog did stink and now with its belly partially open and its legs mangled it was as if all the hardships it had tried to overcome could no longer be contained because the seal on the body was broken.

The cars were as unwilling to stop for the man who ran across their path, his chest braced, as they had been for the dog. Sean had picked it up, wrapped it in his coat and cut down behind Southwark cathedral and on to the embankment. The dog was heavier now, almost a dead weight, but he didn't feel he had the knowledge or the right to make this final pro-nouncement. He had a horror of burying something when there was still the possibility... He needed to see Taff who slept rough in the alley behind Westminster reference library, and who had once been a vet.

Occasionally he stopped and pulled the dog's eyes open, but the pupils lolled at the corners and he could tell that the animal had lost its buoyancy. He half thought of throwing it in the river, still wrapped in his coat, but he believed things never disappeared, that they always came back to you in the end. People avoided him even though it wasn't clear whether the bundle he was carrying was a child or not.

When the dog ran out into the road, he had been sat under the railway arch as he was every night, the map spread over his lap. Sometimes he closed his eyes to remember more clearly the sensation of those journeys in taxis with Dr Achilles, whom he hadn't seen for the past four months. She had stopped looking for him, and now it was time for him to look for her because she had taken his face with her.

He knew, instinctively, that the taxis had driven northwards, that they had left the river behind them. Going to Dr Achilles's they had driven uphill and coming back, on his own, they had gone downhill. Primrose Hill? Hampstead? He had walked to both these places once a week for the past four months, but could feel that he wasn't even close. He had never seen the man, Ludwig, at Amy's again either.

Every now and then he saw the fur on the dog's back moving as if it were waking up and trying to fit itself over the skeleton again, but it was only the wind in its hairs. This fake movement made the dog seem even more dead.

He crossed over the river, through the sound of frazzled parties creeping off the boats moored there. There was a fair on in Leicester Square and the cables he walked over didn't seem capable of containing the light and sound that filled the square. The horses on the carousel had a music of their own that competed healthily with the heavy sounds blaring from some of the other machines; machines promising vicious pleasures, which boys went on to prove themselves, and girls to scream.

Taff wasn't down the alley which was also backed onto by a cinema. Often on Fridays he managed to get into late screenings. Sean found himself in a street that smelt overwhelmingly of food refuse. After a few moments he noticed a tall gothic-looking building whose colour was difficult to determine, but looked as though it might be blue in daylight. He saw the word 'Hospital' and walked straight in.

Usually in hospitals you could only smell steel and lino, but here there was a scent of heavily polished wood as well, and he wondered if this was why people paid for private healthcare. The nurse on reception couldn't take her eyes off his face, and he knew it wasn't the eagle she was looking at. Her eyes weren't curious, just steady and professional. She was considering him, and hadn't noticed that he was carrying a dog in his arms until he laid it in front of her, still partially wrapped in his coat. She flew out of her seat when she saw it and stood back with one hand over her nose and mouth, and the other over her belly.

'Is he dead?' Sean asked.

She nodded and, once this was confirmed, she took her hand cautiously away from her mouth.

He noticed the lipstick print on her palm and thought that she must have had it spread on pretty thick. The dog's head hung over the edge of the reception desk and he had to hold it to stop the whole animal from falling. It was stifling inside the hospital and he tried to wipe his arm over his forehead. He had laboured more than he realised at the time under the weight of the dog.

'A car?' she said at last.

'Yes. Did he die immediately?'

'Probably.' She looked up at his face again. 'Yes,' she said more softly, to assure him.

'Thank you, it's all I wanted to know.'

He turned to go, hoping she wouldn't call him back to collect the dog; he was happy to forsake his coat.

'Excuse me,' the nurse called out.

He turned round, bracing his arms for the weight of the animal again.

'Are you one of Dr Achilles's patients?'

36

Douglas liked to listen to clean music: Buddy Holly, The Shadows; especially The Shadows because there weren't any words. The nights were really closing in now and by the time he left London and Maggie, who he knew was crying her first tears, it was already dark.

Outside London, England shed its skin and he felt as though he was sharing what was left of it with one piece of road heading north and a pair of frantically searching headlights. The only remaining claim to a spine the country had were the Pennines; indecipherable humps in the darkness.

People were their most openly private behind closed doors and he stared into window after window as cars passed cars, prickled by the intimacy of the scenes inside. Sometimes he could even tell what people were thinking as his headlights picked up the backs of their heads. He carried on further and further north, past the Midlands and into a part of the country where towns were either allocated blue or brown signposts depending on historical significance. Nottingham was laboriously brown, but then they had to account for Robin Hood, the Industrial Revolution and D.H. Lawrence.

Just before the Blackpool turning he pulled in at a service station. This was one of the reasons they wanted to colonise Mars, he decided, in order to build service stations on it. Douglas wasn't a cynic he just despaired at the lack of responsibility with which men imagined their imaginations. Things became tedious before they were even properly born.

It took a while for people to become accustomed to using their legs after being in their cars for so long, but the strain on most people's faces wasn't from the fact that they had to bear their own weight again, but that they had to resume disguises once more. He watched person after person reassemble the skin they had made for themselves in order to take part in everyday life, under the bland but interrogative lights of the service station. Those who could barely accomplish it gave the shop a miss and went and stood instead in the corner where the game zone blared, whether they intended to play or not. While others sat at tables for two by the windows staring at the cars passing by, wondering why they were travelling so fast, and how they had ever reached such speeds only minutes before.

The staff in these places were impenetrable and sloth-ful and the tables he had sat at all over an England mapped by Granadas and Welcome Breaks had been strewn with cups where the imprints of lips were rarely washed off properly; lips that had sworn, lips that had kissed, lips that had screamed, lips that had no idea; lips that had behaved with intent or against their will. He knew what they were all capable of, even those that basked under the spotlights in the centre of the restaurant. Then there were his lips, he thought, pouring himself another cup of tea from the red plastic teapot. He slurped his tea whether it was hot or cold because it made him feel as though he had done a hard day's work. He could only rest properly when he slurped. When he finished he sat staring at the chair opposite him that was welded to the table which was welded to the floor, then got up and walked to the phones.

He waited until the family, whose every member had stared at him limping stiffly to the phone, had passed (curious, probably, as to where wood ended and skin began), checked his pockets, then dialled. It was answered immediately. This was something Douglas had always wondered about, and never taken for granted. The other end was never engaged, never not picked up on the second tone; Mack was always there.

'Hello . . . No, I'm just outside Blackpool . . . I know you like Blackpool, but I'm not staying there. I'll get you a postcard or postcards.' Then he paused. 'I've found him.'

'Good.' The voice was pleased but not surprised. 'I thought he might come looking for me, but now he's disappeared and we're looking for him. Again.'

Douglas could feel the sand of the desert and the casino walls that gave you shocks if you leant against them because of the voltage, coming down the line. 'See if you can manage it,' the voice continued. 'Nima couldn't.'

Douglas held the phone away from him so that he wouldn't hear him breathing. It was a long time since he had heard Mack mention Nima's name. He dropped the phone back down on to the receiver as the one-armed bandit opposite dropped a feast of copper coins into the hands of a skinny fourteen-year-old kneeling in front of it who was laughing and stuffing his pockets.

He picked the phone up again; this time it rang for ages.

'Hello?' the voice said at last, and he could tell that she had just wiped her nose on the back of her hand.

'Is that you, love?'

'Yes.' She waited. They both knew he never rang when he was away from home.

'Everything all right?'

'I'm lonely,' she said.

'I know you are, I'll be home soon.'

'You will?'

'Definitely.'

He could hear her moving the ornaments about the side table where the telephone stood.

'I've had to put the heating on.'

'You have?'

'It's getting cold.'

He watched the units left flick down.

'Have you seen the stars?'

'No.'

'They're really clear tonight; you can see all of them. Have a look out of the window before you go to bed.'

'I will,' she said eagerly. 'I'll do that.'

He knew that he had her already twitching at the curtains and that she was craning her neck to see out even though the glass in the window by the phone was frosted.

'Where are you?' she said suddenly.

'Just outside Blackpool,' he answered without hesitating.

'I'd better let you go,' she said after a while.

'Goodnight then, love.'

She waited a moment without saying anything, then hung up.

It was the first time she had ever known where he was when he wasn't with her.

37

'Aesop,' Dr Achilles said, brushing her legs against the side of her bed.

Ludwig watched her move over to the window and look out. She – like him – had a view of the palm house, the top of the dome and the small orthodox cross there.

'Don't.'

'What?'

'Close the window. The dust in here makes my face itch.'

She sat down on the edge of the mattress looking out through the window.

'He has Eastman's; the infant borealis.'

Ludwig touched his face gently and came to sit next to her on the mattress. They weren't afraid of being close to each other and, in the silence, forgot to listen out for scuffles on the carpet outside or floorboards squeaking under human treads, or breathing trying to disguise itself as something else.

'When will Eastman's become the borealis?' he said, pulling a handkerchief out of his pocket and wiping the palms of his hands with it.

'It won't. Children who have Eastman's never grow up.'

'At the moment,' Ludwig put in.

263

'What do you mean "at the moment",' Achilles said defensively.

'I mean until you find a cure.'

'I can't be responsible for other men's passions.'

He flinched suddenly as two moths flew in through the window watching warily as they settled by her bedside lamp.

'He has to leave,' she said ignoring him. 'There's a better chance if he's kept at the hospital. I have more equipment there, better access to other specialists.'

'I can't go back to London,' Ludwig said.

'Why not?'

'I'm supposed to be in Jara for another two years.'

'It's his only chance.'

They were each so involved in their own silence that they failed to hear, above the sound of the moths immolating themselves, the floorboards creaking outside. Then for the first time, Ludwig touched her hand, not the palm of it like most people but the top where the veins grew down from her fingertips. He brushed it slightly with his knuckle.

'Will you let me take him?' she asked, as if intimacy gave her permission.

'And Beatrice?'

'Of course,' she said, sighing.

'Will he live another two years?'

'I don't know; I don't know that I have the power to heal any more. I can't feel it with Aesop,' she said, rubbing her hands down her legs.

Then she looked up at him, waiting for more, expecting more, knowing that after this moment and the words they had spoken, they would find it difficult to speak to each other again, to acknowledge each other even. They had put themselves in each other's hands and were resting there uncomfortably, unable to decide whether they had just started something or just ended it.

38

Douglas walked past the old customs houses where men had stood in frock coats and clasped their hands until the nails went purple, waiting for cargoes of sugar, tea or worse; cargoes that swelled the north of the country and lent it a stocky affluence of hard money earned through trade. Leaving the quayside he climbed the hill to the priory that overlooked the bay, renowned for its treacherous tides. At night you could see the lights at Blackpool, but in daylight the eye could see no further than the headland where a monastery had once stood, then a Butlin's Holiday camp now abandoned, and recently, a nuclear power station, ugly and dangerous with impenetrable functions. The bungalows stretching out along the cliff were already breeding a much higher proportion of twins as well as – increasingly – the sort of offspring that were never paraded in prams or push chairs, but were instead born on to paper as surreptitious statistics.

Douglas had too much time on his hands, of his own making. He should have done the job by now, been out and back home. Mack hadn't rung him yet; he knew. He stopped in front of a shop just round the corner from the hotel that specialised in artificial limbs, and stood with his hands in his pockets, staring up at some of the most technically advanced plastic prostheses available, tapping his wooden leg nervously as he took in the knee and ankle joints. If I stand here long enough, he thought, I might see muscle and blood. It was the soft stuff that intrigued him, he knew enough about the hard stuff.

'What did he want?' Rose said from inside the bus shelter.

Jake looked at her for a moment then turned back to the road, his attention on Blackthorn's disappearing car until the letters and the numbers on the registration plate were out of focus.

'They're taking him away.'

'Who?'

'Aesop.'

'I thought they already had.'

'No, from Hornby Hall.'

He sat down on the bench as the rain started, the sound spreading heavily across the polythene.

'Aesop must be very ill,' Rose said, looking at him hunched in the back of the shelter.

'Maybe.'

'You don't believe him?'

'I don't know, but I do believe they're taking Aesop away because he says he wants me to get there first. I believe him because he doesn't love Aesop, in fact he hates him.'

Rose came and sat down next to him. 'He could be ill,' she said again.

'He could,' Jake said absently.

'When are they taking him?'

'A week's time.'

'What are you going to do?'

'Jake?' a voice said from outside. 'There's a man coming.'

Jesper was stood at the doorway to the shelter

266

wrapped in a shawl with tassels.

Jake wondered if it was Dr Blackthorn, come to tell the truth this time.

'We're going to get him,' Jake said.

'At Hornby Hall?'

'All of us.'

Rose took hold of his hand briefly. 'This is what we were waiting for, Jake. This is it.' But he had already left.

Jake watched as the wholesale food truck that delivered to the Institute pulled away past the shelter and the man it had dropped off walked towards them, turning to look at the hills on either side of him as he did.

Jesper pulled the shawl tighter around him when he saw the man's face and Jake could tell by the smell of him that he hadn't seen the inside of any building for years. He stood in front of them, the eagle tatooed on his face raising its beak slightly as he tried to decide whether to smile or frown, and Jake realised, looking at him, that the tatooist had fitted the entire wingspan of a golden eagle across his cheeks without making it look cramped.

'I've come to be cured,' Sean said after a while. 'I've come to be cured,' he repeated, tracing his fingers slightly over his face as if the rain were irritating it, then walked past them both into the shelter. 'Do you mind if I stay here?' his voice said from inside. 'I can see the Hall more clearly than from the town.'

Jake watched the truck pull in through the Institute's main gate then followed the man into the shelter. 'What's your name?' he said.

39

Her nails were painted with clear varnish and had never been bitten. Beatrice watched as she filled the fifth test tube with blood. Not even the light shining through the glass diluted it. It always surprised her to see how red blood was. Red, as a colour, could suggest orange, the deeper sorts black, and even sometimes blue. But blood was an absolute red. It was one of the few substances the body secreted that wasn't ashamed of itself. She could tell from the way Dr Achilles leant forward over the desk into the light that she wasn't only watching the blood as she transferred it to the tube, but smelling it as well.

She saw Aesop struggling to unroll his sleeve, managing to scratch his elbow before smiling at her as he did his cuff up. He always put his hands on his knees afterwards, to stop himself from rubbing his arm where it was sore and permanently swollen. His skin was so white it wore every bruise, cut or wound with great ostentation whereas Dr Achilles's blood–sucking did nothing to her. If anything it seemed to relieve her of an excess, but it caused a severe imbalance in Aesop, who couldn't relax his muscles enough to let the needle slide in painlessly.

Beatrice had sat that afternoon on the stool by his side, taken his hand in her lap and run circles round it with her fingers, occasionally stroking his pulse point. She could see that for the first time it bothered Dr Achilles that she was the one wielding the needle and she handled it that afternoon as a weapon rather than an instrument. Afterwards she took his hand as Beatrice had done and touched him in the same place as she swabbed his upper arm.

She wrote the dates meticulously on the labels, as well as a whole series of symbols Beatrice couldn't understand. Sometimes, when she stuck them on, the ink ran because the blood was so warm and often the blood seemed more alive than the boy it had left behind. She fingered the tubes not with self-assurance, but the confidence of a believer; the blood wasn't something you tested, it was something to be read and ultimately understood.

'You're not wearing shoes, Beatrice,' Dr Achilles said without looking up from the samples she was fitting into their container.

She never spoke the word 'Beatrice', she always chanted it and it bothered Beatrice a lot that Achilles could make it sound so melodic. The ability to sing was never something she had credited her with.

'They get dirty.'

Dr Achilles raised her head sharply, pulling it out of the arc of light over the desk, and Beatrice knew immediately that she was suspected of the most forbidden of transgressions, of having stepped outside.

'I mean', she added laboriously, 'that the soil in here is very damp and heavy when you go walking about in the trees. That the palm house is, in fact, much bigger than it seems when you first start walking,' she concluded, noting for the first time as the light caught it that Dr Achilles was wearing a chain round her neck, a chain with a small cross on it. She wasn't the sort of woman to decorate herself for pleasure's sake. Beatrice had to stop her hand from going out to it; Aurelius had worn one of these.

'So you walk barefoot,' Dr Achilles said, looking among the trees as if hoping to understand why.

'It's easier to clean skin than leather.'

Dr Achilles locked the sample case with one of the miniature keys she kept on a bracelet on her wrist. Beatrice wondered who it was she was afraid of.

'How's the reading going?' she said, turning to Aesop. She hardly ever said his name.

'Fine,' Beatrice said before he had time to speak. 'We need more books. Better books.'

Dr Achilles looked at her trying to remember how she had subdued her in Jara, then realised that it was merely that Beatrice had chosen to – momentarily – lapse her will.

'Are you still using these?' she said loudly seeing the misshapen stack of flash cards.

Aesop shook his head without looking at her and they watched as she re-laid her trolley, then walked away taking the sample box with her. She had never referred to the missing scalpels.

'Tomorrow I need to speak to you about arrangements for London,' she said when she reached the fountain, looking down at herself in the water. She said it as if warning them to be there, as if there was somewhere else they might be, as if they had a choice.

'Are we leaving soon?' Beatrice asked.

'Yes.' She leant further forward, sniffing again. 'This water's stagnant.'

'Is it?'

Achilles dipped her right hand in. It was a deliberate act; she knew she was contaminating something sacred to them – she acknowledged this much. She dried her hand on her shirt.

'I was wondering,' Beatrice started, sitting in the chair

270

Dr Achilles had just left, 'if Eastman's is hereditary.'

'Hereditary?' Dr Achilles held the blood samples tightly against her belly.

'I mean,' she said, tracing the lines Aesop had drawn on the desk top, 'if I were to have a baby, would that baby have Eastman's? That's all.'

Aesop stood up and for a moment Beatrice thought he was going to walk over to her but he didn't, he sat down on the bed, flicking his fingers at the metal frame.

Dr Achilles didn't look at her, watching Aesop instead.

'I don't know,' she said lightly. 'Eastman's is contracted by children so it's never been an issue.'

'Are we children?'

'Of course you are.'

'Children can bear children.'

She looked past them both and through the window.

'It'll be the shortest day soon,' she said quietly, then left, not even brushing the leaves of the trees as she moved along the path.

In the silence afterwards, above the sound of the water continually regenerating itself, they could hear the sound of feet running. Aesop lay back on the bed, his hand grasped round his left arm, and knew that there were things Beatrice didn't tell him because she was afraid that there wasn't enough space inside his head to contain them.

40

The majority of the settlement was crammed into Jesper's bus and six lucky people had been given coffee to drink (even a toddler had some in a bottle, sweetened with sugar). Jake wasn't one. He was aware that he should have been holding a cup of coffee between his hands and that people should have been able to watch the steam rise into his face. He was also becoming uncomfortable about the fact that the bus shelter was camp HQ because any gatherings of more than three people were held in Jesper's bus. In fact, looking about him, Jake laboured increasingly under the impression that he had been invited to someone else's meeting as a guest speaker, but people weren't even necessarily waiting for him to speak. So he sat, himself waiting, staring at Rose's ring which was large and made of plastic with some anonymous flower incarcerated inside it. He could tell, from the way her fingers strained over her knee, that she wanted to take hold of his hand. He looked at the white knuckles with their unavoidable freckles and suppressed the urge to knock her sideways, at the same time trying not to seek refuge in the memory of feeling another person's hair, thick oily hair, falling over his cheeks. He no longer knew what it felt like to be warm and dry, and Jesper had decorated the floor of his bus with carpet; Jake wished he hadn't.

'Aesop,' he whispered by way of a beginning.

Then Rose's hand did go out for his and he saw the paint under her fingernails; there was nothing immaculate about her. He pushed his hands between his legs, against his groin.

'My brother has been found,' he said more loudly.

'At last,' somebody muttered.

'Was he missing?' one of Jesper's girls asked, concerned.

Jake had hoped, when he started to speak, that an inherent joy would send him into an inspired monologue and that cheering lay on the other side of this. Instead he spoke haltingly, repeating himself because of a sudden lack of words and the need to avoid Rose's hand.

'The Institute?' someone demanded, suddenly.

Even those with their backs still turned to him, lifted their heads at this.

'They've got an Olympic-sized swimming pool inside there. Ever seen one of those before?' one of the dockers from Liverpool said, pulling the child with the bottle of coffee down into his lap.

'We're campaigning for Aesop's innocence. That was where he was incarcerated.'

The chant 'Aesop Whitmore is innocent' tapped its way round the group like a blind man with a stick.

'Aesop's ill,' Rose whispered.

'We don't know that for sure,' Jake insisted.

'You saw him getting taken away by the ambulance, Jake. You heard what Blackthorn said.'

'If we're getting Aesop out we should get all the bloody sods out, empty the place in one night,' someone else put in.

'But Aesop's not at the Institute any more,' Jake persisted, unable to hear what it was they were all listening to.

Rose took hold of his hand as she stood up behind

273

him. 'They abducted Aesop and now we know where he is.'

'Abducted' was the word he had been looking for; he didn't speak any language they understood. These were the words he needed to learn how to use, 'they', and 'we', 'them' and 'us', but he disabled himself every time with his need to define and he left a gaping hole between definition and interpretation while Rose was injecting them with emotions that were hardcore and absolute, and which left no room for anything but the most vigilant dreams of violence. She had the gift, he realised, that some speakers had of being able to take hold of people's chins and raise them upwards; she could stop people from looking down at their own feet.

The inside of the bus was as noisy as it had been when he had spoken, but this was the noise of a group of people finding focus, slowly lifting the speaker on to their shoulders. As the soles of Rose's feet came into view he realised that he was sat in front of a group of people who were complete strangers to him. They would never be any more than this; he wasn't interested in loving them or saving them, and his arm was beginning to ache because of the angle Rose was holding his hand at. Nobody here even knew Aesop.

'Set fire to Hornby Hall,' one of the socialist workers yelled, provoked, the skin stretching over his triumphant face his mouth was open so wide.

There was a group of people already stood by the windows of the bus, looking out across the valley.

'We could set fire to the whole fucking place,' one of the girls said, giggling.

The door to the bus was kicked open and people filed out, unable to conceal this new elation that made them want to take in lungfuls of fresh air.

Jake heard a can being kicked and somewhere, for just a moment, the sound of a cot mobile or jewellery box

274

playing 'Frère Jacques', then 'Blaydon Races'. Matthew, one of the socialist workers, came and knelt beside him, the child high on coffee and sugar barely restrained in his lap. Matthew was an ethics student on the philosophy course at the university and everybody in the settlement left their children with him. The fists clenched tightly round the boy's belly had the words WORLD'S ARSEHOLE STARTS HERE tattooed across the knuckles, which Jake found oddly soothing.

'They're going to set fire to the Hall.'

'I know; I heard,' Matthew said, nuzzling the boy's head. 'They will as well,' he added.

'And what about you?' Jake asked him.

'Of course, can't wait.'

'But Aesop.'

'They won't get to him; they've forgotten him already. Their heads are full of fire now. Don't worry, your brother will be fine.'

'We'll smoke her out,' Sean said from the corner of the bus.

'Who?'

'Achilles, we'll smoke her out.'

He got up and stood by the window staring out. 'And your brother, Aesop Whitmore. Is he innocent?'

'I don't know,' Jake said, quietly, not looking at either of them, 'but I taught him to swim.'

A few days later the camp had repositioned itself so that the first thing most people saw in the morning was the valley opening out towards them and the Hall opposite. The bus shelter was left with its back to the rest of the settlement which seemed to have edged forward so that there was a gap between it and the bus shelter whose polythene entrance was now too far away for most people to visit.

41

'He doesn't love you,' Ludwig said.

The voice wasn't hard, but it was long and reached her very definitely although she didn't know from where. Beatrice looked to see if it had woken Aesop, but he was still fast asleep. This was often difficult to tell because he slept with his eyes half open, so she had to listen to his breathing instead. The sound of somebody unconsciously breathing was very different from the sound of somebody consciously breathing. He was asleep.

She took her skirt, jumper and shirt off while still listening to see whether the voice would speak again, then folded them neatly and put them under the pillow. She had noticed that since they both stopped sweating they liked to have something that smelt – even faintly – of them close by.

She sat for a while on the bed in her pants, then put her Vegas T-shirt on. Her breasts must have grown since the last time she had worn it because it seemed tighter, and she had to pause as she pulled it over her head because it smelt still of the sheets on Mack's bed. For a moment she saw Aurelius lying on it, uncomfortably naked, waiting for her to love his body, then she banished him forcibly, leaving him forever waiting. She looked down, still enjoying the fact that her nipples rose at the

276

touch of cotton and that they jutted out in almost manufactured symmetry.

Standing up, she raised her arms above her head, rose on to the balls of her feet, then walked into the green. The metallic smell of the pipes that carried the water was heavier at night, and she could even smell the details of the invention, the gauges and dials, pumps, cogs and even further back, behind these, the facts and figures that made the whole of the structure possible.

The soil was wet beneath her feet and she wasn't the only thing moving between the trees. Ludwig was somewhere in the palm house as he had said he would be.

'How do you know Mack doesn't love me?'

'He never intended to,' came the immediate reply.

She paused, but still couldn't determine where the voice was coming from. 'When did you last see him?' She carried on walking, waiting for the answer. Often walking at night she forgot about the glass. 'When did you last see him?' she demanded again.

'Ten years ago.' The voice was begrudging. It wasn't that the ten years had taken a long time to calculate but that they had taken a long time to admit.

'Ten years is a long time. Has he stopped loving you as well?'

She looked up to check on the position of the moon and then she saw him underneath the dome of the palm house, standing on the balcony that ran around the circumference. He was leaning over looking down at her. Ludwig watched as Beatrice looked for the bottom of the stairs in the dark, eventually finding them where they grew out of the ground near the banana tree. He could feel the balcony shaking as she climbed, unsure of the sounds the iron structure made. The iron on the balcony was wrought into ivy and this, like the swan's head on the door, re-established the imperialism of a temperate climate in case visitors, losing consciousness, forgot the iron, the glass.

Beatrice suffered very bad vertigo; she even suffered it staring out of the window at the hills beyond; the thought of their height was enough. Her vertigo was based not on the fear that she might fall, but on the presumption that she would, so she climbed slowly, her calves and arms aching with the desire to hurl herself over the edge and have the inevitable over and done with. The mechanical parts of the structure were barely concealed the higher she rose. They were ticking even now, maintaining a constant temperature and this archaic machine sustained her and Aesop in a way Dr Achilles was unable to, she realised, as she shakily reached the top of the staircase.

'He failed,' she said, her cheeks pressed against the warm damp wall, her eyes shut. 'Jara cost him US$180,000 a day.'

'How do you know?' Ludwig was genuinely roused by this figure and her assertiveness with it.

'It wasn't a secret. He told me.'

'Why did he fail?'

'He made a prophecy that didn't come true.' She turned her head slightly to look at him, but kept the palms of her hands pressed tightly to the wall. She could feel the bricks grazing her knees.

'Maybe it wasn't paper he was dreaming of,' he said.

She turned round slowly keeping her back against the wall. 'I remember you.'

'You can't.'

'I remember sitting in his bed with Effie doll watching you. You were there then,' she said, forestalling any more false claims on his part. 'You never spoke to me. Nobody ever spoke to me, but he told me that you were the man who made thunder. I remember watching you at the window, watching the sky and wondering what words you were speaking. After you left it always started to thunder. Every time.'

'I don't remember.'

'You do. I knew it as soon as I saw you again.'

She turned her face back to the wall as he walked over to the edge and leant over conspicuously to watch the sleeping boy.

'You didn't have your face then,' she said quietly.

'Listen,' he shouted suddenly, turning round and taking hold of the tops of her arms and finding that he still had enough room left to press her further back into the wall. 'Mack made you in one night he can't even remember. It took him years to make me; years.'

In the dark the borealis made his skin look as if it was moving, shifting and growing.

'It wasn't even that he didn't love you – he didn't even think to want to.'

'He asked me to kill you,' she shouted back at him, trying to push him off. But he wouldn't let go and she felt the slam as his back hit the balcony railing passing through his pelvis into hers. 'That night, in Jara, in the horticultural nurseries . . . I followed you to kill you.'

Then she felt her feet rising up off the ground as he leant back over the railing further and further until her body was lying along the length of his.

'But you didn't. Because of Aurelius,' he said, and Aurelius's presence in the nurseries that night seemed suddenly overwhelmingly protective.

'If we fall over, we'll fall on to Aesop. We're directly above him,' she said, her eyes closed.

He lowered her back on to her feet, but carried on holding her tightly around the waist.

'Tell me about Mack's death,' he said quietly.

'There was a state funeral.'

'I need to know more than that.'

'Well imagine it. He spent a lot of time planning his

funeral; had very definite ideas. You know how much it preoccupied him.'

'Everyone had to be there?'

'Everyone. Aurelius was hysterical that day. The day of the emperor's funeral.'

'But there was someone who wasn't there.'

'That's right.' She could feel her ribcage trying to move in order to escape his fingers.

'The only person who didn't attend the emperor's funeral was the emperor. Where's Mack?' he said pushing her back against the wall.

She pulled something out of the top of her pants and held it out towards him. It was warm and crumpled from where it had been pressed against her belly. He turned it over expecting to find himself looking at Mack, presuming it was a treasure she had carried round with her either since her birth or his death, but it wasn't. The photo had been taken inside the lobby of Mack's Las Vegas apartment next to the curving velvet banquette and fake palm trees. The gaudy colour of the décor was apparent, despite its being black and white. He was looking at himself before the borealis.

He watched her hands clutching at the railing. Her love was even lonelier than his. He left her alone, not attempting to follow her back down the stairs, and watched as she pulled at the covers not on her own bed, but on Aesop's, arranging them around them both on the narrow bed whose springs he could hear and which sounded familiar although he couldn't think from where.

Then he started down the stairs himself, the photo held tightly in his hand. The existence of such a photo had never bothered him before, but he knew now that it was imperative he didn't lose it because it was the only proof he had of his reflection. He wondered how long she had had it for and how long it had taken her to decide to give it to him.

He stopped at the third coil in the stairs and pressed it against his chest to try and smooth out the creases. The photo looked big in his hands. He stopped at the foot of the bed. Beatrice was feigning sleep and, looking at her arms which lay carefully over Aesop's shoulders, it occurred to him that this might be the last time he would ever see him.

42

Deirdre pulled the net curtains back. She could see the coach parked outside, the one that had brought them up to Liverpool, Blackpool and then here: *TIM'S TRAVEL in pursuit of happiness*. Next to the coach was the minibus they also used. Beyond this there were some cement bunkers from the Second World War, a beach that was dark brown because of the frost, and then the sea. The horizon was mucky with tankers and floating islands.

'What you doing up at this time?' her mother said from the bed.

'You don't even know what time it is.'

'It's early that's what time it is. That's what it is in my book.'

She turned round as her mother started farting – something she did about this time every morning to get rid of dreams she hadn't got round to dreaming, and to give her body the chance to fit itself again.

'It's started to snow.'

'Didn't think it snowed at the seaside.'

'Well it does here. I'm going down to get breakfast.'

Even in the dark she could still pick out the royal purple walls and the wardrobe that had tanned unevenly in the sun. The room smelt of the trapped scents of nylon counterpanes that had never hoped – spread separately over twin beds – to aspire to happiness.

Downstairs everything that had been dreamed of in the past two decades was crammed into one room also filled by the better half of the gospel choir she had travelled north with: shag-pile carpet, velveteen fleur-de-lys wallpaper, memorabilia from Spanish holidays, and in the corner the mirror-tiled bar that the ginger-haired husband of the proprietress served tea from every morning. Deirdre couldn't help noticing when he did the tea that the zip on his zip-up cardigan was rusted, and wondered what could possibly have caused this if it wasn't dribble.

The sausages were very pink and the bread very white. They looked raw and premature, but she ate them anyway even though the man behind the bar looked as if he didn't expect her to or even particularly want her to and she saw him looking at the fork and knife she had eaten with when he carried them through to the kitchen. He smelt strongly of menthol and she only saw the wife once as she pushed her head round the kitchen door and was able to catch a glimpse of her blonde and black hair and bruised face.

'Is there a Young Offenders' Institute near here?' she asked him when he came back.

'Got family there then?' he said without gallantry.

'I thought there was – sure I read about it.'

He gave her a quick look that suggested she had no sense of humour.

'They were going to use the old Butlin's holiday camp – that was a camp for evacuees before Butlin's bought it, but they built a new site instead up there near the abbatoir,' he said nodding his head up towards the ceiling where his and his wife's bedroom was. 'Terrible amount of money they spent on it. Terrible. People say it's like a five-star hotel.'

She didn't know how to sympathise with him, or

283

demonstrate that she shared his point of view exactly, which was what he was looking for, so she just shook her head instead.

'Got family there – or just curious?' he said, now antagonistically suspicious.

'Just curious.'

'It's a nice drive up there towards the Pendle Hills. We went the other Sunday.'

Deirdre didn't say anything, she just reached for some more toast off the rack and started to hum the hymn they were opening with that night, a tune soon taken up by the other tables in the room. The ginger-haired husband arranged the cups on the bar and started to pour out the refills, listening to the rude echoes that bounced around his carpets and walls and wondering how the world had ever been allowed to come to this.

43

'What is it?' Beatrice said.

'Snow.'

It was falling so heavily that they could even see it in the dark.

'Will it stay?'

'Depends on how cold it is.'

Neither of them dared put their hands against the glass, afraid that it would burn with the cold, but Beatrice's fingers hovered just above it. The nail varnish she had painted on last night was already chipped and there was dirt again under her nails.

'It used to snow in November and stay till April.'

'That long?'

'When King Arthur was alive.'

'Who was King Arthur?'

'Some king, long time ago,' he said remembering the illustration on the page that described the snow when Jake read it to him. There was a castle in the background and a lady in a red dress on a horse being led through a grove of trees. There was snow still on the ground and the man leading the horse looked more like a woman than the woman did, had long blond hair and looked as though he would never need to shave.

'What does it taste of?' she said, not turning round, but

her back was warm from him standing so close.

'When it snows and it's sunny, it tastes of the North Pole,' he said, very sure of himself. 'But when it's grey and all shitty outside and you've got the buses and stuff spunking out at you all the time, it tastes of the sky.'

He saw the balcony running out in front of him with the rows of painted doors and Ludwig's heels, and every time he looked up they still seemed to be stood in front of the same door no matter how fast they walked.

'Thames used to freeze over as well,' he said quickly. 'They used to skate on it. I've never seen that though. Never seen snow this white either. Nothing like lying in snow, softest thing. People die when they fall asleep in snow.'

They were exactly the same height. He took hold of her hand lightly and walked over to the fountain, pushing her hands down into the water and pressing his own down on top of them to stop them floating back up to the surface.

'Your fingernails are filthy. Don't look after yourself, do you.'

She could feel him running his nail beneath hers, trying to get the dirt out.

'Why aren't yours?'

'I don't spend every night up to my elbows in mud, do I. What you digging anyway, a tunnel? Never had any trouble keeping clean,' he added.

After a while he lifted his hands out of the water and started to wipe them across her T-shirt. He laughed but she was too busy watching him to laugh back.

'You're making my T-shirt dirty.'

'I want you to take it off.'

'No you don't.'

Then she did laugh, but she didn't find it as easy as she expected to because his hands were pressed against the tops of her legs and then after a while he put his thumb in her mouth. He was waiting for her to bite on it as a sign that he should begin, even though he didn't know what it was he was meant to be beginning. They each undressed themselves and by the time he came to stand in front of her again and take her hand, half crouching and using his spare arm to cover himself, the scent of his erection lay heavily along the length of both of them.

Jake took the poster out of his pocket. He could hear the snow falling on the ground around him and he could smell the leaves, bark and soil as they secreted their final burst of odour in the knowledge that they would soon be buried. He lay back on the ground as the shadows of branches passed across the picture of Aesop, the badly smiling portrait. Then the paper began to get wet and he had to fold it carefully back into his pocket. He had forgotten what his brother looked like and was half afraid of coming across him here in the forest. It was a long time since he had been in a forest.

When he got near the brow of the hill he whistled quietly and the others from the camp raised themselves up unsteadily from the forest floor with a rush of staleness, the staleness of bodies trying to keep themselves warm rather than clean. They climbed up over the hill, trying to bend where it hurt the least, wary of themselves and the violence they were about to commit, wary of how it would look, how it would be seen, but intent on it now, intent on fulfilment, and excited to be outdoors and trespassing in the middle of the night, enjoying hearing the breath of the others and feeling their bodies hit against them as they ran. Jake ran ahead towards the Hall.

Douglas, who had left the hotel at dusk that evening, parked his car at the bottom of the hill, and climbed up through the forest close behind the campaigners watching them from the edge of the lawn as they ran across, bent (in a jangling fashion) on destruction. The air, once they had passed, was filled with the stench of alcohol. He sniffed at it heavily, then walked on, his foot tapping slightly on the hard ground. He looked back when he was half way across the lawn and could see from his footprints the efforts of his right leg to sustain those of his left.

They smashed five of the large windows at the front of the house and threw the lit bottles through. The heat from inside wheezed quickly out through the broken panes, making it momentarily difficult to breathe. Jake stood still and watched through the broken glass for a while. They stepped back and it was as if something, a certain tautness or heaviness that had been there for as long as any of them could remember every morning when they woke up and every evening when they went to sleep, was now at last lifting.

'We need to find Aesop,' he said, but nobody was listening.

Jake watched them move around outside the house, close to the flames, and the way their jewellery and loose clothes swung about them made them look even more inflammable. A couple of the professional riot-mongers were running, getting as close to the heat as they were able, and letting out sounds that didn't even resemble words in their rawest form; they were no longer trying to communicate. With their arms stretched out above their heads, they were celebrating, perhaps nothing more than the fact of the fire. Their faces were strangers' faces and he suddenly had no notion of how they got to be here with him. His sole intention had been to elevate himself and them above the human condition.

'We have to go inside,' he said, as the realisation of what was really happening reached him, frantically. At this, one of the campaigners shouldered his way into the flames, but soon came out again, choking and nursing his arm. The look on his face, however, was something close to laughter.

'My brother's somewhere in there,' Jake said at last. 'We have to find my brother; then we have to stop this fire.'

This made the campaigners stop for a moment and stare, as if he had mentioned something that was forbidden, something taboo. They looked at him long enough to let him know that he would never be forgiven for that, then they started to move closer to the house in search – he could tell – of death. Men and women who had refused to eat meat since the age of their reasoning, now went off in search of it, and he wondered how they would reconcile the fact afterwards that, despite refusing to eat it, they were able to hunt and kill it. He began to see the fire as something that was protecting Aesop, something he could hide him behind.

The flames took hold quickly and as they finished with the curtains and moved on to the table that stretched the length of the dining room, they started to make a high-pitched whistling sound. Watching them destroy, Jake no longer felt the need to feel responsible for the history of others, the history of his country, that he had listened to out of his own free will. He looked for Rose, but she was already moving with the rest of the group along the front of the house smashing anything that looked as though it were made of glass. The sound of their feet on the gravel made it sound like a game. He wrapped his coat round his fist. Aesop was somewhere in there and he had to find him before they did.

He hadn't seen Sean climb through the window next to him.

44

Achilles thought it strange that she had been given a key and wasn't prepared to believe that this had been an oversight on the part of Blackthorn. She turned it in the lock and tried the handle herself, then lifted the key to her nose; it smelt of wood and baize, and faintly of paper.

After a while she sat down on the edge of the bed, dragging a pillow out from under the covers and holding it tightly against her stomach. She could think of nothing to do but watch the door. It was the first time in her life that she had ever suspected herself of being under attack; it had never come to this before and she disliked such direct concentrated violence. There was nothing of hers left in the room. The case on the floor was packed, shut and locked as well, ready for tomorrow's departure. She watched a piece of silk that had been trapped outside the case as it flapped jerkily in the draught from the chimney and had no inclination to help it.

The round black handle turned first clockwise then anti-clockwise and she was sure she could hear it wheezing with laughter. There was a silence followed by a short sharp bang as Blackthorn kicked the door on his side and she watched the lower left-hand corner of it bulge momentarily as a streak of light from the corridor outside ran into the room. She had only been able to lock the inner door. There were two doors to most of the bedrooms at the Hall. She waited, feeling safer with the room in darkness, afraid that once she switched the light on she would lose her ability to see in the dark. The kick, however, was not necessarily something to despise. There was nothing intentionally or unintentionally impotent about it, and he became in that instant someone who was capable rather than incapable. He became suddenly limitless and she was no longer able to determine him. It seemed to her that Blackthorn wasn't just beyond her bedroom door, but was everywhere, even outside, wrapped around the house which had become nothing more than a parasite feeding off the most intimate parts of his body. She was terrified of looking out of the window in case she saw nothing but the empty gaping pores of a flesh magnified beyond proportion.

'Are you still there?' she called out after a while.

'Yes.' He pushed himself several times against the door.

'Won't you go?'

'No.'

She waited for the next bang, but there wasn't one. Instead she could hear the tentative ringing sound of metal against china which made her doubt the door more than any of the physical force hurled at it had done.

'Blackthorn.'

There was no answer this time, but after a while she heard a slight thud which must have been Blackthorn closing the outer door. Unless he had somehow managed to stand between the two. She remembered his face at the station the day she arrived and this feat – momentarily – seemed possible. She loosened her grip on the pillow, waiting for the handle to turn and the door to open, but it didn't. Then she heard the sound of a key being turned in the lock. It wasn't until she heard his footsteps faintly disappearing down the corridor that she realised he was no longer trying to get into the room. He had locked her in.

The room seemed darker now and she was afraid that if she tried the electricity it wouldn't work. It was better not to know than to have a fear confirmed so she sat very still on the edge of the bed, aware of how cold her body had become. Then she noticed that the room was slowly becoming lighter, something outside was shining directly on to the faces of the Toby-jugs lined up on the mantelpiece and the glass that covered the embroidered Chinamen hung on the wall. It was a blind light rather than a light that illuminated.

At last she moved from the bed and went to look out of the window. She drew back, but could still see the flames of a fire, which had divided themselves into many tongues, and were making their way along the length of the Hall, towards the palm house.

The flames distorted the darkness so that it felt as though this was all happening a long way underground, and the darkness above wasn't night but a ceiling of earth which was able to bear the flames because this was a place where there were always flames, where fire raged incessantly. She looked at the fireplace in the room as if in the knowledge that soon there would be earth by the ton falling down it, and that it wouldn't be long before it started to spill out of the hearth on to the carpet; she could see herself already, crawling about on the bed with a sea of mud about her.

She knelt down on the old-fashioned eiderdown which – she noticed this now – smelt damp, the damp of something that was beyond repair, beyond love. She crouched there unable to lift her face from it, until through the damp she began to think of Aesop. She threw her legs from the bed and ran back over to the door, lifting both her fists and hammering them against it, her shadow with its raised arms yawning over the ceiling and opposite walls in the light from the fire.

'Blackthorn,' she screamed. 'Aesop's going to burn, Aesop's going to burn. Blackthorn.'

She could smell the paint on the door, and the wood; the tree the door had come from, and the forest the tree had come from; she gave a consciousness to everything in the room so that they could all scream in unison and her fists banging on the door in the end sounded like nothing more than echoes of themselves.

45

The light coming off the television was blue, a hazardous blue which lit up the sides of Preston's head as well as his ear lobes. You could swim in light or you could sink in it and he wasn't sure which of these he was achieving sat in his armchair. The armchair was covered in a fabric that displayed shepherds and shepherdesses doing anything but watching their flock, sailing through the Age of Follies in boats padded with silk. It also stank of urine, from imagined trips to the toilet that he had never made. Mrs Jay, who sat on the pouf by his side, was on a level with his groin and could smell the urine clearly. It was a smell that had brought them closer together over the years.

They were watching the snooker and stared at the screen as the slim brown cue slipped across the green baize and the coloured balls rolled around in simple patterns without meaning. The bow tie and waistcoat had always struck Mrs Jay as being an uncomfortable outfit to play the game in.

Soon he would ask her to turn the television off and they would put the Bush gramophone on instead, some Mantovani, Ken Dodd or Vicky Leandros, something that they could listen to in silence. The walls were hung with calendars – the earliest dating back to the seventies

– that chronicled Preston's dwindling contact with the outside world. Most of them were from the Malton Farmers' Association or grain merchants, which came through the post smelling of the unbearably sweet smell of grain, a smell that was sweeter even than rotten meat. Mrs Jay hung calendars up that she had been given as well so that there was a more female, glossy element to the wall hangings. There was a calendar for 1985 whose December picture showed a rockface with naked women swarming over it. They all had hard hats on, rubber boots and rope coiled round their arms. The positions they assumed on the rockface, which would have been professional if they had been clothed, were nothing more than graphic. If they had had to choose a favourite calendar it would have been this – neither of them could remember who had been responsible for sending it.

Then above the sound of the television they heard the cheering start up, loud and victorious, and the reflection from the television was no longer blue, but warmer, a less stable light. They were both remembering the night his father closed the lino factory down and the men came up through the trees to the Hall in search of blood. The gravel on the driveway and round the house had danced that night under the men's feet in the same way they could hear it moving now. He had sat in the same room with his father in the chair he was sitting in now, and they had known that not even the authorities would interfere. The men were to be left alone with their intentions and were not to be interrupted. Up until then it had been the quietest night that either Preston or his father could remember. The sounds of the machines making flooring for the Empire had always filled the valley, rolling among its trees, along its rivers, even out along the pier and into the sea; just as the nights had been lit by the light shining through the factory windows rather than the moon. When they went to bed they could smell the lino in the creases of their counterpanes and even in their pillows when they should have smelt nothing but the scent of their own hair and dreams. He remembered Mrs Jay, fresh from India, and unafraid, who had fallen asleep night after night in India to the sound of rioting knowing that she would wake next morning and the world would be a different place.

There was the sound of glass splintering.

'Are there rioters among us tonight Mrs Jay?'

'They're burning the east wing of the house down,' she said quietly.

'Just the east wing?'

'I don't think so. Not specifically. No one's trying to put it out.'

Preston leant awkwardly forward and turned the television off.

Mrs Jay walked over to the window and had a look out, then pushed her hand over the light switch, turning all the lights in the room out.

'Mrs Jay,' he said, beginning to tense his hands on the arm of the chair in case he needed to stand up quickly.

She looked out at the sky around the gables of the house.

'They've started,' she mumbled, then turned round.

'What was that?'

She could see him just as clearly with the lights off.

Preston sat up in his chair. 'Are you sure?' he said tentatively, hoping that disbelief would give reason time to reveal itself.

'They're burning us down all right,' Mrs Jay said going back to the window, and this time they both saw the straggle of smoke coming down over the top of the house and moving past the window from above.

'Who is?'

Neither of them had any idea.

296

'It's that woman,' Mrs Jay said at last, weakly.

Preston got himself out of the chair with effort. He went to the writing desk and knelt down on the floor beside it, lowering his belly on to the carpet and feeling underneath. When Mrs Jay turned round from the window, he was stood up, wheezing, a shotgun held under his arm. The gun had been hidden under the writing desk during the Yorkshire Ripper murders. Both him and Mrs Jay had had a fascination for the Ripper at the time and he was the person they felt closest to after old Preston's death. He was caught only nine miles from Hornby Hall, in his forest. Both he and Mrs Jay knew that it wasn't for her that he had the gun in the room, it was kept there for his mother and two sisters, all long dead. After old Preston's death, the Ripper threatened them in some way.

He snapped the barrel shut and pushed the toupé made from his dead brother's hair back into place.

'There are children in there,' he said suddenly, waiting for Mrs Jay to fall in behind him.

It had taken Beatrice and Aesop a long time to find a way of making it possible on the narrow iron bed which they had dragged closer to the trees. Beatrice didn't want to lie on her back with him above her, the length of her, so she knelt over him, balancing her knees on the ridges, waiting until his eyes calmed down and she was able to take his cock in her hand.

'Don't start laughing,' she warned, knowing how afraid he was. 'If you start laughing we won't be able to do it.'

When she slid him inside her he gasped as if short of breath and she knew that it was hurting him more than it had ever hurt her, and she leant forward so that he could calm himself by sucking her breasts. Then she sat very still, feeling him grow up inside her until he spread his fingers over her thighs and his body started to move, taking a jerky responsibility for his pleasure. As she hung her head slowly forwards she noticed, when he had his eyes closed, that there was what could only have been sweat on his forehead, and looking down, a rash, a heat rash, spreading across his chest. She sat back up slowly, wiping her hand across her own forehead, but before she had time to think about it, she noticed through the windows that the front of the house was bowing outwards and that it was no longer solid, but a moving mass of orange. 'Fire,' she whispered, but Aesop's eyes were still shut, and he smiled a wide smile as if he had just heard her speaking his name.

Dr Achilles knelt by the door, her ears now full of the fire. The walls and floor were much warmer and the sky was orange, the same as it was over London every night.

'Blackthorn,' she shouted, her voice now hoarse, and no longer sure that she wasn't the last person left in the house.

After a while she became aware of footsteps in the corridor outside, but they sounded confused. They stopped and she could hear someone trying the outer door. She raised her head and looked through the keyhole only to find herself looking at the face of an eagle, a golden eagle painted blue, its beak raised because of the wrinkles on the forehead it sat on.

'I've come to be cured,' the voice whispered through the keyhole.

'Sean?' she said and, as she said his name, she remembered the ceiling in her flat and him lying looking up at it. She had never thought about it before, but this was where she always saw him, where he had his place. 'What are you doing here?'

'I need you to cure me,' he repeated.

'Is the house on fire?'

'Look out your window.'

'I don't want to,' she said quickly.

'You have to let me in.'

'No, you have to let me out. You need to find Blackthorn; there's someone here called Blackthorn, Dr Blackthorn,' she added as if this might make a difference. 'Find Blackthorn,' she said again, 'and if you can't find Blackthorn go to the palm house, go to the palm house as fast as you can before the fire reaches it. There are children in there.'

46

They turned their faces towards the windows and Beatrice felt her hair rise in this new heat, not just the hair on her head but the hair on her body as well. She felt a stinging in her right arm as Aesop's nails cut into her skin and she started bleeding, and she knew that not even Dr Achilles was behind this.

In the sudden light she could see Aesop's swollen lips and, looking down, the skin between her breasts was shining. She pressed herself against him and, as she put her hands up towards his shoulder blades, she could almost feel them stretching out and growing as if the skin on his back was splitting and turning into feathers. His cock had completely shrunk, but it left the wet trail of its intentions across the top of her thigh, like a tongue trying to taste, and she imagined it straining blindly at its root.

They watched as the back wall of the palm house began to bulge towards them, as if the particles in the bricks were draining away and the wall which had always been solid was now liquid. Then it was sucked suddenly back in and became solid once more, and there was a sound which should have been sharp, but was more fluid than this, more instrumental. It was the door that led to the kitchens, the door Achilles and Ludwig used. The door buckled and then the wall blew in with a howl as the flames rose up, climbing the iron framework. They could hear them scratching at it as they clawed their way to the top and the edges of the palm house were lost.

The trees seemed taller on fire and, because of the smoke, the glass and framework couldn't be seen, and the palm house no longer finished. Neither of them could remember the lawn outside or the house behind them, all their memories became this: a jungle on fire. Beatrice could even hear thunder behind it, whenever there was fire there was thunder – there always had been.

She had to let go of Aesop's hand, even though he hadn't stopped crying since the fire began and he started screaming again as soon as she left him. When she reached the camp bed she caught the metal frame with her shoulder. It was already too hot to touch and she knew that the heat would soon make the mattress burst. The vanity case was still under there, still pink, but the plastic on top was bubbling slightly.

As soon as she got back to where he was standing he took hold of her hand and arm and held it to him, looking down at the vanity case as if it were going to save them.

'Are you cold?' she asked.

'No,' he said.

'Neither am I.'

'We can't leave,' he said understanding her immediately.

'We have to.'

'We'll die.'

'A better death. Do you want to be eaten?'

'No.'

'Eaten by this?'

'No,' he said, finding a new defiance at the edges of his fear.

'Do you want to die in an animal's belly?'

301

'No.' He looked expectantly at the pink vanity case again.

'Then we have to leave.'

She picked up the regulation shirt he had worn at the Institute from where he had dropped it, and saw him watching her as she wrapped it round her arm.

'Think of the sea,' she said, walking over to the window that faced across the valley.

He watched the top of the vanity case which was still bubbling in the heat and had no idea where she was going. 'You've never seen the sea,' he said.

'Tell me about it.'

'I can't.'

'What is it?' she demanded, stopping and turning round.

He was crying again, looking over his shoulder.

'It's water, water, water, water. It's grey.'

'I thought it was blue.'

'It's grey in England and it tastes dead.'

'Tell me about the fish.'

'Never seen any. I hate the seaweed.' He wiped his arm over his forehead. They were both filthy with smoke.

'Why?' she said. 'Why do you hate it?'

'Because it won't leave you alone. All you're trying to do is swim and it wraps around your legs and arms and even though it's in the water it's wetter than the water. It's like something with arms and legs, and . . .'

She swung her arm out towards the window, but nothing happened.

'Stop,' he screamed.

She swung again, bringing it down at an angle rather than striking. The glass bowed outwards slightly. She felt Aesop's arms round her waist, as he tried to pull her away.

'Anything's better than being eaten alive,' she reminded him. 'Anything's better than loving me,' she

302

added starting to chew on his arm.

She ran back towards the table where their books were, hardly noticing that she was dragging his weight behind her, and picked the lamp up off it, smudging the brass base with filthy fingers. On the third try, with the lamp, the Victorian glass cracked and she pushed her arm through so that only a few splinters tore at the underside of it. She felt Aesop's forehead pressing into the top of her spine as the first flurry of snow blew in through the window on to her upturned face.

The cold outside was a still cold, not a moving one, something you walked into, but there were sparks in it and there were pockets of warmth that shouldn't have been there as well as layers of smoke much higher up in the sky. The snow was up to their ankles. They ran for a while, then stopped so that Beatrice could look down at her feet.

'Are you cold?' he said watching her.

'Freezing.'

'Me too.'

She let go of his hand and started to walk round in a circle. After a while she began scooping the snow up and rubbing it into herself so that it quickly became nothing more than dirty water falling blackly into the snow about her. Then she lay down.

'Come and lie down beside me.'

He watched her for a moment wondering what it was her eyes were trying to pick out.

'At least five minutes,' he said.

'What?'

'We've been at least five minutes.'

They looked at each other.

He knelt beside her without trying to lie down, waiting for her to pass judgement on this. But she kept silent and in the end he couldn't wait any longer.

'I don't think we're ill, Beatrice.'

He tried to put his hands under her head and lift her up, but it was too heavy. 'We're not ill.'

Then they looked back towards the palm house seeing the fire for the first time, not only as something with an appetite, but something they could outrun, and as they watched, it was as if the trees were no longer burning, but had decided instead to walk out of the fire as they had done, and were now following them, in their footsteps.

Preston knew that there were intruders in the house. He could hear them running about blindly and could feel their excitement rushing through objects they had passed. He shuffled along as quickly as he could, aware of the fact that people who don't know what it is they're searching for are far more dangerous than those who do. The sounds reverberating around his now unfamiliar kingdom were filled with the fury of those making history on behalf of others.

He pressed his thumb against the gun, thinking specifically of Mrs Jay, then passed down into the kitchens, where the flagstones began. This was the part of the house that hurt him the most. Upstairs where it was carpeted, the midriff of the house, he had never been sure how many people there were, or how few, but down here there had always been one hundred exactly. This was where the silence was most noticeable, where he saw clearly how minute his life had become, and how people at large had taken to living – at the end of this century – in rooms rather than houses.

He reached the corridor with the door at the end. It was the smallest whitest corridor in the house and as he got older he often wondered why the entrance from the house into the palm house had been through the servants' quarters. He had never loved anyone enough to understand this move of his grandfather's. Somewhere high above he heard a woman screaming and he thought he recognised a name in the scream. The smoke was growing thicker by the second and was now the fuller smoke of established mayhem. It occurred to him that he was treading the fire's path, a fire belonging to broken people who hadn't found love and were still waiting for a new set of Ten Commandments to be issued. He left the house by the kitchen door.

Two naked children, holding hands, ran past without seeing him. They seemed to emerge from the fire itself and he watched as the girl lay down in the snow and the boy knelt next to her. The girl lifted the boy's hand to her mouth and kissed the knuckles, not taking her eyes off him.

The flames were growing and beginning to breathe. He almost wanted to walk into them and was suddenly afraid that this was what the children, silently, unanimously, had decided to do. But then, without looking back over their shoulders at the fire, and with the boy's fist still pressed close against the girl's mouth, they got up and ran on.

As he stared after them it occurred to him that he should have asked Blackthorn more questions, that he had allowed him an unaccountable freedom and that Mrs Jay should have been involved from the beginning. Mrs Jay would have known what to do. He thought about her for a few moments, then clicked the gun shut stalking out across the lawn in front of the house with it raised to his shoulder, cocked, assuming a posture that was as close to a crouch as he could come.

Ludwig's face was already severely burnt. When he used his muscles he could feel that the skin was raw and wet – people would no longer be able to see whether he was crying or not. The fire had already passed through the old ballroom and the room at the far end which backed on to the palm house. Even above the flames and smoke he could still smell the heavy damp heat that housed more than one man's dreams.

'He's burning,' he shouted, under the illusion that either the palm house was already full of people or that they had followed him in there. He presumed that the palm house was the centre of everybody else as it was him and so thought that he would have to fight the crowds or at least Dr Achilles to get in. But he hadn't seen her for hours and was alone now as he had been since the fire began.

He couldn't see either Aesop or Beatrice, or hear – even – any echoes of their death. There was only a high-pitched whistling sound that slowly evened out until it became a note, sung. The fire seemed to stop spreading, gathering itself together in a column that started to twist upwards. It used the banana trees and sugar cane as its centre pulling the leaves upwards and spiralling up to the roof. He watched, unable to leave, expecting the column to crash through the top of the glass ceiling and up into the sky, but it didn't. It lingered near the top for only a few seconds before the singing sound got lower and lower until it became a sigh, and the column blossomed out, spreading itself across the roof and down the sides of the entire palm house.

Ludwig ran blindly towards the centre of the fire as if hoping to pass through it and out the other side, only stopping as he saw through a window to the right of him Douglas stood there, his arms stretching through the space where the glass had been with hands wearing driving gloves. He had on a dark coat whose edges weren't defined in the confusion of light, and he was wearing his chauffeur's cap. Ludwig could only see the top half of him framed in the window as he called out, 'Ludwig, Ludwig, over here.'

'Douglas.' He ran towards him. 'Where is he?'

'Who?'

'Aesop. Did you kill him?'

'I couldn't have. The fire . . .'

'He's already dead?'

'Probably.'

Douglas stretched his arms further through the window, reaching out for Ludwig's coat. 'I didn't come to kill him.'

'Why did you come then?'

'I came to kill you.'

Ludwig stopped in front of him and he could see that Douglas was afraid he would start to walk backwards into the flames.

But he didn't. He stood watching his chauffeur for a few moments more, then took hold of his hands. The leather of his gloves felt more like skin than his own hands ever had to him.

For the third time Blackthorn walked past the old vegetable patches which looked more like unmarked mass graves. He hadn't given himself time to put his coat on before leaving the house and, although snow didn't usually make him feel cold, he was cold tonight. He passed along the kitchen garden wall, trying to imagine what it would look like in the summer, but couldn't. He was unable at that moment to conceive of himself reaching another summer, let alone living through one.

He had expected his work at the Institute to daunt him, he had always expected this from the moment Preston first phoned him, but he had never expected it to devastate him as it had. It made him realise that he had taken the Institute on board because he had been in search of a saint; or if not a saint, a humble devil with the makings of one. What he had discovered instead was that he didn't have the faculty to deal with or even

307

acknowledge evil and certainly not on a daily basis. He wasn't able to tread the same fitted carpet as it, the same linoleum, the same water; he wasn't made for war as some men – even unexpectedly – were.

He stopped when he reached the end of the wall and looked up at the sky which was much lighter tonight, an orange sky; a London night. London had terrified him the last time he was there; it had made him feel like a forgotten emperor returning from exile to find that the streets were no longer named after him.

After a while he heard the noise of snow being pressed down under running feet. Then something shot past. At first he thought they were skinned rabbits, he didn't know why they should be rabbits, but they had the stoop of something hunted and he had recently lost all perception of things. He looked down at the footprints in the snow: only four and he had seen two rabbits, so there should have been eight prints. He was finding it easier to think in numbers whose meaning was absolute (if abstract). Kneeling down and counting again, it occurred to him that they were, of course, footprints and not paw prints. Two children had run past him, two naked children, and not rabbits as he had supposed. There was a light spattering of blood around some of the right-hand tracks.

He looked up at the sky again and realised that it sounded orange as well as looking orange, and that the air was thick with the smell of smoke. He wondered for a moment if he was on fire himself, but felt nothing, so looked behind him in the direction the children had come from. He didn't know what he expected to see, an ogre, revolutionary mob, twelve-foot witch, or a forest that had grown legs; he believed in all these things. The Hall was on fire and he couldn't see the palm house any more for flames, and the children must have been Aesop and Beatrice. They were running through the snow.

He started to walk back towards the house, treading in their footsteps to cover their trail although he didn't know why he felt he needed to do this. He wanted to know why they were running, why they weren't dead. Had Achilles cured them?

The fire was steadily growing through the house which was more crowded now than it had probably ever been, with people or the shadows of people at every window. He felt in his pocket for the key, pausing only a moment before breaking into a run; he was going to save her. As he ran on he started to move his hands about as if her head was already lying in his lap, and he could feel her hair, burnt and coarse, filling his hands. The only thing he couldn't see were her eyes.

47

Singing in a choir had seemed like a good way to spend the murky period between being born and dying. She used her voice to fill the space Jake had left, and was lucky that it was as loud as it was. Singing, Deirdre thought, looking at the lifted faces around her, was a way of experiencing joy on a (virtually) daily basis, which was more than most people ever hoped for. People's lips grew swollen and trembled when they sang; sometimes they cried.

They were packing churches out all up the west coast of England, making them temporarily full and swelling them with people until the echoes vanished. She supposed people came because word got ahead that if they heard the choir singing they would know what it was to feel joy, they would be able to put the word back into their lexicon again. So the gospel choir started to tour in their marine-blue minibus that had been given them by the Swedish Seamen's church in Rotherhithe and a coach, donated by TIM'S TRAVEL. The only detour they took was round a tide-ridden headland where the black slave Sambo's grave stood, and where they had gathered to sing without animosity. In the minibus afterwards she heard that Sambo had tried to escape, not his master's wrath, but his master's love. She still couldn't decide whether he had been buried facing out to sea as an act of malice or kindness.

After this they arrived in Lancaster, and she realised that she had found Aesop without even looking for him.

That night they were singing on the site of St Peter's monastery on the cliffs overlooking Heysham Nuclear Reactor and Morecambe Bay. Their purple tunics were stretched to the hilt over jumpers and coats as they sang in the snow.

After a while they realised that everybody in the audience was beginning to look at the sky and she could tell from the looks the choir exchanged that they were afraid their singing had been heard as incantations. With their eyes turned silently upwards they all looked as though they were waiting for something to land or fall.

'It's burning,' someone said above the singing.

The singers closed their mouths and turned round. The valley behind them was on fire. Deirdre saw her mother take hold of Kilroy's hand.

'It's the Young Offenders',' someone else shouted. 'The buggers have set fire to themselves.'

'They'll escape then. The fence will burn down and they'll escape.' They pushed themselves together in a circle.

But the singers, who had the ability to believe reverently in any form of damnation, read the sign and started to sing again. Fire and damnation were something to be fought, and they all lived in the hope that one day they would be given the chance to prove themselves in spiritual arm-to-arm combat.

'It's not the Young Offenders', it's Jack Preston's place. It's Hornby Hall,' someone said, and the silence was the closest thing to a crowd cheering that she had ever heard.

The choir was singing louder than before, but this time the listeners came and stood among the singers so that, after a while, they were all stood in a semi-circle facing the fire that was rising up on the hill in front of them.

Deirdre started to run through the snow away from them. She had driven the minibus that evening and the keys were still in her coat pocket. She did something she had never done before. She abandoned twenty-five people on a cliff top, not even sure if she would be able to come back for them, and started to drive along the cliff road and inland towards the fire. As she drove she felt at last that the two hands she had been waiting to feel the pressure of all her life were now resting on her shoulders.

48

Douglas took hold of Ludwig's hand and pulled him across the lawn. Away from the fire it was snowing again and Ludwig ran with his arm across his face, as careful of the snow as he had been careless of the fire. With every step he took he seemed to grow smaller until after a while he felt as though he had to stretch beyond his limit in order to keep hold of Douglas's hand.

They knew if they turned round now that the house behind them would be full, that there would be people at every window. Ransacking was a dance that always took place in the aftermath of violence; the reward of the initiate. And those people that now were nothing more than shadows dancing at the windows would wake up strangers to themselves tomorrow morning after discovering themselves capable of cannibalism in the night. And this feeling was nothing that vomit or bile would dispel.

Ludwig was starting to stagger and Douglas could smell him burning still. They stopped at the edge of the lawn where it dipped down into forest and the valley proper. Douglas tripped him up quickly and started to roll him about in the snow.

'My face,' Ludwig said over and over again, sometimes a shriek, sometimes a whisper, and when Douglas pulled him to his feet again he was crying.

'Where's Achilles?' he said, starting to unbutton Douglas's coat so that he could get inside it as well. He was cold now.

'Was she in there?'

'Yes.'

They looked at each other and Douglas only flinched slightly as Ludwig's hands pressed into his chest.

'I didn't see her.'

'Did you look for her?'

'I didn't know she was there.'

'You did.'

Douglas tried to pull Ludwig off him, but he had buried himself too deeply into his coat. 'I didn't think to look for her – why should I?'

Inside the coat Ludwig could feel Douglas's back folding over his waist band in two folds that felt so much part of his anatomy he half wondered if they weren't gills.

'Come on, we have to go down there,' Douglas said, managing to pull him away at last.

'Down where?'

Then he saw where they had stopped and where the line of trees stood, dark and wet, but unable to describe their brittleness in the face of the fire now raging across the lawn. Ludwig knew that trees could run, that they moved as soon as you were amongst them, that they grew, that they could spread like a carpet so that you grew smaller and smaller.

'No,' he said violently, now managing to loosen one of his hands from Douglas.

'Come on.' Douglas was trying to stay soft.

'No, I'm not going in there.'

'The car's parked just on the other side.'

'But they've started to move, look.'

Douglas didn't bother. He grabbed hold of Ludwig's other hand instead.

'A handful of trees, then the car.'

'I can't,' Ludwig said, terrified now of being hit about the face, which he was sure Douglas was going to do.

'We need to get to the car.'

'Is Mack there?' he said suddenly.

'No.'

'I'm not going,' he said again, already beginning to try and walk backwards, convinced that the trees were advancing, lifting their roots up out of the snow and walking up the hill towards them. He was crying with fear and no longer saw Douglas standing there or the small gun he held in his steady hand.

'Ludwig.'

They both stopped and waited.

Preston watched as a man with long hair separated himself from the other figures on the lawn and ran towards the forest, flinching at everything that touched him, the snow, the heat from the flames. Preston took the toupé, that was gradually getting singed, off his head and pushed it into his trouser pocket, then took aim and fired.

The man fell forward automatically into the snow, then turned round, unable to believe the sound the shot made. Preston carried on staring at him but didn't lower his gun even though his shoulder was beginning to ache and he knew he had already bruised it badly. He watched as the man pushed the hair out of his eyes and started to walk away, afraid, but with the lope of wounded pride.

'What's your name?' he called out down the gun, across the lawn, just as the man was about to disappear over the edge.

'Jake Whitmore,' the intruder said without hesitation, loudly.

'You're trespassing.' It was the first time he had ever used the word. He could tell that the man was looking beyond him and the gun now, back towards the house.

'So? They've burnt it all.'

Preston fired again. This time the man fell forward and didn't get up for a long time, but Preston carried on waiting.

Eventually he got to his feet, but he was clutching his left shoulder. He felt the cheer rise up in him, the cheer at the wounded rather than the dead; now they could begin properly. The man disappeared over the edge and Preston heard him rolling over in the snow and down into the forest. He lowered his gun and started to follow; he had forgotten the fire.

Beatrice ran through the last of the trees straight on to the road and the vehicle coming towards them only had time to stop because it was going uphill. She got straight back to her feet and would have run into the trees on the other side, but the driver had already got out.

'We're not dead,' Aesop said automatically, walking into the road and in front of the headlights. He watched as the driver took Beatrice into her arms, and he was suddenly afraid because she was naked. The driver was wearing a purple tunic and was looking at them both. She knew his name.

Douglas was grinding the gears of the car as he had never done before and he was driving without his coat which was wrapped around Ludwig, lying in the back. The car had taken ages to start and he was worried that the snow might get worse and that they would be stuck.

Ludwig had quietened down and was now staring at the ceiling of the car which was stained slightly with rust, speaking in a language Douglas recognised but didn't understand. He was flinching as he drove because of the snowflakes which were falling heavily on to the windscreen and he didn't trust the glass to stop them.

'Shut up,' he said after a while when Ludwig didn't

stop mumbling. He could hear the leather in the back squeaking as Ludwig shoved himself backwards and forwards across it, trying to find something to hold on to. He remembered, in the early days, helping a Ludwig who stank of excessive fucking into the back of the car where he vomited copiously, on and off, all the way home. The vomit, then, had been a sign of triumph if not conquest, now it would be nothing more than the ravings of an ill body.

He was about to tell him to shut up again when he noticed something rolling out of the forest on his right and straight in front of the car. He slammed the brakes on and waited.

'Did we hit him?' Ludwig said.

'I don't know.'

He didn't want to unlock the doors and get out of the car, and was about to drive round the body when it got up hesitantly. The man pushed his hair behind his ears and tried to stare into the headlights. Douglas didn't dip them, but carried on waiting. The man didn't move and after a while he realised that it must have been one of the campaigners because he had blood over his left shoulder which hung much further down than his right. He was standing very still now and Douglas could feel Ludwig's fingers round the top of his seat, pressing into his back. He put the car into gear and drove slowly round the figure where he stood in the middle of the road, afraid that he might try and throw himself under their wheels again.

'We didn't hit him,' Ludwig said, looking back through the rear window.

He was so intent on looking out through the window at the man and the fire, which was still content to burn, that he missed the van they overtook at the brow of the hill, and the faces of the two children pressed against its back window. Douglas no longer had his eyes on the road as the car and the van drove abreast over the brow of the hill.

Coming down the hill Jake could see mountains in the distance across the bay. It was that time of morning when sleep and the quality of the light made headlands into other countries. He didn't know whether he had stopped bleeding or not, but the canvas of his coat was hard and his left shoulder was the only part of his body he could feel. He smelt the fire in his hair and on his skin although there was no sign of it now on the hill behind him, and no sign of any of the campaigners either. He couldn't conceive of people going home or going to sleep after the night that had passed, but that was what happened, he supposed; at the end of a day man sought sleep.

He noticed with surprise and alarm that some of the houses he passed on his left, which had been built for prison wardens and their families, had Christmas decorations strung up across the windows. Countries and not people were brought to their knees he remembered, for the first time feeling something close to defeat.

On the scale of things the fire had been big and, in light of the night that had passed, life should have stopped or at least halted in some way, but here was daily life staring him in the face again. It was maddening and relentless. Even the cemetery he passed on his right was making some effort for the new day and lorries with freshly laundered linen for the terminally ill were pulling into the hospital forecourt.

He tried to think of fires that raged for more than one night, of shops broken, ransacked, empty, of cars that had lost their meaning and lay turned on their sides so that they became barricades; of tanks; of people unbound from all known codes of conduct, of chaos in all its depravity. But he still couldn't get out of his mind the

318

picture he had once seen of a family of six sitting cross-legged around a cooking pot in the ruins of their home, Leningrad, 1945. The family supper, taken at the same time as usual, and he wondered who really won the war.

He carried on walking, able to hear his boots scraping on the road, but not able to feel them. He kept his eyes on the road, not looking to the left where the perimeter fence of the Institute for Young Offenders began. He didn't even have the reassurance that he had failed because he didn't know whether he had failed or not, or whom he had failed. All he knew was that his boots were walking in a definite direction.

The only thing he stopped for were the abbatoir gates which were computer-operated and opening as he passed. These were blue, complicated-looking structures and as they opened he saw a group of boys in the yard standing, oblivious of the gates, in puddles of liquid. They were wearing white rubber boots and the blue shirt and trousers that he quickly recognised as uniform from the Institute. The boys were standing in a loose group passing a cigarette around, but it took him some moments to realise, above the bleating of a reversing lorry, that they were laughing. They were so busy laughing they hadn't noticed that the gates to the yard were opening.

There was one moment when they broke up the group and lowered their voices, gesturing, and Jake thought with a sudden lightness that they were going to make a run for it through the open gates. The tallest one even dropped the cigarette stump in the puddle. But they didn't. Instead one of them disappeared into a corner and came back into the light kicking something. This boy paused for a moment as the others began to clap and yell, their backs to the gate, then he ran towards the pig's head and kicked it clean into the air, across the middle of the yard and over to the other side. Then looked up at Jake.

'At least you didn't drown,' Jake said out loud, as it occurred to him that he hadn't once tried to stop the fire.

49

'Do it so that while you're doing it I've got something to look at.'

'You don't like needles?' Blackthorn said.

'You know I don't,' Dr Achilles answered, tired.

Her arms had grown larger, looser, more capable of absorbing a needle. He pushed her over to the window which was too tall for her to see anything other than the immediate skyline out of. She rarely saw any people, but got an impression of them from the thick smells – even in winter – that made their way through the sash windows.

The treatment room they used at the top of the Institute was one of the sparsest, just a trolley, some chairs of various heights and a fridge which was large, walk-in size and American-looking, from an era when furniture and domestic appliances suggested not only outer space but the extra-terrestrial life that might inhabit it. Inside on the top two shelves were rows of blood samples, graphically annotated, but mostly with figures: there were no names. They contained nothing more than Eastman's Syndrome. A few shelves down were samples of her own blood.

Initially Blackthorn had treated her only for burns which, she noted, looking at herself in the mirror for the first time afterwards, had disfigured her completely.

Afterwards, when it became clear that her face wasn't healing due to the presence of a legacy other than that of the fire, Blackthorn stayed to treat her. Later, when it became worse and they started to discuss a biopsy, he helped her to sell her flat and move the contents of it to the upper floor of the Institute where he also moved some things of his own. It was a marriage of sorts, or this was how the children saw it at least. Now Blackthorn was the only reason they stayed.

The children were the only thing that had really surprised her. She had smiled at herself before making her first tour of the ward again, anticipating not only love, but more love than before. She saw figures kneeling at the end of beds, arms flying over the iron railings, their pelvises bruised from the efforts of their hands to reach her skirts. But instead they had got back into bed and the younger ones had even pulled their covers up until most of the beds looked as though they were occupied by corpses in shrouds. She missed their hands; she had never mourned anything as much as the touch of their hands. At first she thought it was Blackthorn, but knew as she reached the double doors at the end of the ward with their wire-mesh windows and posters of New England in the Fall, that it was because of her face, and her arms (which she had purposefully made no efforts to cover). Getting burnt was unforgivable and she couldn't bear them to look at her after that. She also noticed for the first time that the ward smelt and that the children didn't smell of children.

Blackthorn watched the front of her throat quiver as he stuck the needle into her arm and knew that she was mouthing the words 'a bee sting', 'a bee sting'. He was the only one who treated her and she hadn't asked for anyone else, although he wouldn't have objected.

'How was Ludwig today?' she said once the needle was in.

'Same as usual,' he said not taking his eyes off it for a moment as if he distrusted its presence in her body.

He held the syringe upright and leant over to look out of the window. The needle even managed to reflect the drab light coming in, and she looked at her blood with something close to disgust.

'Lift me up,' she said, watching him. 'I want to see him leave.'

'I can't, you're too heavy.'

'Lift me up.'

He put the syringe on to the window sill, then placed his hands under her arms.

'You're the only person who has always, consistently, treated me like a child,' she said.

He paused for a moment then lifted her to her feet, his fingers touching the sides of her breasts as she leant forwards, her arms outstretched towards the window.

Even with her forehead pressed against the glass she could only see half of the car's black roof. She didn't hear the feet running down the hospital stairs or the slamming of the car door. But she saw the car leave. She had never felt as heavy as she did in Blackthorn's arms with her whole body pulling down towards the floor.

The chair rolled slightly as he sat her back down in it.

'I've found the cure,' she said quietly, trying to pull her skirt down where it had got caught.

'For the borealis?'

'Yes.'

'And Eastman's?'

'Not yet. Not that.'

Blackthorn went over to the window to catch a glimpse of Ludwig but he had already left.

'I don't want him to know,' she added.

Blackthorn turned round and looked at her.

'Ever?' he asked.

'No. Just for a while.'

She could feel her left arm throbbing where he had given her the injection, but still managed to push the wheelchair over to the fridge.

'Cures don't always come in a bottle,' she said to him before opening the door.

50

As soon as Ludwig stepped outside, he heard the sound of a car door slamming and after a while Douglas's voice shouting his name. Inside the car it didn't feel as silent as it had in the hospital. He sat next to Douglas in front because of the other passenger in the back. He didn't like the smell of the bandages on his lower arms and had to take them off at night in order to sleep. But every morning Douglas came in and put them back on so that he spent the rest of the day with his nostrils full of surgical spirit.

The leather on the back of Douglas's driving gloves had cracked and peeled in places and now looked blistered, but he wouldn't let Ludwig buy him a new pair. Ludwig heard fire now wherever he walked; he could be turning a corner, jostling on a crowded street, or walking up the middle of an empty one. He could be in Whitechapel, on Leadenhall Street, in Stoke Newington, on Hampstead Heath, Ealing, Bloomsbury, Putney, Greenwich, it didn't matter, the crackling and spitting of an appetite embodied in flames never stopped licking at him. Sometimes, rushing up from behind, he heard the long high note that was sung before the fire roared, and then the sigh that came afterwards.

'Are you ever going to get your cure?' the man in the

back of the car said, sighing.

Ludwig, who didn't answer, heard his clothes crackle as he turned his head to look out of the window. He thought of Aurelius in Jara and wondered how tall the crop of eucalyptus and Caribbean pine would be now, but didn't say anything.

Douglas couldn't see Mack in the mirror because the shadow he cast was so immense and when the car stopped at some lights on the Strand the shadow, in only a few seconds, spread on to the road and buildings around them.

Ludwig looked out of his window at the stained wall of the building next to them. It was Charing Cross police station and, as he looked, he noticed a poster stuck to the wall that had obviously been there for some time: another child missing. Then he saw. It was the picture of Aesop.

Douglas slowly followed his stare, then put the car into gear before the lights changed. If they hadn't had the third person in the back he would have taken his left hand off the wheel and held one of Ludwig's. Even now he knew he would never tell him that two children had passed him on the night of the fire, running across the lawn holding hands. At last Ludwig looked up again, and he felt the passenger in the back relaxing when he did.

'Still missing then,' Mack said.

A SELECTED LIST OF CONTEMPORARY FICTION
AVAILABLE IN VINTAGE

☐	THE MERCY BOYS	John Burnside	£6.99
☐	DISGRACE	J M Coetzee	£6.99
☐	LIFE & TIMES OF MICHAEL K	J M Coetzee	£6.99
☐	BY THE SHORE	Galaxy Craze	£6.99
☐	MEMOIRS OF A GEISHA	Arthur Golden	£6.99
☐	EVERYTHING YOU NEED	A L Kennedy	£6.99
☐	AMSTERDAM	Ian McEwan	£6.99
☐	ENDURING LOVE	Ian McEwan	£6.99
☐	BELOVED	Toni Morrison	£6.99
☐	PARADISE	Toni Morrison	£6.99
☐	MASON & DIXON	Thomas Pynchon	£7.99
☐	AMERICAN PASTORAL	Philip Roth	£6.99
☐	THE GROUND BENEATH HER FEET	Salman Rushdie	£6.99
☐	THE LIGHTENING CAGE	Alan Wall	£6.99

- All Vintage books are available through mail order or from your local bookshop.

- Please send cheque/eurocheque/postal order (sterling only), Access, Visa or Mastercard:

☐☐☐☐☐☐☐☐☐☐☐☐☐☐☐☐

Expiry Date:_____Signature:_____

Please allow 75 pence per book for post and packing U.K.
Overseas customers please allow £1.00 per copy for post and packing.

ALL ORDERS TO:

Vintage Books, Books by Post, TBS Limited, The Book Service,
Colchester Road, Frating Green, Colchester, Essex CO7 7DW

NAME:_____

ADDRESS:_____

_____

_____

Please allow 28 days for delivery. Please tick box if you do not
wish to receive any additional information ☐

Prices and availability subject to change without notice.